CUT OUT.

SERVICE
UNIFORM

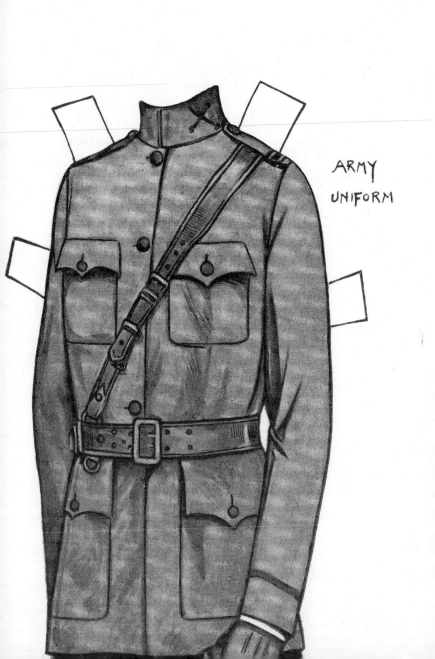

ARMY
UNIFORM

The Red Tunic

Kate Wiseman

The Red Tunic

Kate Wiseman

NEEM TREE
PRESS

Published by Neem Tree Press Limited 2024
Copyright © Kate Wiseman, 2024
Kate Wiseman asserts her rights under the Copyright, Designs and Patents Act 1988 to be recognised as the author of this work.

1 3 5 7 9 10 8 6 4 2

Neem Tree Press Limited
95A Ridgmount Gardens, London, WC1E 7AZ
United Kingdom
info@neemtreepress.com
www.neemtreepress.com

A catalogue record for this book is available from the British Library.

ISBN 978-1-915584-13-7 Paperback
ISBN 978-1-915584-14-4 Ebook UK
ISBN 978-1-911107-18-7 Ebook US

Printed and bound in Great Britain

Imagine their skirts 'mong artillery wheels,
And watch for their flutter as they flee 'cross the fields
They would faint at the first drop of blood, in their sight.
What fun for us boys,—(ere we enter the fight)

"The Women Who Went to the Field"
—Clara Barton, 1821-1912
Civil War Nurse, Humanitarian,
Founder of the American Red Cross

CHAPTER ONE

Near Passchendaele Village, Belgium, September 1917

Corporal Knowles is in full flow this evening, trying to get us to write letters to our loved ones, "just in case the worst happens". He says this with a pursed-lipped smile, embarrassed at having to mention something so inconvenient. *Hello and welcome to the Western Front.* According to Knowles, we're supposed to say that we're happy to make the "ultimate sacrifice" for our beloved country, or some such rot. That'll make our families feel better, won't it?

Dying in battle is choked with euphemisms, I've discovered. It would be funny if it wasn't so pathetic. They make it sound peaceful. Pleasant, almost. A well-aimed shot to the heart and you waft gracefully to the ground, your eyes nicely closed and arms already crossed over your chest. Amen and thanks for trying.

I've not been here long, but I saw through that comfortable lie within five minutes. This battle has been going on for months, and the men who've died instantly are lucky. Most aren't so fortunate. Their dying has been drawn-out and messy.

Knowles says something or other that's intended to give us heart, I imagine, but his words are drowned by the thunder. It's a storm made by men—from shellfire, flying in both directions. We've been transported to the front line from the reserve trench and the bombardment that always precedes an infantry attack is in full force. Our enemy, out of sight across the craters and thickets of barbed wire of No Man's Land, is returning the shellfire, waiting for ours to stop: a helpful signal that we are about to go over the top.

Two weeks ago, when we boarded the train at the huge military camp at Étaples to journey to the Front, we were full of bravado—sounding off about giving Kaiser Bill a good kicking. I was among the most boastful.

It wasn't long before the rumbling began, distant at first, but getting closer and louder. So what? We weren't scared of thunder; not the natural sort, anyway. This wasn't natural.

As the noise swelled, the landscape we were travelling through became more bleak. We passed villages where every house was devastated by shellfire, but people were still living in them. I saw two children—girls in clean pinafores—playing with a hoop outside a roofless brick shell. There was no glass left in the windows, yet fresh yellow curtains still billowed and a woman leant out of one of them to wipe the frame. Chickens were pecking for worms in gardens and streets. Pigs foraged. Cows were milked. Not much further down the line we saw forests blasted to matchwood and rain-filled shell craters so vast, you could go across them by boat. All the while, the thunder grew and grew.

When we stopped at the Belgian town of Ypres, I wondered whether we had been whisked to hell by some mischievous demon. It had been laid waste. An archaic phrase, but the right one. Centuries-old houses and the once-imposing medieval Cloth Hall were now charred and spiky ruins. Beyond it was a thin, green-tinted cloud that was, a seasoned sergeant told us, the final remnant of a gas attack.

"Don't worry: there's not enough to harm anyone," he reassured us as we exchanged worried glances. "I daresay you'll get used to it, soon enough."

Ypres wasn't deserted, though. A market was in full swing and housewives examined potatoes and apples. Tommies like us were stretching their legs for a few hours before continuing their journey, gathered in noisy groups outside half-destroyed bars, swigging beer and wine in spite of the early hour. Horses and motor cars picked their tedious way through the rubble-strewn streets. And still the rumble of battle was getting louder.

By the time we reached the reserve trenches, the thunder terrified us and my bravado had shrivelled. It's monstrous; the clash of warring gods. First, it echoes in your brain. Then, your eyeballs begin to vibrate. Then, it surges through your whole body, and into the trembling ground. It's not just the water in the shell holes that vibrates, it's the mud that clogs your boots and legs and everything else. In the end, you *are* the noise.

Now, we only register the thunder when it stops.

Corporal Knowles is trying to grow a moustache. He thinks it makes him look manly and imposing, something certainly needs to. The moustache seems to quiver on his upper lip. It looks like a furry caterpillar with a touch of mange. It's adding nothing to his masculine image and I should know; I'm the expert. Maybe I should offer him a few tips.

"Of course, these letters are just a formality," Knowles clears his throat and repeats his words more loudly. "I'm positive that they won't be needed. In fact, I'd lay money on it." I assume he's talking about gambling a shilling or two, not his life savings. That would be the height of stupidity.

There is an unexpected break in the shellfire and his voice blares out like a braying donkey.

"You can expect minimal resistance in the morning. The hard work's already been done for you. Their wire will be in shreds and the enemy will be grateful to surrender to you. It'll be a walkover!"

I lift my eyebrows and wipe my nose on my sleeve. "A walkover." The "walk" part is certainly right. We've been ordered to *walk* towards the enemy trench. If we run, we risk being shot by our own men, for failing to obey orders. I wonder if our commanders are in cahoots with the Germans; they seem equally dedicated to wiping us out.

The silence is scornful. I like the way Corporal Knowles bundles the entire German army on the Western Front into one figure. One enemy. That sounds much more manageable. One enemy should be easy to deal with. Anyone here should be capable of that. Even the rookies. Even me.

Knowles hands out pencils and sheets of paper made limp by relentless rain.

We slosh through yellow mud to collect them. Judging by the stench, it must have seeped in from the latrine trench. I perch on a wooden firing step and stare at my paper. What do I say? When you're faced with the prospect of putting down your final thoughts, no words seem adequate.

And who do I write to? Not Father; that would ruin everything and, anyway, he and I have never had much to say to each other. It will have to be my twin. The other half of me.

Dear N. What to say? I don't want to instil guilt. This was my idea, after all. I wore down every objection. I always do. I've always been the stronger one.

How are you? I hope you're settling into nursing life nicely. You'll make a MAH-vellous nurse, you know.

That's our shared word. Between us, things have always been MAH-vellous, even when they're not.

Now comes the hard bit. *Tomorrow morning, we're going over the top. We've been told that Fritz has had enough, so it shouldn't be too tricky. Let's hope our generals know what they're talking about.*

Better leave it at that. If I criticise the powers that be—suggest that no one believes for a second that we'll stroll unopposed into the German trenches—it'll be redacted. The censors watch like hawks for anything that might damage morale at home. I would also draw attention to myself, and that's the last thing I want. N will know to read between the lines; we've been communicating like this for as long as I can remember.

In a strange way, I'm looking forward to it. In the end, action is better than hanging around, thinking about what's coming, getting worked up over it. I've always believed that. It's better to live something once in reality than a thousand times in your head.

The words are coming more easily now.

In case the worst happens, (what was I saying about euphemisms?) *I want you to know that nothing was your fault. We both know that I pushed you into certain things. It was all my idea. My responsibility. And I'm happy with it.*

I'm glad things turned out this way. It's for the best, for both of us. Do you remember the very first time we dressed as a soldier and a nurse? That was ten years ago! Can you believe it? Ever since then, we've been preparing for these roles. We're destined for them, and you can't fight destiny.

I'm afraid it will be up to you to break the news to Father if I don't come back. I don't envy you that task. Whatever you choose to tell him (and I'll leave that up to you), we both know that he won't understand. I suggest that you say whatever makes your life easiest. To hell with the truth.

I blow on my chilled fingers. I'm finding it hard to hold my pencil and I grasp it more firmly. I don't want the lads to think I'm shaking.

Be happy and, with a bit of luck, I'll be seeing you soon.

Your loving brother (ha ha) A. xx

The ending might raise a censor's eyebrow but they'll just assume we're not that close. Or that we're not actually related at all—friends rather than siblings. I'm positive that they won't guess the truth.

I address the letter to Miss N Mullins, c/o The Royal Pavilion Hospital, Brighton. Around me, men's heads are lifting. They're looking but not seeing as they grasp for words to their wives, sweethearts, mothers. All those women, left at home to worry and wait; to dread the sound of someone in uniform knocking at their door.

Others try to catch someone's eye. If they succeed, they crack a joke. We greet even the lamest ones with loud laughter. I understand why. We all think that if we smile and joke like normal, Death will pass over us in search of those who are resigned to their fate. Men like that make easier prey.

I look at my pal, Liam. He has straight black hair and a nose like a bird of prey. I flick him an approximation of a smile and wonder who he's writing to. One of his girls at home, probably. He's a bit of a Jack the Lad. In Aldershot, if there was a group of Tommies eyeing up a barmaid, it was always Liam who sauntered over and got her smiling and chatting.

I try not to think about that too much.

Liam is a conscript, like me, but his experiences of life have left him better prepared for war than most of us. He's London born, a few years older than me and what Father would label "something of a ruffian". His mother and father are market traders and not exactly outstanding examples of parenthood, from the little he's said about them. They knocked him around a great deal and when he was twelve, he ran away for a while. He went travelling with a fair and got into lots of what he calls "scraps and scrapes". He went back after he'd learned to handle himself and his parents never touched him again.

We're so different: chalk and cheese, as Gertie would say. Liam is that rare being: a person who seems completely at ease with himself. I wonder what that must feel like. I often find myself wondering why he bothers with me, but I'm glad that he does. In my old life, I was never very good at making friends. The new me seems to get the best of everything. But I knew there would be a price to pay, and now it's time to pay it.

I get up and walk over to Corporal Knowles, drop my letter into his hands and walk off without a word.

Now there's only the night to get through.

And everything that the dawn brings with it.

CHAPTER TWO

Cambridge, Easter Saturday 1907

"I can't, Nina. Don't make me…" Alfie's voice trails off into a tremor.

"Yes, you can. Look—it's easy! Watch me!"

We're at home, on the stairs. I'm on step number seven, which is exactly halfway up. Alfie is crouching behind me on step number nine.

I flap my arms and make cawing noises. I don't exactly know what kind of sound eagles make, but that doesn't matter. It's a rainy day and I'm bored. After being shooed out of the kitchen by Gertie, our maid, who's up to her neck in dough and chicken feathers, I've decided that we should play at being eagles.

"Just like the painting in the dining room," I coax Alfie. "Here I go!"

I throw myself off the stair and for the briefest moment I'm soaring through the air. I land with a jarring thud on Mother's precious Persian rug. I skid a little, rucking up the rug's soft green weave. The landing hurts one of my knees, which is already covered in purple bruises, but I stand up without rubbing it. That might put Alfie off, or prompt him to rush downstairs and fuss over me, offer to fetch the arnica or make a compress. I make sure to straighten the rug. Mother treasures it, which is why it's on display at the bottom of the stairs, where every visitor gets to admire it. I don't understand this. A rug is a rug.

"Nothing to it," I claim, fixing Alfie with my gaze. With his wavy red hair, so like my own, he reminds me of a scared fox cub that's been left to fend for itself. "Your go."

Alfie creeps down a single stair and stops. His eyes never leave mine. With utmost reluctance he takes another step. Beneath his smattering of freckles, his skin is pale.

"Off you go." I give him a smile to encourage him. I'm confident that my twin can do this. After all, I've just done it, and we're so similar.

Alfie shuffles forward.

"Will I be all right?" he asks me.

"Of course. I wouldn't let you do it, otherwise!"

He nods. He trusts me.

He's bending his knees and stretching out his arms when the door to the kitchen opens. It's Gertie, red faced and perspiring. She's pushing damp strands of salt and pepper hair back into her top knot when she spots Alfie and me. Her hands drop and she starts forward.

"Lord above and Lucifer below, *what are you doing?* Alfred, do you want to kill yourself? Nina, you don't have to tell me—this was your idea."

She glares at me, which doesn't daunt me in the least. Gertie loves us and her bark is always worse than her bite.

"Do you want to disturb your ma? You know she's not feeling too chipper… What would your father say if he came home and found you like this?"

These are two very different questions with very different answers. The easiest is the one about Father. There is absolutely no chance that he'll come home and find us. He's far too busy, selling ribbons and buttons and fake flowers and other bits of nonsense to the wives and daughters of Cambridge dons. The only time he has ever left the shop early was last year, when his mother—our Grandmother Mullins—died. On that occasion he'd taken exactly a week off, "to maintain the correct conventions," as he put it, but he was back at the shop as soon as he decently could, looking dapper in his new black mourning suit.

The question of Mother is harder to think about, and even harder to answer. Mother has been unwell for a long time and she seems to be fading into the background of our lives. Although she insists on joining us for dinner every evening, she eats hardly anything. Even Alfie and I, wrapped in our bubble of mutual self-absorption, have noticed this. We choose not to talk about it.

As for whether we *want* to disturb her, my honest answer would be yes. She spends so much time in her room, and when she emerges Father takes most of her attention. A little more recognition of our existence would be welcome. I even miss the way she used to shake her head when I embroiled Alfie in some scrape or other.

"Nature seems to have gone topsy-turvy with you two," she'd say with a sigh. "Or did the fairies swap you at birth? I think you're changelings!"

But that's not the answer Gertie's hoping for, so I keep my mouth shut.

Gertie sighs.

"Go up to your rooms, the pair of you. Find something *quieter* to do."

She turns and plunges back into the kitchen, leaving behind her unique aroma of sweat and spices.

"That's a shame. I was just about to jump," Alfie claims.

I don't contradict him, although I would if it was anyone else. Instead, I stomp up the stairs, past the gilt-framed photographs of Mother and Father, and the smaller ones of grim-faced Mullinses (many of them thankfully dead) and push open the door to my room. Alfie trails after me.

After sitting on my bed, kicking my legs and feeling wronged for a few minutes, I get up and head into our old nursery, next to Alfie's room. There's a wooden trunk in there, painted white but very scuffed. Our dressing up box. I lug it out of the nursery and along the landing, making an unholy scraping noise and scuffing the skirting. I cross my fingers that Gertie won't notice.

I drag it to a halt a couple of feet from my bed. Then I open the lid, turning over the contents and holding them up without much interest. I pull out a faded mauve silk gown—one of

Mother's cast-offs. I never like wearing this dress. It makes my springing red hair look too wild. Too strong.

For Alfie there's a soldier's tunic in heavy red wool. The twisted gold braiding on the shoulders reminds me of coiled snakes. I think it's wonderful, but Alfie's no keener on it than I am on the gown. Usually he ignores it, preferring the dusty old bowler hat that always seems to be right at the bottom of the trunk.

I look at the gown, with its missing buttons and its limp lace collar, and wrinkle my nose. Gertie's always telling me that I'm not a pretty sight when I pull this face.

"One day you'll get stuck like that. Then where will you be?" she says, shaking her head. But I don't care. I already know that pretty is something I'll never be.

Alfie inspects the soldier's outfit and dumps it on the floor without interest. He returns to the box and rummages around, in search of something more promising. He pulls out a ratty white feather boa and flourishes it in the air. When I giggle, he wraps it round his neck and strikes a stiff pose, like an outraged matron.

"You look MAH-vellous," I say. "Try something else."

He hesitates, shooting me an uncertain look. Then he grabs two strings of beads—one purple and one amber coloured. He drapes the purple beads around his neck and the amber ones around his forehead, looping them over his ears. They glitter against his hair.

"Beautiful," I say. He grins his usual grin and then seems to stop himself. He wrestles with the muscles in his mouth and the grin turns into a demure smile. Despite the fact that he looks so much like me—all elbows and freckles and pale skin—he's pretty. He gets up to close the bedroom door, then grabs the gown and steps into it.

"I feel wonderful!" he says, pulling the tight sleeves over his arms. "Your go."

I go straight for the soldier's tunic. I've always been drawn to the bright crimson, brighter than a young girl like me is allowed to wear, and to the brass buttons with their little emblems of crossed rifles. There are even a couple of toy medals dangling on the front.

As soon as I slip into the tunic and button it up, I feel different. Strong and free. I could conquer the world. I give a smart salute, which sets the medals swinging and jangling.

"Ready for duty, Sah!" I click my heels together. Then I pull the wooden rifle out of the dressing up box and aim it at Alfie. I'm surprised at how heavy it feels, how unfamiliar. I don't think I've ever held anything like it.

"Surrender, villain!"

Alfie's hands shoot into the air. "Spare me," he flusters. "I'm a noble nurse, back from tending the victims of the treacherous Boers!"

The Boer War finished a few years earlier and my hero is the young soldier-aristocrat Winston Churchill, who made a death-defying escape from a Boer prisoner of war camp. Alfie's heroines are Mrs Seacole and Florence Nightingale who is half dead and, according to newspapers, as cranky as an old nanny goat.

We have a grand time. I march around the room and then kneel at my window to snipe at people on the way to the Botanical Gardens. I take extra careful aim at Miss Shelby, the miserable excuse for a woman who lives next door but one. She recently reported me to Mr Jakes, the sweet shop owner, after she saw me accidentally drop an extra humbug into my little paper bag.

"Bang! Enemy disposed of! Her guts are all over the pavement!"

Alfie's nose wrinkles.

"That's horrible, Nina!"

I give a wicked smile.

"You're the nurse. Get down there, pick them up and stuff them back inside her! You can sew her up with your bootlaces." I know the idea will make him go green.

When Alfie has recovered his composure, he glides around like a swan on a still lake and then sinks gracefully onto my bed. He throws me an excited smile.

"We really *are* changelings!"

Before I can reply, we hear the scullery door open and slow, heavy footsteps approaching the stairs. Panic surges through my body—Gertie mustn't catch us like this. I don't know how we know this. We just do. If she sees what we're wearing, Gertie will tell Mother, who will look helpless and wait for Father to come home. And then we'll be in real trouble. Father hates anything that isn't usual.

We're tearing at our clothing. In my hurry I pull a loose button off the tunic. It rolls under my bed. Then I turn to help Alfie, who is just throwing the last string of beads back into the box when the door opens and Gertrude's broad face appears.

"You pair all right? You're mighty quiet," Gertie huffs. She's looking from Alfie to me, and back again.

"Of course, Gertie," I say, sweetly. "We're playing quietly, as you asked us to. So that we don't disturb Mama." I give a saintly beam.

"And I'm just tidying up. To save you a chore," Alfie says.

Gertrude blinks. "Easter truly is a time for miracles," she says, turning away. We hear her heavy tread on the stairs again.

I look at Alfie and Alfie looks at me. We smile at the same time.

"We'll do it again," I promise. "Soon."

CHAPTER THREE

Near Passchendaele Village, Belgium, September 1917

"This is madness! They'll get us all killed. I thought that was Fritz's job, not our own bloody commanders." The speaker is a weary-eyed man of about thirty called Walter Warmsley, the veteran of several battles. He is shaking his head in disbelief.

It's 4.30 and a timid light is heralding the start of the day on which some of us will die. None of us have slept. We haven't tried. We've been waiting for the command to attack, doing our best to ignore the knot of sick dread fizzing in our stomachs.

Because death feels so imminent, I find myself remembering the day that Mother died. Her murmured request for me to look after Alfie. I've been doing that ever since.

And I still am. That's why I'm here, now, about to go into battle, about to face something I can't even imagine.

There comes a moment when fear turns to desire to get on with whatever you're dreading, when the compulsion to do it and get it over with becomes almost overwhelming. For me, that time has come and gone several hours ago. But still, we're here.

There's a penknife in my trouser pocket. Without taking it out, I manage to unclasp it and dig it into my leg. Warm blood trickles down my chilled skin. I concentrate on the pain; it's a relief from my thoughts. How much longer will I be able to wait?

Now Knowles is telling us that the attack has been postponed until 7.30.

"It'll be broad daylight. We'll be sitting ducks," Warmsley gasps. He is clenching his fists, as if he's having difficulty stopping himself from grabbing Knowles by the front of his tunic and throttling him.

Knowles has no answer for Warmsley. He just rubs his feeble moustache and gives a sick smile.

I turn away and wonder how I can survive three more hours at the mercy of my imagination. I try with all my might to think of something positive, something or someone good in my life.

Well, there's Alfie, of course—the reason I'm here. And Gertie, bless her heart. The only other person I care about is Aunt Julia—staunch and outspoken. Determined to do what she believes is right, even if others don't agree. I'm glad she has been a part of my life

Would I have had the courage to become a solider without their influence? I don't think so. And now I am waiting to do what soldiers exist for.

Booze is passed around and the men chug it. I do too. It's disgusting. Like drinking paraffin.

"Steady on, Mullins. This is rum. Powerful stuff." Liam smacks me roughly on the back. "We know your tolerance of the demon drink leaves something to be desired."

I smother a cough and swig again. Around me I see pale cheeks beginning to flush. Eyes become brighter. Someone tries an old joke, and suddenly it's the funniest thing I've ever heard. Laughter spurts out of me. I have just enough presence of mind to ensure that it's lower than my real laugh.

This will be a good time to visit the latrine trench, I decide, while everyone else is downing the rum and hoping for more. I've learned to grab such opportunities whenever they come up. The other chaps are used to my shyness about my body and they rag me about it.

"Mullins doesn't want to show off his lily-white goolies. He's as shy as a girlie." That's the usual kind of comment I get. I welcome it. Let them think I'm scared of the sight of my own body. That's a lot easier for them to accept than the truth.

I return, leaving it late to button my fly, the way a man does when he's surrounded by other men and there are no women whose delicate sensibilities have to be considered.

"Been to the shitter again, Mullins? You must be scared. You'll be half a stone lighter by the time we go over the top!"

The speaker is Albert Lacey. He was at school with Alfie for a time. Although they had quite a bit in common, they were never friends. Just the opposite. Lacey's survival tactic was to try to divert attention away from his own shortcomings by highlighting other people's, and Alfie was one of his favourite targets. My brother was quicker-witted than Lacey, and usually able to deflect his attacks. Not always though. Lacey left St George's before Alfie, who was heartily relieved to see the back of him.

When Lacey pushed his way over and introduced himself at the embarkation point in Dover, wringing my hand as if we were the best of friends, my stomach turned over. I'd seen him once before, but I couldn't place him until he told me his name. Then I remembered and took a step back. Fortunately, he decided that my failure to recognise him was due to how much he'd changed since his time at St George's. Has he really forgotten the horrible things he did to Alfie? That they were deadly enemies?

He was a nuisance for a while, hanging around, grateful for a familiar face, which was the opposite to how I felt about it. I started giving him the cold shoulder and, in the end, he'd got the message and left me alone. I could tell that he resented it, though.

His remark rouses a few sniggers. Lacey stands just a bit taller than me. He has thin, yellow hair which he parts in the exact centre of his head. You can see his pink scalp glistening between the strands. He also has little, widely-spaced teeth, like a toddler's or the rose-cheeked girl who advertises Bunter's Tooth Preparations. For some reason his smile makes me shudder. He's such a squirt that I'd feel sorry for him, if he hadn't made my brother's school life a misery. But now he's trying to take out his terror on me and I can't let him get away with it. I've got to nip it in the bud.

I see Liam frown and fold his arms. He opens his mouth to say something—to protect me, I think—but that's no good. If I get known within the first weeks as a chap who hides behind his friends, I'll be doomed. It's up to me to sort this out.

"Then I'll still be a stone heavier than you, won't I?" I curl my lip, looking him up and down. "Why don't you send home for some Mellin's Food? That might bulk you out a bit."

When we were children, Gertie always tried to get us to take Mellin's Food for Infants and Invalids "to build you up". We were neither and we both complained noisily. In the end we simply refused to take it. It wasn't so much the taste that I disliked, although Alfie said it tasted like cod liver oil with cabbage stirred in. It was the revolting picture on the front of the bottle. Fat, naked cherubs with tiny *butterfly wings* merrily wending their way to the top of a bottle of Mellin's, presumably desperate for a large dollop of the stuff. I liked to imagine an altercation between them: snarling cherubs shoving each other out of the way so that they could move to the front of the queue more quickly.

My comment does the trick. An ugly blush stains Lacey's cheeks as laughter rings out. He won't forgive me and I don't want him to. He'll think twice about picking on me again.

At least I hope he will.

CHAPTER FOUR

Cambridge, May 1910

I t's late spring and we are 11 years old. Gertie has just woken me to tell me that I'm staying home from school today. Alfie too. Normally, I'd be pleased. I hate my "school" and I'm hugely envious of Alfie for going to St George's, a proper school right in the centre of Cambridge

My education is in the hands of an ineffectual spinster called Miss Wren, and we're constantly at war. From time to time she sends letters to my parents bewailing my wild behaviour. On the last such occasion my mother, who seldom leaves her room anymore and seems to have diminished a little more each time we see her, simply sighed before placing the letter in Father's hands and closing her eyes. Father turned his freezing gaze on me, looking me up and down as if I was utterly beyond comprehension. I had been reading *War of the Worlds* and I thought that H. G. Wells' invading Martians couldn't have looked less sympathetically towards their human prey than my Father did at that moment.

"I know better than to ask you why your behaviour is so appalling," he said. His voice didn't get any louder. That's not his style. "I suppose I should take some comfort from the knowledge that you would at least *try* to behave if you knew how. But such knowledge is beyond you. You are a savage. Go to your room. Get out of my sight until I can bear to look at you again."

I looked to Mother, hoping for a word of support or understanding. It didn't come. She didn't even open her eyes. She must have felt especially ill that night, and there I was, making her feel worse.

"Mother, I'm sorry," was all I said before turning to leave the room. I meant that I was sorry for exacerbating her illness, not for my behaviour. To Father, I didn't say a single word.

In return, I plotted revenge on Miss Wren. In the past my plans had been simple, like the time I left a toad in her desk drawer, causing her to shriek like a banshee when she opened it to extract her useless lace handkerchief. My idea on this occasion was more elaborate and involved lacing her tea (which she drank from a floral teacup the size of a thimble) with powdered glass. Our newspapers had been full of coverage of a sensational poisoning trial involving this commodity, and I was eager to see if it really worked. That plot, like most of my more elaborate ones, came to nothing, which was probably fortuitous: the poisoner in the newspaper was convicted and hanged.

One of the rare occasions that Alfie and I fell out was the time I conceived a plan to take his place at St George's for a day. I had already looked through his timetable to choose the day when the lessons were most to my liking. Thursday looked best. Alfie had double Physical Education on Thursdays, and I was desperate to try it. Miss Wren's idea of Physical Education was to dress us up like china dolls and make us hop and skip around a maypole, trailing a bright streamer that was attached to the top of it. Even that only happened once a year. For the rest of it, we were expected to sit around on our rear ends, pretending that we were too delicate to move.

"You'd love a day off, especially on Physical Education day. It's football this term, isn't it? I'd love to play football...." It was Sunday evening and I was eyeing up his sports jersey, already knowing that it would fit me just right.

"No."

"No? What do you mean, no?" I shook my head, wondering if I had misheard.

"It's not right."

"What do you care about that? We're always doing things that aren't right."

"That's different. That's important. This isn't."

"It's important to me!"

But Alfie wasn't budging.

"Nina, think about it. I've been playing football for years. I'm not that good at it, but how am I going to explain the fact that I've suddenly forgotten all the rules, and don't know where I'm supposed to be standing and where I'm allowed to go? And how are you going to know who everyone is, or how to get from the science lab to the changing rooms or the Geography room? You'll make me look like a proper Charlie. I'll be a laughing stock, and I'm close enough to that already. It would make my life unbearable."

I flushed with anger, and the fact that I realised he was right didn't help at all.

"It's alright for you! You do interesting things every day. All I get to do is learn the French word for rolling pin and listen to Miss Wren reciting Wordsworth and Elizabeth Barrett Browning in that dreary voice of hers! It's not fair!"

I was working myself up into a red rage, storming around my bedroom, fists clenching and unclenching.

"I never ask you to do anything for me, but the one time I do—"

Alfie got off my bed and stood in front of me.

"If it went wrong—if you got caught—it would mean the end of everything. No more escape into our other selves, ever again. Just because you're bored and you want to play football. If you ever need me—really, really need me, not just to help you with something stupid—I'll be there for you. Nothing would stop me. I'm sorry that your life is dull and that you have to do so many things you hate. Life isn't fair for either of us. Maybe, one day, we'll do something about it. But when we do it, let's do it for a good reason, not just because you're fed up with William Wordsworth."

I hated him for being right, so I stormed out into the garden to throw stones over the hedge towards Miss Shelby's cucumber frames. It took three days of frigid silence on my part, and patient smiles on Alfie's, before I calmed down. I trudged to his bedroom, where he had been going after school while he waited for me to see sense, and entered without knocking.

"Sorry."

Alfie was lying on his bed, studying one of Father's catalogues of frills and furbelows. He jumped up and hugged me.

"Dear Nina," he beamed, "I'm so glad you're talking to me again. The silence in the dining room was giving me a headache. Let's go and ask Gertie for some almonds. It's baking day today, so she's bound to have some left over."

In an instant our quarrel was forgotten and we were the best of friends again.

"By the way," he said, as we were jostling downstairs, "what *is* the French word for rolling pin?"

Now, on this spring morning, with Gertie looking at me through reddened eyes, and Alfie standing behind her with a look of terror on his face, I'd give anything to be sitting in Miss Wren's stuffy schoolroom, pretending to listen to her twittering in bad French. I can think of only one reason for keeping us from school. Something serious is happening, and it has to be Mother. We haven't seen her for days, and Father is looking even sterner than usual.

Alfie joins me in the dining room, pushing unbuttered toast around his plate. We've been forgotten. We drift upstairs and stare at the walls, listening to the murmurs coming from Mother's room.

After what seems like many hours, Gertie appears.

"You're to come and say goodbye. Then I'm to take you out." Her voice is flat and exhausted.

"What?" I jump up. "You can't expect us to go out. Not if she's …"

Gertie gives a weary shrug and says nothing.

Mother's room smells horrible. Vomit and sour sweat from being confined for too long in too small a space. As well as Mother and Gertie, Dr Wain is there, and a nurse. And Father, of course. The heat in here could knock over an elephant. I move towards the window to let in some fresh air.

Father is sitting on a corner of Mother's bed, head bowed, unshaved. He is still wearing yesterday's creased shirt: almost a capital crime in his eyes. When I get up to open the window, he tuts and drags me away without a word of explanation.

"Kiss your mother," he says. "For the final time."

"C-can we talk to her?" I'm struggling to control my sobs.

"No."

I try to remember the last thing Mother said to us. It should have been something full of meaning, something to carry with us for the rest of our lives—"look after each other" or "face life fighting."

Her words come back to me, from sometime last week: "Don't slam the door, Nina. The noise makes my head ache so."

That's not enough, not by a long way. We need more: something to remember when we're lying awake at night, missing her.

I've never liked Doctor Wain. Once he'd dosed me with cod liver oil to calm my wildness, and I'd retaliated by throwing it up all over his shoes. He has no right to look so neat and calm, not while our mother is dying. He should be horror-struck; full of pity for the family she is about to abandon. I launch myself at him, pummelling his chest through his starched-up jacket.

"You stupid, stupid man. She's not dying …"

Father's hands close over my shoulders and he hauls me backwards.

"You're disgracing us, Nina. Behave yourself, or you'll be sent out."

He releases me as if I'm unpleasant to the touch, like a slug or a piece of gone-off meat. I look up at him, hoping for a spark of kindness or concern in his eyes, but I've seen warmer gazes on a fishmonger's slab. I wish that it could be him lying there, struggling to breathe and about to leave his family forever.

Mother's eyes open and she stares at me as if she is trying to remember where we'd met.

"…Nina…" I have to lean very close to hear her. Her lips are flaking and her breath is stale. I try not to flinch from it.

"… Alfie…please…" Her voice trails into nothingness and her eyes close again.

Alfie…please… What did she mean? It must be important. These are her final words.

Biting my bottom lip and tasting the rusty blood, I take Alfie's hand and lead him to the bed. I lean over and kiss Mother's cheek. As I draw back, I see that I've left a red smear there. I reach out to wipe it away, but hesitate. Perhaps Father might allow it to remain there, a physical reminder of me to take to her grave. I dismiss the thought immediately. It won't happen; people would find it peculiar and Father lives and dies by what people think.

Then it's Alfie's turn and I hear the catch in his breath as his lips touch her.

"Good girl. Good boy." Gertie never praises us. "Now go downstairs and wait for me. The doctor thinks some fresh air will do you good."

We leave the room like sleepwalkers. Mother's words are running round and round my head. *Alfie…please…Alfie…please…* She must be asking me to look after him. Her dying wish.

Gertie appears. With a last glance upstairs, we drift through the porch and out into the heartless, sunlit world.

An omnibus rumbles past, too close to the pavement. Alfie is in front of me, wandering along in a daze at the very edge of the path. I grab his shirt and haul him back to safety. I am looking after him as Mother asked me to. She'd entrusted the task to me on her deathbed. It's my sacred duty to carry out her wish.

The omnibus stops a little way up the road. I drag Alfie and Gertie onto it. We sit in silence and get off in the centre of Cambridge. We drift from shop window to shop window, looking but not seeing the wealth of goods on display. All I can see are the reflections of two pale waifs and, between them, the solidly comforting figure of Gertie.

I realise that all the light seems to have leeched out of the day, and look up at a sky heavy with storm and darkness. Perhaps it's God's way of showing sympathy for Mother.

At that moment the heavens open and fat drops of rain splash on my upturned face. God's tears, Gertie always says. Mother has just died—somehow I know it. The thought makes me gasp and hot tears mingle with the water already streaming down my face. Gertie hurries us over to a shop with a striped awning. The rain is so heavy that water bulges in it, weighing it down until it spills over, splashing passers-by.

I don't know how I am supposed to behave. Alfie is looking at me, his face as wet as mine. He needs me to show the way, to take control, as I always have done. But there's simply nothing I can do that will make things any better.

I mouth "sorry" at him. Gertie's lips are trembling too. She looks from me to Alfie, and catches us both into a hug that threatens to suffocate us. Neither of us wants to break away, though. I think I'm not the only one who realises that from now on, affection is going be in short supply.

It's evening by the time we're standing outside our front door, and the gloomiest thing in the whole gloomy street is our house. Every curtain is drawn so that not the tiniest sliver of light can escape.

Gertie fumbles with the doorknocker, which is already muffled in black crepe and white ribbons. Who's done that? Surely not my father. It must have been Miss Shelby, the nosy old cow. She's been circling the house like a vulture for weeks now, hoping to get inside for the death. She must have made this elaborate mourning decoration in advance. If she was here now, I'd force her mouth open and ram the ribbons down her skinny throat.

"Now, you must be *quiet*," Gertie emphasises, her gaze on me.

With a glare that manages to be fierce and sympathetic at the same time, she leads us into the silent house.

CHAPTER FIVE

Cambridge, August, 1910

The summer passes in stultifying misery. After the funeral, at which the assembled Mullinses cluster around Father, who is white-faced and rigid with grief, but barely acknowledge me and Alfie, we are confined to the house. Father decrees that we must wear black at all times and that we should take care not to "engage in anything that will take your minds away from your dear mother. Life is short and precious. That should be at the forefront of your thoughts."

We are allowed to read books, as long as they are not fiction which, I assume, he thinks would lead us into levity. I read of historic battles—Agincourt and Crecy—and dream about being a chain-mailed knight. Alfie reads Mother's books on gardening, and learns about the secret language of flowers.

"That posy of flowers that Father threw…into the grave. I wonder if he knew what they meant? The cornflowers— Mother's favourites—mean delicacy, so I suppose that's all right. But those anemones, they mean forsaken! And the blue columbines mean desertion or folly! He can't have known!"

The idea of a secret language appeals to me and I lean over Alfie's shoulder.

"He'd have been mortified! Look—" I point further down the page. "Ivy—that's what he should have chosen. Ivy for marriage, fidelity and friendship."

Alfie flicks over a few pages

"Marigolds. Grief and despair. They would've been a good choice."

Our heads are close together as we peruse the little book. I'm imagining interesting ways of using this new language. It adds another layer to the secrecy that rules certain aspects of our lives. I must acquire a copy of my own; Alfie can keep this one, and then we will always be able to communicate with each other, even at times when words aren't possible.

My eyes linger for a while on something called glasswort. Its meaning is pretension. Glasswort looks succulent but spiky. I read that it thrives in inhospitable soil and salty marshes. It acquired its name because the ashes can be used in the making of glass. *Spiky. Inhospitable. Pretentious. Brittle. The perfect plant for Father.*

After two weeks, Father returns to work, dressed from head to foot in mourning. It's not the suit he wore when Grandmother Mullins died last year; he has bought a new one. I don't doubt that his grief is sincere: there was always a bond so tight between Mother and Father that we were left feeling like outsiders, but it isn't enough to make him forget his own appearance, or to quell his urge to progress the family business.

After a month has passed, we are allowed to walk but not run in the Botanical Gardens, still dressed in black. Other children look at us as if we are plague-carriers and steer well clear of us.

Finally, on this humid August morning, he has decreed that we may leave off our mourning clothes and go into town.

"As long as you remember to behave with decorum," he says, looking at me, not Alfie. "I will be asking Gertie to report to me. Your mother is still dead, you know."

As if we needed reminding of that.

Both Alfie and I wear clothes based on sailors' uniforms, with square, white collars and blue jackets. Alfie has blue trousers, while I have a tiered blue skirt with a white petticoat poking out underneath. Usually, I would envy Alfie the freedom of his trousers, but after the heavy black mourning we've been wearing through the long, tedious summer months, these feel as if I'm wearing clouds.

With Gertie at our heels, muttering about the work she will have to catch up on when we return, we climb on an omnibus and head into town.

Now that we have been freed, we don't know what to do with ourselves. We window-shop, taking care to steer clear of Mullins & Son. We're mildly interested in the new books in the windows of Bowes & Bowes, and stare without enthusiasm at displays of lace blouses and striped blazers and straw boaters in Parmetter's.

"What now?" Alfie asks, looking at me, not Gertie.

I look around, at a loss. Across the road is a little courtyard, illuminated by dozens of pink and yellow lights. There's an open door and beyond it, a brightly lit corridor. People are streaming inside—men, women and children. They are excited, laughing and talking, removing their hats and folding their parasols. They seem so full of life. After our gloomy summer, that is irresistible.

"What's that?" I point. "Could we—?"

Gertie hesitates. Her face is full of doubt.

"Well, your father wouldn't approve, but Lord knows, you could do with some jollity. If it takes your minds off…"

Her decision is made. She forges across the road and we follow in her wake.

Just outside the entrance to the courtyard is a group of women, only six of them but they're making enough noise for double that number, singing at the top of their voices:

Forward sister women!
Onward ever more,
Bondage is behind you,
Freedom is before…

The tune is "Onward Christian Soldiers" and they sing it like warriors marching into battle. They carry drooping cloth banners. *Votes for women! Deeds not words!*

A man in a cloth cap is heckling them.

"Go home to your husbands! If any man will have you, that is. You belong in bloody jail!"

"Given the choice between prison and marriage to a man like you, bloody jail sounds like bloody paradise!" an elderly woman retorts after looking down her nose at the heckler. The rest of her group and a few spectators cheer her.

I gasp and peer at her. Ladies don't swear or answer back to strange men.

"Bloody…bloody…bloody," I mouth the word to myself. It feels like a challenge to the world. I like it.

The woman who had answered back is tall and thin-faced, with a ramrod straight back and bedraggled grey hair which she doesn't bother to protect with a hat. She is wearing a sash around her torso in green, white and purple stripes. The words VOTES FOR WOMEN are emblazoned on it. Her dark eyes are sparkling with life.

The man mutters something and slinks off.

"Lord above, it's Miss Julia!" Gertie moans, ducking her head as if she doesn't want the extraordinary woman to notice her.

"Who?"

"Don't speak to her. Your father wouldn't like it," Gertie takes me and Alfie by the hands and drags us around the protesting women in a wide semi-circle.

I catch the woman's eye and she winks at me. I wink back.

"Don't tell your father you saw her." Gertie mutters.

"Who is she?"

"Your mother's aunt. The family black sheep. A Suffragette, seeking votes for women. She's at permanent loggerheads with your father."

Votes for women? Surely, women can vote? Why wouldn't they? I can't think of a single reason why men would be able to vote, but not women. No wonder she swears! She must be absolutely furious!

Inside the busy building, Gertie stops at a wooden counter and asks for tickets for the gallery. We follow the stream of people inside and climb a set of wide, bare stairs into an auditorium.

It feels like walking into the great hall of a lord's mansion, albeit one who has fallen on hard times. The auditorium is long and wide with a rounded ceiling, painted with scudding clouds in a blue summer sky. Half a dozen electric chandeliers glisten and glow like huge jewels, throwing shadows onto the flock-covered walls. It's only when you look more closely that you notice that the flock is peeling away and that the chandeliers are coated in dust and cobwebs.

From our seats in the gallery, I look down at twisted pillars, gilded gold, flanking each of the entrances into the stalls. Down there, people are sitting on bare benches. They are mainly young men with their arms wrapped around their sweethearts. Heavy, red curtains shield the back of the stage and give it an air of mystery. The place hums with humanity. Normally, I'm not a big one for crowds, but now all I want to do is be swallowed up by these carefree people. They are so alive.

"Gertie, what is this? A theatre?"

Gertie snorts.

"It's better than theatre. It's a music hall."

"It's a fairy-tale palace," Alfie gasps.

If it's a fairy-tale, it's a rowdy one. The audience is boisterous, singing, rustling paper bags of pungent snacks, calling and waving to distant friends.

Then, the little orchestra strikes up an indolent tune and the world turns upside down for me.

A man strolls onto the stage.

As the audience cheers and whistles, he saunters around the platform as if he owns it, as if he's got all the time in the world. He comes to a languid halt and leans on his long, silver-topped cane. He's slim and pale, with hair neatly parted to one side and oiled against his head. His lips are thin and fastidious. His eyes are well-spaced, with perfectly arched brows. There's no shadow of a beard on his chin.

He's wearing a black evening suit with a mauve silk waistcoat and matching gloves. His top hat gleams in the stage lighting. After tipping the hat to the audience, who respond with a shimmer of applause, he continues his stroll around the stage. He's perfectly at ease, cane balanced against one shoulder.

He stops again. Uses his cane to tip his hat backwards. The orchestra pauses with him.

Then he opens his mouth to sing.

I gasp.

This indolent society gent is no gent at all.

It's a woman.

My head starts swimming. Where are her curves? The rounded hips and swanlike bust that, for reasons that I can't begin to understand, are deemed so essential to women that they cripple themselves in corsets to acquire them? *HOW* can this woman get away with dressing as a man *in public*? Why aren't the audience yelling at her? Telling her to get off the stage and stop disgracing herself and her family? Alfie is craning around Gertie to look at me. We exchange a look of blank incomprehension.

"G-Gertie?" I stammer through dry lips. What I'm witnessing on this stage is turning my concept of the world—of my potential role in it—upside down.

"That's Vesta Tilley, that is," Gertie says, as if that explains everything.

I've never heard of Vesta Tilley, although Gertie's reaction suggests that I should have. I lean forward to examine her.

All of Vesta Tilley's songs are about the fun of being a man. I'm old enough to spot that every song is a little suggestive. She sings about going to the seaside and being tempted by the pretty girls and about the exploits of friends in Paris—gay Paree as Miss Tilley calls it. My favourite one, *I'm Following in Father's Footsteps*, makes the audience hoot with laughter as Vesta Tilley confesses that, just like her father, she can't resist a pretty face. By now they're singing along and stamping their feet at the suggestive bits.

As Vesta Tilley reaches the end of her performance, I spring to my feet and applaud for all I'm worth, not caring about the quizzical looks I'm attracting.

After a few seconds, Alfie pulls me back into my seat. "People are looking," he says. Even Miss Tilley notices. She turns towards me for a moment and gives me a bow. My heart sings.

The rest of the entertainment passes in a blur. My mind is whirling. A woman dressed as a man. And not only does she not have to hide it, she's applauded for it. Loved for it, even! If Vesta Tilley can do it, maybe I can too.

When the show has finished and we file out among the cheerful throng, I look around for Aunt Julia but she has gone, along with her friends. I hope that I'll get to see her again. This is a day I'll never forget: I've seen two extraordinary women who have shown me that there's much more to being female than I'd realised. I had thought that a woman's only prospects revolved around trying to be quiet and pretty and grateful for male attention.

I was wrong. The knowledge exhilarates me.

CHAPTER SIX

Near Passchendaele Village, Belgium, September 1917

It's 7.25 and the wait is nearly over.

With the dawn, our bombardment of the German trenches starts up again. Then, five minutes ago it stopped, which means the enemy knows that we're about to attack. It's the standard sign, Walter Warmsley tells us, understood by both sides. When the bombs stop, the infantry attack begins.

The rum has worn off.

Men I've shared jokes with are staring silently at nothing. I'm doing the same thing. Time has jumped forward. We're seeing ourselves walking across No Man's Land, shying away from shellfire and machine gun bullets. We're imagining the thud as the bullet hits. The searing pain; the tearing flesh. We're seeing ourselves falling. We're imagining oblivion.

I think about our childhood—Alfie and me: two peas in a pod, the leader and the follower. Whatever is about to happen, I'm glad it's me here and not him. I reckon I've got a chance of surviving this. Alfie would have none.

A minute to go and we're lined up by the ladders. Knowles is at the front followed by Venner, who sends frequent cheery postcards to his mum, "so that she doesn't worry too much." A few days ago, I asked him why he took such pains over them. He fills them with awful little poems and snippets of sunny news that bear no resemblance to reality.

"It's for Henry, my little brother, more than Mum," he'd told me. "He's a couple of years younger than me and he's not cut out for war. I'm trying not to scare him. The only good thing about being here is that it gives me the chance to help finish this off before he's old enough to be called up."

I'd warmed to him then and there. Someone else who was trying to protect his brother. Could he be right about the war ending soon?

After Venner comes his pal—the chap with the ears, whose name I can never remember. I'm fourth in line. Knowles has a whistle that he will blow at 7.30, to indicate that the attack has started. It drops from his lips. They're trembling so much that he can't keep hold of it.

Liam is looking at me. I try to smile, but the muscles around my mouth won't comply.

"Stick close to me if you can, Mullins." His voice sounds different—strained and unsure.

Despite my fear, I feel a flush of shame. Why should he think that he has to look out for me? Was I so completely hopeless during training?

I force my mind back to our time in Aldershot.

Every morning, we gather in the parade ground to practise drilling. We march and turn and form fours, again and again and again. It's brain numbing.

"Help me out, Mullins," Talbot gripes one morning, after we've been marching around the square and turning left and right for at least three hours. "Explain to me how this'll help us kill Huns?"

"Obvious, isn't it?" I mutter back, rolling my eyes. "They'll be so entranced by our pretty manoeuvres, they'll forget to fire at us!"

We're weeks into our training and we still haven't been allowed anywhere near a weapon.

"You wait, lads. You'll get your hands on a weapon when you're capable of not killing yourself with it. We wouldn't want to deny Fritz that pleasure," Sergeant Grimes replies when questioned, with a gleam in his eyes that I hope is humour.

Finally, we are allocated weapons and the heaviness of the SMLE rifle, with its solid wooden stock, surprises me. The act of testing its weight and nestling it into my shoulder takes me back to my bedroom, all those years ago, when I dressed up in a child's idea of a soldier's uniform and lifted Alfie's toy rifle for the first time. The sense of excitement and possibility is identical.

Once I've adjusted to the feel of the rifle, I'm pleased to discover that I'm not a bad shot. Not a natural like Abbott, the blacksmith, who never seems to miss a target, but still I can handle a gun.

No, I think now. I can look after myself and I refuse to be a millstone round Liam's neck. If he's worrying about me, he won't be concentrating on protecting himself and if anything happened to him...that is something I don't want to think about.

"Thanks, but you look out for yourself," I say, through lips that still feel frozen. I stick out a cold hand towards him. He grasps it and shakes it. I don't want to let it go. He opens his mouth to speak.

But there's no time for more.

Knowles sticks his whistle back in his mouth. He manages to control his lips sufficiently to blow it. It gives a pathetic little shrill, then peters out. He tries again and it lasts a bit longer. All along the trench I hear other whistles, some clear, others shaky.

"Good luck, men," Knowles calls over his shoulder as he climbs the ladder.

CHAPTER SEVEN

Cambridge, October 1910

Father's grief has changed him, and not for the better. He has always been remote, but he's started to look as if he doesn't understand what we are doing in his house. When he does notice us, it's to order us to be quiet—me especially. I have never felt that he loves me, but I begin to think that he positively hates me.

My suspicion is confirmed a few weeks after Mother's death. Angry and still aching with the need to see her, I storm into her room one evening. The stink of her deathbed has long been cleaned away, and the sweet scent of lily of the valley—her favourite perfume—has re-established itself. I slam the door behind me and take deep gulps of it, dashing away my useless tears with the back of one hand.

"Oh."

Father is lying on the bed, holding one of her dresses to his face, drenching it with his own tears. Stripped of all its careful layers of pretence, his face is a picture of naked grief.

He sits up, glaring at me.

"What are you doing here?"

Panic clutches at my heart.

"Sorry! I didn't know you were home. I– I just wanted to be with– to smell– I miss her so much!" It's a cry of anguish.

"Go. Leave me in peace. You don't belong in here."

I reach out one hand to him.

"But–Father– please, I–"

"You heard me. Go. GO!" The final word is a roar. For a second, I think he's going to leap to his feet and hit me.

I flee, gasping at the realisation that, to all intents and purposes, I am now an orphan.

Then on a Sunday, about five months after Mother's death, we are sitting at the dining room table, half-heartedly attempting a jigsaw puzzle.

The picture on the puzzle annoys me. It depicts a girl of about my age in a white lacy dress. There's a wide sash around her waist and her hair is streaming around her plump face. She is grinning like an idiot, sitting in front of a pond and dangling a length of wool with a twist of paper tied to one end in front of a bored black and white kitten, with a pointless pink bow tied around its neck.

I look at the girl and imagine her learning to knit, imagine her cooing over reels of ribbon and lace and being good all the time. I know I would hate her, and she would hate me back. I'd probably end up pushing her in the pond and freeing the kitten of its constricting ribbon.

Out of the corner of my eye, I half notice someone striding up to the front door. The person knocks with too much energy and we all look up. It's a Sunday, so Father isn't at work. He is poring over a catalogue of next season's fashions, making pencil rings around the items he wants to order for his shop.

Gertie trudges from the kitchen to open the door.

"Oh," she says, flustered. "I'm not sure—"

"There's nothing to be unsure about, Gertrude," a gruff woman's voice replies. "I've come to see Cedric. He's bound to be in because his shop is closed and he has no other life."

"Oh, lord." Father's face falls and he stands up as if he's been cornered by a man with a rifle. "Aunt Julia! What does she want?"

The outspoken lady outside the music hall! I jump to my feet as she barges into the dining room. She is carrying a large carpet bag and wearing a long, purple coat and a man's bowler hat, into the hatband of which she has stuck a few purple and white flowers. There's a lorgnette on a gold chain around her neck, which she lifts to examine Father as if he's a germ under a microscope.

"Cedric. My commiserations. You look miserable."

She's taller than him. Father grabs her claw and bends over it as if he's going to kiss it. She snatches it away.

"Don't be ridiculous." She turns her lorgnette on me. "One of your twins. Nina, I believe?" Then she examines Alfie. "Peas in a pod! You two couldn't be any more similar."

Unbidden, she dumps her bag on the floor and turns to Gertie, who is hovering behind her.

"A cup of tea, please, Gertrude, and take that up to the spare bedroom."

Father's jaw drops.

"Aunt Julia—I– we– there's no room at present, I'm sorry to say."

"Sorry, my eye! I've come to take care of your twins. It's what Susanna would have wanted, even though you didn't bother asking me to her funeral! I hear you're wedded to your wretched shop and that Nina and–" she looks at Alfie "–and whatever this boy's name is are being shamefully neglected."

Gertie's gaze drops, and I wonder if she was the one who informed on Father.

"Alfie," my twin pipes up, walking up to her with one hand outstretched. "My name is Alfred, really, but you can call me Alfie. It's very good to meet you." He grabs her hand and shakes it.

Aunt Julia had been looking at him as if he were something nasty stuck to her shoe, but now her face softens.

"Alfie. A pleasure to meet you too." She turns back to Father and her gaze hardens again.

"It's poppycock to say that you don't have a room for me. And if it isn't, well, I shall just have to stay in yours, repulsive as that thought is to me."

Alfie and I both gasp. She's talking about sharing Father's bed! His face flushes as red as the soldier's tunic I loved to wear.

"Julia! Please! Show some decorum. There are innocent ears listening."

"Decorum be hanged," she replies. "Children are robust. They're not going to swoon away at the thought of a shared bed. The world would be much less populous if that were the case. Now, are you going to show me to a room, or will Gertrude be taking my things to yours?"

Gertie is trying not to smile.

"Gertrude, please find a spare room for this lady," Father says. "Just for the night. She won't be staying any longer."

"Hmmmm. We'll see about that. You don't get rid of me that easily," Aunt Julia replies. "I'll go when I'm satisfied that Nina and Alfie—" she smiles at him again, "are being cared for properly. Lead on, Gertrude!"

Father totters back to his chair, but Alfie and I follow Aunt Julia out of the room. As she goes to mount the first step, I tug on her sleeve. She lifts her lorgnette and looks down at me.

"Aunt Julia," I whisper. "I'm *bloody* glad that you've come."

For some weeks afterwards, before Aunt Julia is called away to appear before a London magistrate for breaking the windows of a department store that has been unsympathetic to the Suffragette cause, our lives improve immeasurably. Aunt Julia cares little about decorum and rules. She takes us punting on the Cam, raising eyebrows when she declines the offer of a male student to propel us down the river.

"Certainly not," she says, examining the blushing young man with her lorgnette. "If you can do it, so can I!"

This turns out to be rather optimistic. She gets the pole stuck in the mud several times and almost capsizes us in her attempts to retrieve it. By the end of the outing, all of us are soaked to the skin and roaring with laughter.

"Next time you can both try," she says, wiping the river water from her lorgnette with a man's handkerchief. "We'll master it, eventually. We only fail if we give up."

She also tells us about the Suffragette cause, pouring scorn on the idea that women lack the necessary judgement to vote wisely.

"Who would you trust in a real crisis? Me or your father? Or that wishy washy shop assistant of his?" Frederick, the assistant in question, has incurred Aunt Julia's wrath by trying to sell her some lace gloves to keep the sun off her hands. He is lucky to escape with his life.

On the subject of suffragists, who try to obtain votes for women using legal methods, she simply says that they are on the right track, but need to be more realistic. "This government will never give in to polite petitions and genteel meetings in church halls. We should join forces and storm the Houses of Parliament!"

In the evenings she reads aloud to us, using action and accent to bring the stories to life. Her portrayal of the dastardly but charming Long John Silver makes Alfie shiver with delight and he watches her, wide-eyed, from behind a cushion.

After that, I decide that I want to be a pirate, especially after I find a book in the library about a female pirate called Anne Bonny, and I try to persuade Alfie to run away to sea with me.

"Not likely," he tells me. "You'd end up as the pirate captain and the minute I disagreed with you, you'd have me walking the plank."

"Not you," I assure him. "I'd happily make anyone else walk the plank, though. Well, not Aunt Julia or Gertie. I'll tell you what: we can take it in turns to be the pirate captain. You can do it for special occasions like pirate dinners and parties and things, and I'll do it when there's fighting to be done and ships to ransack. No one will ever know we're two different people."

"We're not. Not really." Alfie smiles. "Just one person with two different brains."

Yes, I think. *That's true.*

CHAPTER EIGHT

Near Passchendaele Village, Belgium, September 1917

As soon as the first men show their heads over the parapet, the bullets start: the *phut* of rifle fire and the stutter of machine guns. Shells howl and scream. A few fly over us but most explode in No Man's Land where, any second now, we'll be making our way towards the enemy trench. The noise is a weapon in itself. Hell must sound like this.

As Corporal Knowles goes over the top, I glance behind me at my companions, in case I'm looking at human faces for the last time. My fear must be pathetically obvious because when Liam meets my glance, he frowns and shoves his way in front of me.

"Stay with me. *DO it!*" He spits the words at me.

There's no more time for arguments: he's up the ladder and I'm following behind him.

Knowles is lying perhaps ten yards from the trench. He is on his back. A bullet or shell shard must have caught him under the chin, travelled through his skull and out through the top of his steel helmet. The helmet is lying next to him, full of bloody brain matter. His face is obscured by more blood and I'm grateful for that.

He won't need to worry about that moustache any more, I think, stupidly.

Somehow, the men are remembering their orders and are walking towards the German trench. I see Walter Warmsley plodding on as if he has all the time in the world. If it weren't for the rifle in his hands and the steel helmet on his head, he would look as if he was walking home after a hard day at the plough. An evil splutter of machine gun fire peppers the earth a few feet in front of him. He stops, turns his head to one side and spits into the red mud. He waits for a few moments and then, once the volley is over, trudges on again. When his head turns, I realise his lips are moving. The thunder of battle drowns out his words, but I think he's praying. I wonder if it helps, whether I should be praying too, so I grope for the words of the only prayer I know.

"Our Father, which art in Heaven—"

It's pointless: words have no power against this deadly storm of metal. If God really is in his heaven, then his attention is somewhere else at the moment. If I'm going to die, I want my final words to mean something, so I abandon the prayer and repeat my brother's name, over and over again. *Alfie…Alfie…this is for Alfie. As long as Alfie is safe, I can do this.*

Albert Lacey weaves as he walks, trying to make himself harder to hit. A shell explodes. A strong gust of wind blows away the smoke and I see that the boy in front of him, a fair lad called Grindley, who was training to be a tailor, has disappeared. He's been vaporised into red rain. Lacey lifts up his face into the obscene shower and closes his eyes for a second. He's bitten his bottom lip and the blood is staining those wide-spaced little teeth of his. The front of his trousers is soaking wet.

Liam moves on steadily, crouching as he walks to minimise the target he presents. I try to focus on the polished blade of his bayonet, attached to his rifle and ready for action, glinting in the weak sun.

My body is screaming *run!* at me, but somehow I manage to keep it in check. I don't know if I'm capable of running and, anyway, it would draw attention to myself. Not only from enemy fire, either; there are so many crimes for which a man may be shot by his own side. Desertion, cowardice, disobeying a command by running rather than walking…

My shaking hands tighten on the butt of my rifle and it's only then that I remember that I'm carrying a weapon. But it's useless. Even if terror hadn't obliterated my rifle training, I would hit the lads in front of me: Liam and Warmsley and

Venner, and the others whose names I haven't had time to learn. As for my bayonet, I'd have to be in hand-to-hand combat with an enemy soldier to use it, and I haven't seen a single one yet.

I remember bayonet training in Aldershot, jabbing at swinging sacks filled with sand, filled with horror at the prospect of sliding that long, cold blade into living flesh. When it was my turn at the sandbags, I'd jabbed once and dropped my rifle. I couldn't do it. The images of screaming mouths and gaping wounds were too strong.

Sergeant Grimes placed an understanding, calloused hand on my shoulder.

"Never mind, lad. You'll get used to it. Believe me, if it's Fritz or you, you'll be surprised what you can make yourself do."

Was he right? I'll know soon enough.

My terror becomes a knot of pain in my stomach, twisting around my back and down my thighs. I thank the gods that I made those visits to the latrines.

Something hot whizzes past my ear. It's followed by a searing pain that spins me around and knocks me off my feet. I flounder in the mud for a few seconds. Could it be a few hours? My ears are ringing. I raise a hand to my right one. It's hot and ragged, pulsing with blood.

Bullets puncture the mud all around me, and the spatters spit in my face. On my belly, I slither into a shell hole. It's half full of water and the remains of a German soldier. He must have been here for a long time because he no longer stinks. He's mainly bone and stretched skin. He is still wearing his helmet with its ridiculous spike on the top—a relic from an earlier, more optimistic stage of this bloody war.

Liam's back is swallowed up in the smoke of what must surely be all the weapons in the world. He hasn't realised that I've been hit, that I'm no longer following him.

The world fades to black.

Who knows how much time passes before my consciousness swims back to me?

To my right and to my left, I muzzily watch wave after wave of men moving through No Man's Land. Many don't get to take more than a few steps before they crumple. Piles of corpses mount up in front of our trench.

More bodies lie ahead of me where the German barbed wire remains largely intact, in spite of the confident predictions of our commanders. Living men use the dead as platforms to climb over the wire. A gift of a target for the German snipers, who wait until our men reach the top of the mounds before picking them off.

My ear won't stop bleeding. I'm amazed at the amount of blood that seeps from it. Slowly, the grey water I'm lying in becomes stained with crimson. For a few moments, the swirling patterns mesmerise me.

More time passes.

I'm thirsty but my canteen has been damaged. It's empty. Drinking the water I'm lying in is unthinkable—my companion will have poisoned it with his decay. The thought alone makes me gag.

I wonder where Liam is—whether he is still alive. Venner—at least I think it's him—is dead. He's hanging on the barbed wire like a scarecrow. I remember the dreadful poems he writes for his mother about the primroses blooming in England's leafy hedgerows and twittering blackbirds: nonsense like that. His pal—the chap with the ears, whose name I can never remember, and who sings filthy songs in a choirboy voice—lies wounded a few paces from him, screaming for help in a cracked soprano.

A shell blows Warmsley off his feet. A miracle: he looks unscathed. But then, as he staggers to his feet, I see that his left arm is missing. Shards of white bone jut gruesomely from a tattered curtain of charred skin and flesh. He walks back to our trench like a man in a reverie.

Suddenly, I can't stay put any longer. I need to move. To survive. Have the bullets died down a little? I think so. Now is my chance. I grasp my rifle and feel for my helmet, but it's nowhere to be seen. I have absolutely no idea how long I've been without it.

I need a replacement. The only one within reach is on the head of my German companion. Ignoring my revulsion, I grab at it. As I remove it from the German's head, I release a powerful stench. Maggots drop to the mud like fat, white raindrops. Hot vomit surges into my mouth. I can't put that on. I can't.

Without allowing myself any time to think, I clamber out of the shell hole and move towards the German wire. All around me are bodies and dismembered limbs. Men mutilated in every possible way. Men crying, groaning, whimpering, screaming, swearing, vomiting. Trying to live. Or, if their injuries are bad enough, trying to die.

A volley of machine-gun fire to my right causes me to pick up my pace. To hell with walking! Let General Allenby come out here and try walking through this.

Through a roll of smoke, a figure comes into sight, holding a rifle with a red bayonet. It reaches the uncut barbed wire, runs along it perhaps twenty yards to a rare gap and gets through.

He's heading for me, covered in mud and blood. His helmet is missing and his face is so filthy it's impossible to make out his features.

This is it. Time to kill.

Time to do the deed I came here to save Alfie from doing.

I drop to a crouch and take aim. My hands are shaking. I try not to wonder what the man's name is. Where his family is. Whether he has a brother. I shift my fingers and try to force my hands to cooperate. The shaking subsides. I nestle the butt of my rifle more securely into my shoulder. I realise the soldier hasn't taken any steps to shoot me. Why not? He must have seen that I'm aiming at him.

His mouth opens and closes. Opens. Closes. In the noise and chaos, I can't hear his words. The inside of his mouth, red against his filthy face, startles me.

I can't wait any longer. The same horror and revulsion I'd felt during bayonet training is growing within me. I can't let it get any further. I need to kill this man. Now.

My finger tightens on the trigger.

"–lins! It's me!" At last, some of the soldier's words reach me, carried on the changeable wind. "*Mullins!* Don't shoot me, you bloody idiot!"

"*Talbot?*" I lower my rifle and stare at him, stupidly.

Liam reaches me and spins me around.

"Come on, we're going back. It's a slaughterhouse over there." He's pulling me back towards our trench.

We slide in among a handful of others. Liam tries to take my rifle from me to stow it safely, but my hands refuse to loosen their grip. Eventually he manages to unfasten my fingers, one by one. We exchange a look of understanding. We survivors take off our helmets, those who've retained them, before dropping into exhausted heaps, wherever we can find somewhere dry.

Liam reaches out one hand towards my ear but drops it before he touches me. "What've you gone and done to yourself?"

"I didn't do it to myself," I say, hotly. "It was a bloody Hun bullet!"

His face is stiff with exhaustion but he manages a smile.

"Are you injured?" I ask him.

He shrugs. "Dunno, to be honest. Don't think so, but if I'm not it's a ruddy miracle." He looks around and drops his voice. "Those bastards…"

"Which bastards? The Germans or our butcher leaders?"

Liam finds a space big enough for both of us—a shallow funk hole, abandoned in favour of easier excavation spots when the diggers came across clusters of thick tree roots. The rest of the tree must have been blasted into oblivion some time ago. He sinks into it and shuffles over to make space for me. He closes his eyes, giving me the chance to examine him.

He's not a handsome man, not like the square-jawed, brilliantined gods from the newspaper advertisements. But he's a little taller than average, sturdily made, with an air of lazy confidence. His green eyes open and I look away quickly.

"Back in a sec." I get up. I need the latrines again.

I'm in luck; they're deserted. I pull down my breeches and squat.

And stop. "Oh."

Another injury. Blood is smudged over my thighs, drying into stickiness. Wet blood between my legs.

I pull up a handful of moss, spit on it and wipe surreptitiously. No injury. I check in another place. Still nothing.

Then I realise, and reach into my pack for the field dressings I keep with me at all times.

My period. I'd hoped—ridiculously, it seems—that I wouldn't be bothered with them while I was at the Front. But why would the gods make things easy for me? When have they ever done that?

Anyway, it makes sense, I suppose. Today is a day for blood.

CHAPTER NINE

Cambridge, April 1912

"I just couldn't contemplate marrying my dearest Philip without poor, dear Nina in attendance as one of the bridesmaids," my cousin, Esme, simpers.

From my seat on the sofa next to Father, I glower at evil Esme. I can't abide her. She doesn't have a brain in her head. What she *does* have is a collection of bizarre and hideous hats that I want to rip off her head and jump up and down on. Today's offering features two poor little dead birds on a useless nest and enough netting for a North Sea trawler.

"No," I say, folding my arms and hating her even more than usual because of her pity. *Poor, dear Nina!* She has no right to feel sorry for me.

Esme's little pink mouth falls open.

"Pardon me?"

"She'd love to, Esme," my father interjects, after a swift glare at me. "She's joking, and in very poor taste. It will do Nina good to get involved in something feminine. She spends far too much time with her brother."

"Father– please–," I stutter.

He runs his eyes over me for a mere second. That's all my anguish is worth to him. Then he turns back to Esme.

"I'll make sure she behaves herself," he says to Esme, as if he's talking about a badly behaved dog.

Alfie fled into the garden as soon as he heard the commotion of Esme's arrival. When she and her fish-faced groom finally leave, I seek him out.

"I won't do it." I kick at the stones in the rockery, sending showers of earth flying into the air. "She wants me to carry a shepherdess's crook. They can't make me! I'd rather die!"

Alfie gives a little sigh.

"And I'd love all of it!" he says, dreamily.

I look at him and he looks back at me. The idea hits us at the same time.

"Well…."

"Dare we…?" Alfie breathes. "We're the same height. And we're pretty well the same size…"

"It's a chance for both of us to test how far we can go with our other selves…. And it would be a wonderful way to get back at evil Esme." *And at Father*, I think to myself, *for not loving me. For not even liking me very much.*

I give a decisive nod.

"We dare!"

We plan it meticulously: I drill Alfie on what happens during rehearsals, on what he's expected to do, on the names of the other bridesmaids and how he can tell them apart. I incur Father's eternal anger by cutting my hair short, a day or two before the wedding. I regret this too: my hair is my only beauty, but it has to go.

"No nonsense, today. Don't let me down." He's looking straight at me for a change. So often, he seems to focus his gaze a few inches above the top of my head. Then he turns to my twin.

"Are you sure you're well enough to attend this wedding, Alfred?" Father's face relaxes a little as he speaks to my brother. "You're rather pale."

"Yes. I'll be fine. I've got a bit of a headache. It'll be gone by the time of the wedding," Alfie says, with a wan smile.

Immediately after breakfast, Alfie and I disappear upstairs to start our preparations and, at 11.30, two open carriages promptly pull up outside our house. I wedge the hideous floral bonnet onto Alfie's head and give him a thump on the arm, for luck.

"Don't forget this!" I thrust the shepherdess's crook into his hand. Wrapped in pink and white ribbons, it looks for all the world like a huge stick of Brighton rock or the maypole that Miss Wren used to make us dance around.

"How do I look?" As he twirls in front of the mirror, there's a breathless catch in his voice that I recognise as fear. I'm feeling it too, although I'll never admit it. I'll always summon up courage to help Alfie.

I examine him. On me, the dress with its puffed sleeves, tiny, pearly buttons and looped up skirt looks ridiculous. On Alfie it's pretty. Maybe it's his enjoyment that makes the difference.

"You look MAH-vellous!" I meet the reflections of his eyes. "I know you're scared, Alfie. But some things are worth being frightened for. Agreed?"

"Yes! I'll never get this chance again and I'm going to make the most of it! I'm so tired of trousers and starched shirts."

With a stab of pity, I watch him descend the stairs towards Father. I love dressing in boys' clothes and I wouldn't give it up for anything, but I know in my heart that to Alfie, it's so much more than that. I'm always me, but Alfie only gets to be truly himself when he's a girl.

"You look very nice, Nina. Surprisingly nice," says Father gruffly. "Make sure you keep your bonnet on—we don't want the whole world seeing what you've done to yourself. Stay in the background and everything will be fine."

I wonder if Father is talking about the wedding or my life in general. How he'd love it if I could somehow merge with his fussy wallpaper and stay there forever. Out of sight, and out of mind.

Walking down the stairs in Alfie's new grey suit, with Father waiting for me at the bottom, my heart is beating so loudly that I'm surprised he doesn't mention it. My palms are sweaty and I wipe them on the sides of my trousers.

A sudden frown descends over Father's face.

My breath catches in my throat. He knows it's me!

"Don't wipe your hands on your clothes, Alfred! Do you know how much that suit cost?"

Barely able to put one foot in front of the other, I follow Father out of the house. Perhaps it's fortunate that he is distracted as we make our way to church; his silence gives me the opportunity to check the reactions of passers-by. I feel as if there's a sign above my head proclaiming **THIS IS A GIRL!** Miraculously, it seems that no one has noticed my imposture.

A few minutes later, Father finally looks at me.

"Alfred, I apologise for my silence. I was thinking about your dear mother, and praying that Nina won't disgrace us. Sometimes I think that she is quite mad. At least I have one normal child! … You're very quiet. Are you feeling quite well?"

My heart is turning to ice.

"My head…" I whisper. "It still hurts a bit."

Father stops and peers into my eyes. I have to force myself not to turn my head away, especially when he reaches out a frigid hand to feel my forehead.

"Hmmmm. Do you wish to return home?"

I shake my head, ignoring the craven impulse to say yes and hide at home. That would be letting Alfie down. "I'll be fine."

He pats me on the shoulder. "You're a good lad. No trouble at all. How different from your sister! That girl will be the death of me yet." He gives me a sidelong look. "You must never mention our little talks about her, Alfred. You know that, don't you? If you did, it might destabilise her even more."

I nod. Alfie obviously knows that only too well: he has never breathed a word of Father's criticisms to me. I wish that I had my penknife with me. The next time Father leant over to examine me, I would stab it into his heart. He probably wouldn't even notice. It's cold and dead, anyway.

We arrive at church and slip into our pew, Father nodding at the ranks of Mullinses, all decked out in ghastly wedding finery. I note several hideous hats that evil Esme will love.

Perhaps a minute before the bridal procession appears, a figure in lavender bursts through the door. She ignores the ushers, who do their best to bundle her into a seat at the back, and after peering rudely at the congregation through her lorgnette, makes a beeline for our pew.

My heart leaps with joy.

"Oh lord," Father mutters, backing into the far corner.

It seems like ages since Aunt Julia left us, but we've never forgotten her kindness and crackling vitality. She looks thinner than before, and her silver hair is swept upwards and secured under an extraordinary black fur hat, which even I know isn't remotely suitable for a wedding. It reminds me of the bearskin hats worn by the guards at Buckingham Palace. A long, emerald green scarf is wound around her neck like a boa constrictor. She barges into our pew, knocking hymnbooks to the floor. Father looks terrified.

"Cedric, glum as ever, I see. Alfred, how lovely to see you again," she says in a loud voice.

"*Shhh!*" The reproof comes from several places at once.

"The bride," someone else hisses.

Aunt Julia raises her lorgnette in the direction of the bridal party.

"Another fool sacrificing her freedom for the sake of a gold ring, and a honeymoon in Torquay," she mutters, very audibly.

The assembled Mullinses titter with embarrassment.

As the gaggle of older bridesmaids passes, she shakes her head.

"Good Lord, how many of them are there? Not one of them looks as if she has a brain in her head…"

Finally comes Alfie, fear obviously forgotten, trying to look soulful but having the time of his life.

"Ugh! Poor Nina! That bonnet is frightful! And—a shepherd's crook! How ridiculous! I suppose we should be grateful that we were at least spared the sheep!"

She subjects Alfie to intense scrutiny as he passes. He obviously feels it—it would be hard to miss—and he turns towards us. We exchange a look of panic. Now his whole face is exposed to Aunt's Julia's lorgnette.

She looks at me again and then back at Alfie. Her lips tighten. I can almost hear her brain working, making connections. My knees turn to water. I try to collect my wits. I need to prepare my defence for the storm of accusations that is about to break.

But then Julia does something unexpected. She makes a point of looking away from Alfie. Her lorgnette comes into play again as she examines Philip.

"My goodness! Is that the *groom*? Is she marrying a man or a fish supper?"

For the rest of the ceremony she closes her eyes as if she's sleeping. But no one could sleep in such an upright posture.

Feeling sick to my stomach, I spend it wondering when the hammer will fall.

As soon as the happy couple have left the church, I push my way outside, incurring disapproving tuts from various Mullinses who believe that children should wait for their elders to lead the way. I need to reach Alfie, to warn him to stay away from Aunt Julia. But before I can get him alone, we have to gather in the churchyard to shower (or in my case, pelt) the new Mr and Mrs Pettifer with rice and rose petals. It's not the right time.

Straight after that, the bride is expected to throw her wedding bouquet. All the unmarried ladies except one are gathering in a group around Esme. I stand with the men, a spectator of the little ritual, wondering if there is glasswort for pretension, or columbines for folly, among the profusion of wilting flowers in her hands. Aunt Julia refuses to take part in this humiliating tradition, of course. She stands with us, glaring at the bride as if she is daring her to send the bouquet her way. I think, if she caught it, she would trample it into the ground.

Alfie is there among the spinsters, pushed to the rear of the group. Strictly speaking, he is too young to take part in the little procedure, which is supposed to identify the next girl to secure a husband. But perhaps he reasons that he'll never have the chance again, and he wants to make the most of it.

"Ready?" Esme teases.

Excited squeals confirm that everyone is ready and waiting. They sound like a pen full of piglets.

Esme turns her back on the group and tosses the bouquet over her shoulder.

A minor skirmish commences as the older bridesmaids barge each other out of the way, all desperate to catch the bouquet. Judging by their inexpert little leaps into the air, none of them has done a minute of physical exercise in their entire lives.

There are wails of disappointment as the bouquet sails over their heads.

Alfie has been forced to participate in a punishing exercise regime every school week since he was seven. Among the gaggle of bridesmaids and single women, he is an Achilles. His leap into the air is magnificent. He snatches the bouquet to his chest in a rugby catch and drops to his feet.

I gasp. Alfie has forgotten himself.

There is a ripple of applause and a few discontented murmurs from the older bridesmaids.

"Oh! Nina's caught it. How unfair. She'll never get—"

I seek Aunt Julia in the crowd. She is raising her lorgnette and examining Alfie like a botanist might inspect an uncommon orchid.

I flash him a look of warning. He catches it and his face freezes. He thrusts the bouquet into the arms of the nearest bridesmaid and scuttles over to me.

"Idiot!" I hiss at him.

"I'm sorry. I couldn't resist—"

"Nina. Alfred. A word with both of you, please."

Aunt Julia sails over to intercept us.

"Oh, but I think Father is calling us," I begin, grasping Alfie's wrist and starting to drag him away.

Aunt Julia extends an arm to cut off our escape.

"Cedric can wait. Come with me."

She steers us towards a quiet corner of the graveyard.

"An explanation, please."

"For what?" I'm not going to give in without a fight.

"You know very well what for. I might be old, but I'm not an idiot. Please don't treat me like one."

We're struck dumb.

She sighs. "Very well, I'll be specific. You–" she glares at Alfie "are not Nina and you–" she bends her eagle-eyed gaze on me "are not Alfred. I know you, remember. It's a clever deception but a deception nonetheless. I wish to know why."

My mind races. What should we say?

"We're happier this way," Alfie falters. "We're not doing any harm. I like being a girl and Nina likes being a boy."

"Hmmm," is all Aunt Julia replies.

"I didn't want to be a bridesmaid, but Esme and Father made me." I think my mention of Father is quite clever. Aunt Julia delights in upsetting him.

"Look at the outfit she picked out for me," I continue, pointing at Alfie's bonnet and shepherdess crook. "She deserves to be ridiculed for those alone!"

Julia nods. "I agree about the dreadful costume. What was she thinking? But what were you going to do if you got caught? You would be in very serious trouble. Your Father would probably die from shame…" She can't quite prevent a small smile at the thought.

"We didn't think we would get caught," I say. "We've been doing this for ages and no one has a clue. Except you."

"You're fortunate that it's me who spotted you. You should learn a lesson from this. If you're going to do this, you must stay in role no matter what. Understand? You must *become* who you are pretending to be. Otherwise, you're lost."

We give sullen nods.

"I've had theatrical training, so I know what I'm talking about. The moment you step out of role, the illusion you've created is shattered."

"Are you going to tell on us?" Alfie whispers.

"Do I look like a telltale? I'm simply passing on some advice. Now go." She waves us away.

We don't need to be told twice. We thank her and hurry away. But before we've taken more than a couple of paces, she calls us back.

"One more thing … until that moment with the bouquet, you were both doing magnificently. Never be afraid to be yourselves! If you ever find that you need a friend–" She fishes around in her ugly bag, locates a calling card and hands it to me, "–this is where you will find me—unless our delightful family has succeeded in hurrying me into my grave by then!"

Torn between relief and exhilaration, we nod our thanks and flee.

CHAPTER TEN

Near Passchendaele Village, Belgium, September 1917

Yesterday's slaughter wasn't enough. We've been patched up so we can do it all again. Ours wasn't the only section to suffer severe losses, so we've been banded together with a lot of chaps we've never seen before.

Our objective is the same—get through the gaps in the wire if we can find any, take the enemy trench and this time, hold it. Now that Knowles is a goner, we're given our orders by Sergeant Cox. I've never seen him before, but he's older than Knowles—mid-thirties, at a guess, and he looks as thin and nervy as a whippet. This must be misleading, though, because his eyes are steady in his bony face. A soldier I've never met before tells me that Cox is a veteran—he's been here since the war started. When we hear this, Liam and I look at him like a species of dinosaur that has been newly discovered, living on some remote island. How is such survival possible?

"Take it steady, lads. No unnecessary risks. It'll be slippery out there, what with all the overnight rain, so don't try and sprint. I'm not expecting you to stroll though," there's a gleam of ironic humour in those grey eyes, "no matter what the brass says. Find your own pace. Stick to it."

We all nod, encouraged by Cox's astonishing longevity. If he can survive for so long, why shouldn't we be able to, as well? I feel a squirm of hope in my stomach. When Cox moves away to take up his position at the ladder, Liam nods at me. "At least it's stopped raining," he says. "Stick with me if you can."

This time I don't argue. "Good luck," I say, wishing I could think of something more meaningful. It could be the last thing I ever say to him.

Liam nods. For a long moment he examines me. "You too," he says, unsmiling. Then he turns away.

Shrilling whistles pierce the din of shells and bullets.

Sergeant Cox mounts the ladder in a crouch, turning his body sideways as he gets to the top. He moves off and is lost to my sight.

When it's my turn and I've managed to force myself up the ladder behind Liam, I see Cox again. In spite of his own advice, he is being forced to walk. He's past his ankles in mud. It's worse than it was yesterday—churned up by feet, shellfire and overnight rain. Actually, he's not walking, he's wading. Painfully slowly, trying to keep his rifle clear of the muck, as the bullets fly around him.

I adopt a similar sideways crouch and take a step forward. I sink. Not as far as Cox—I'm lighter than he is—but the mud sucks at my boots. I lift a foot. The sludge feels like lead under my soles. The noise of shellfire is deafening but I can imagine the long sucking *SHMOOP* noise that my foot must make as I pull it clear of the mire. For some reason this strikes me as exquisitely funny and I feel a bubble of laughter rise in my throat. I swallow it.

A soldier to my right loses his balance. He skids forwards like a music hall comedy act, dropping his rifle into the mud. As he leans over to pick it up, a burst of machine gun fire slices into him. I turn away as the puddles around him flood red.

Liam isn't looking my way—that would be madness. It's up to me to try to keep up with him. By stepping lightly, he is managing to keep going. I try this technique too. It works, more or less. I still can't run, but by throwing my weight forward and avoiding bringing my heels down as much as possible, I manage to keep moving.

The air is grey with bullets and streaking shells. It reminds me of a book that I read as a child. It was about Henry V's triumph at the battle of Agincourt. *The sky was black with English arrows,* it crowed, as if that was something to be proud of. If I knew then how it felt to look up at air filled with death, I would have thrown that book on the fire.

The thunder of shellfire hurts my ears. It's impossible to predict whom the bullets will hit, where the shells will fall. That's in the lap of the gods, if such beings exist. If they *are* real, they must be heartless bastards. All we can do is keep going until they decide that it's our turn to crumple into the mud. I start to almost wish for it. When *my* bullet or shell comes, this deadly terror, this feeling of time slowing down, will be over.

I don't know how long I've been going, but I've got further than I did yesterday. There's the gap in the wire and there's Venner, still hanging there too exposed to be retrieved by our recovery parties, even at night. His face is going black.

I'm through, following Cox and Liam, whose backs are shrouded by smoke and spattering mud. Others are clambering through too. I think I see Lacey's fair hair off to one side. He must have lost his helmet.

Time no longer exists. I am a creature in a vacuum, in space, moving in my own world.

I stumble onwards.

I'm becoming better at moving through the mud, allowing my foot to sink to a certain level, judging when to pull it up and replant it before it sinks too far.

My foot strikes something soft. I look down. I'm standing on the body of a soldier. He's on his back, his mouth gaping open. Every inch of him—his uniform, his hands, his face, even his eyeballs and the inside of his mouth—is coated with yellow-brown mud. I can't tell if he's one of ours, or one of theirs—death has obliterated such differences. Whatever he was and whoever he fought for, now he's just part of this quagmire; a stepping stone for those of us who are yet to join him.

Yesterday, this would have made me sick to my stomach. Today, I just step off him quickly and move on. How quickly we learn to accept horror!

It's a surprise when I realise that I've reached the enemy trench. Some part of me expected to be stumbling on forever.

I crawl down, steeling myself for the thud of bullets into my body. But every German I see is dead. This is the first time I've seen the enemy up close. We have been told that they are godless demons, but the only difference between these dead men and our own is the colour of the uniform they died in.

The German trench zigzags sharply. Perhaps fifty yards ahead, I see men in British uniforms disappearing around a sharp bend. I follow them.

I've nearly reached the bend when I sense rather than hear a movement behind me. I spin around.

A boy. Not much older than me. A boy with fox-coloured hair, like Alfie. Like me. A boy in a German uniform. He's crying. I notice bubbles of snot, inflating and deflating around his nostrils. I'm reminded of a toddler I once saw in the Botanical Gardens in Cambridge, crying because he'd dropped his ice cream onto the gravel path. His desolation had seemed absolute, out of all proportion to his predicament. This time, it seems spot-on.

It's only then that I take in the fact that he's aiming a muddy gun at me.

I clutch my own rifle and point it at him, willing my hands not to shake. I realise that I'm crying too.

We stare at each other. For a moment it feels like some stupid, childish game that will end when one of us backs down and looks away. Then the loser will hunch his shoulders in shame and slink away to tell tall tales to his friends about how he could have won the little encounter, but….

My finger is edging towards my trigger.

I hear a click. And then another. He's squeezing his trigger. But his rifle is jammed, clogged up with mud by the look of it.

I shake my head.

"Don't," I whisper.

My own finger seems to be frozen.

He gives a sob of despair and lunges at me, jabbing his bayonet towards my heart.

I feel my eyes widen at the same time as I sidestep. I don't retaliate. It just doesn't seem real. I can't be fighting to the death in this trench, against this desperate, snivelling boy.

He pulls back.

I crouch.

We wait.

"Don't," I say again.

He attacks again. This time, I read his intention in his face.

I'm not quite quick enough. As I jerk away, he alters his aim and I feel the shocking sensation of cold metal piercing my skin, breaching my torso.

Although it hurts, the pain isn't as bad as I'd imagined. But my warm, seeping blood feels like an insult and I react.

Reflexively, I pull back my arms and jab.

My bayonet hits home, into his left side, quite high. It feels nothing like jabbing that sandbag back in Aldershot. The boy takes a sharp breath.

As he falls forwards, I'm staring at the red tip of my bayonet. It seems so wrong that his blood is staining my blade. Blood is private. Seeing it on display like this is as shocking as reading his intimate thoughts or seeing him naked.

It seems to take me forever to shift my gaze to the boy on the muddy duckboards. I stare down at him, willing him to move. He can't be dead. How can he be dead? He was alive a second ago. Death shouldn't happen so easily.

I kneel down and pat his shoulder. "I'm sorry," I say. "You shouldn't have—" Shouldn't have what? Tried to kill me? Tried to defend his family? His country? His life?

It's not until the blood from his punctured heart congeals that I look down at my own tunic. My blood is on display too. A wet stain has spread above my wound, turning the rough khaki fabric reddish black.

Somehow, I find the strength to clamber out of the trench. I see that my hands are slick with blood but I don't know whether it's mine or my vanquished opponent's. When it comes down to it, all blood looks the same.

I stumble onwards until the world turns black.

CHAPTER ELEVEN

Cambridge, October 1912

"Ineed to talk to you," Alfie says to me when he storms in from school one day. He doesn't wait for my response. I follow him to his room.

He sits on his bed, dropping his head into his hands. "I'm dead," he says, dully.

"What? Why?"

"There's a chap at school—Moody—who's been giving me a hard time. He's ragging me about my dislike of sports. Saying I'm unnatural. Lacey's egging him on, as usual. If he's goading some thug like Moody into picking on me, nobody picks on *him*."

Alfie has mentioned Lacey before, always for the same reason. He's the worst kind of bully: a weak boy who'll do anything to save his own skin. I hate him, even though I've never laid eyes on him.

Unnatural. We both know what that means. Boys are supposed to love girls and girls are supposed to love boys. Anything else is wrong. But what does it matter who you love? The important thing is to love *someone*. A few months ago, Alfie confided to me that he was in love with a boy in the year above him. I've forgotten his name—Simpson or Simpkins—something like that.

"I just need to tell someone," he had said, glaring at me through tear-filled eyes. "It's *agony*. I hate it."

I had wondered if I envied him. The only people I loved were Alfie, Gertie and Great Aunt Julia. I had never felt a twitch of attraction for anyone, boy or girl. I wondered if I would ever feel the passion and pain he described. Perhaps I was missing out, but love sounded too tricky for me to desire it wholeheartedly. I knew that Alfie would never care for women in the way that convention prescribed, and that he dreamed of living as a woman, but I didn't have a similar conviction. I loved the freedom of wearing trousers and the knowledge that I was doing something shocking, but would I prefer to be a man? I didn't know. I only knew that I would be happy if I was just allowed to be *me*. Before I fell for someone else, I needed to know more about myself.

"Don't look at me as if I'm going to hit you," I'd said to Alfie. "I don't care who you love, as long you love me too. Perhaps he loves you back? Have you asked him?"

Alfie gives a short laugh.

"Of course not. When I'm tired of life, I'll ask him. I may be short of muscle, but there's nothing wrong with my brain!"

Now, I put down the book I'd carried in with me and grasp his shoulder.

"Don't listen to Lacey or Moody," I say, hotly. "It's not important. They're idiots."

Alfie stares at his feet. "It's too late. He's challenged me to a duel. If I'm not—unnatural—he says I'll fight him to prove it."

I'm on my feet.

"A *duel?* What kind of duel? This isn't *The Scarlet* bloody *Pimpernel!* Tell him he's an idiot."

I'm imagining the worst—swords at dawn. Pistols even, and Alfie lying on the green grass as it changes colour.

"A boxing match. He's put up signs announcing it. You know how much I hate violence. I don't think I can do it."

I feel a rush of relief. Boxing looks nasty, but I suspect a lot of it is show. I've seen amateur boxers in singlets and drawers, having a go at each other at a Summer Fete on Parker's Piece, and I've always thought that it was something I'd like to try. The ducking and weaving around. It was like a strange dance. Somehow, boxing encapsulates what attracts me to the idea of being a man. If a girl drew attention to herself like that, she'd be in trouble for being too forward. If a girl stripped to the waist like that, she'd be beyond redemption—a shameless hussy—the worst label I know.

"Well, perhaps you should try it. You're light on your feet. You can weave about and tire him out. Then you go in for the attack. An uppercut to his chin and a jolly good thump in the eye and bam! He'll be flat on his back and you'll be a hero!"

Alfie shakes his head. "No. You know I can't do that."

I look at my brother, sitting on his bed with his head in his hands. I wonder how we can be so alike physically and yet so dissimilar in other ways. I look at the dust-covered model motor cars and lead soldiers, lying untouched around his room, and I feel a twinge of distaste for him.

"Alfie, life is a battle. Don't give up so easily. How will you cope when you're grown up if you don't fight?"

He shrugs.

"I don't know. Maybe I won't have to fight. Maybe I won't grow up."

"There! You're at it again. Lying down and playing dead. You've got to *try!*" I'm on my feet, raising my voice. I'm surprised at the strength of the emotions surging around my body. I hardly ever get angry with Alfie.

He jumps up too.

"I *CAN'T.* That's it. End of discussion."

"Can't, can't, can't. That's all you ever say. Well, I say you *CAN, CAN, CAN* and this time you'll jolly well have to."

I hear the thump of Gertie's feet as she surges upstairs to see what the fuss is about. I head for the door.

"Alfie, be a man for once in your life."

I stomp to my room and drop onto my bed. I open a book, close it again, pick at the hem of my skirt, stand up, walk around the room, go to the window and stare out at Miss Shelby, weeding in her garden. My heart's already twisting with guilt. It's my job to look after Alfie, not to goad him into bloodshed. I must apologise to him and tell him that it's all right to refuse to fight.

I fly out of my room and knock on his door.

"Alfie?" I open the door and peer inside. He hasn't budged. Still on his bed, face set and stony. He doesn't look up as I creep in.

"I'm sorry. I shouldn't have said that."

Still no eye contact and no answer.

"Alfie, please…"

At last he looks up.

"What?"

"I was wrong. Angry. I'm sorry. Of course you don't have to fight."

"Yes, I do. You said so. My own sister is ashamed of me. I'm doing it." His voice is low and determined.

"No—I was wrong—angry—being a bully."

"Yes, you were. But I'm doing it. Go away. I need some peace."

"Please, Alfie—"

He stands up, hands on hips.

"Go away."

"But—"

"GET OUT!"

With a gasp, I turn and run.

The "match" is scheduled to take place after school the next day and I'm sure that we both spend a sleepless night. I feel floored by guilt. Alfie is going to be hurt and it's all my fault.

In the morning, he won't meet my eye. After a few fruitless attempts at an apology, I watch my brother push his breakfast around and leave without even a word to Gertie.

I make a vow. I can't stop the fight but I'll be there. I'll hide myself away so I can bear witness to Alfie's bravery.

Mother would expect it of me. It's the only thing I can do for him. And it's my punishment.

After an endless day of imagining bloody scenarios in which Alfie is seriously injured, maimed—killed, even, I put on some of his spare uniform, tuck my shoulder-length hair under a cap and slip out of the house.

It feels strange to be dressed like this and outside without Alfie. Strange and a little frightening. But as I slouch along and realise that no one is sparing me a second glance, my fear dies. When I reach Alfie's school I pull my shoulders back, hold my head up and walk in as if I belong there.

My worry for Alfie doesn't stop me admiring St George's. It smells of beeswax, cabbage, suet pudding, fresh mown grass, and of the boys themselves. Lessons have just ended and they're milling around in the corridors, talking, pushing and shoving at each other, laughing at jokes and each other.

I know where the playing fields are. I've passed them often enough, stopping to watch the boys as they dash around in liberating shorts. I pull my cap low over my face and lounge out through the double doors, heading for the carefully tended expanse of green.

Moody is waiting amid a gathering crowd, and he's not what I'm expecting. In my mind he's a muscle-bound bully, with narrow eyes and greasy hair. But he's just another boy. Taller and more muscular than Alfie, it's true, but so are many boys in his year. Moody has a wide mouth and springy, light brown hair that he brushes up and away from his face.

I examine his physique from the edge of the crowd. With the exception of his face and lower arms, which are a reddish brown, his skin is white. His shoulders are broad and promise strength in future years. There's a smattering of red spots on his back. His arms are lightly muscled and so are his legs. He has big feet.

One of Moody's most vocal supporters is a thin boy with floppy blond hair and restless blue eyes. I hate him on sight, and that's before I work out who he is.

"Teach him what's what," the blond boy urges. "There's no room at St George's for pansies. Smash his face in!" I just know that this must be Lacey, who picks on Alfie as a form of self-protection.

I stare at the boy so hard that he seems to feel it and his eyes flicker over to me. I pull my cap further down and look away. Two Alfie Mullinses at the same event would raise suspicions. Before I shift my gaze, he gives me a little smile. Ingratiating.

Complicit. He's inviting me to share his opinion. I close my eyes and imagine a long, agonising death for him.

When Alfie appears from the pavilion there are a few cheers—or jeers—I'm not sure which. I feel a pang of fierce love for him. He's alone except for a short man of perhaps forty with an opulent moustache. He's talking to Alfie, and giving him last-minute instructions.

"Remember, Mullins, duck and weave. Weaving is key for the lighter fighter…"

Duck and weave? Wasn't that what I told Alfie to do last night? Now it sounds like pure nonsense. He isn't making a rug. I hate myself for giving my brother such facile advice

In his shorts, Alfie looks almost pathetic. Unlike Moody, every inch of Alfie is white. It's an important part of his female self; ladies don't tan. The big leather gloves on his hands look as if he's stolen them from his much older brother.

Someone has stretched out some ropes on the grass, to form a boxing ring.

Moody watches Alfie's approach. There's no mistaking who is the crowd's favourite—there must be forty or fifty boys of all ages clustering behind him. I wonder if Simpson or Simpkins—I still can't remember the name of Alfie's first love—is among them and pray that he isn't. Alfie's side of the ring is deserted. I wonder if I dare drift over towards Alfie, to show some kind of voiceless support, but I can't risk it. Alfie might see me and that won't help him one bit. Just the opposite.

The short man with the moustache struts to the centre of the ring. Moody is to one side of him and Alfie the other.

"Now, I want a clean fight. We play fair, irrespective of our differences. We're young gentlemen, remember."

"This is the final chance for apologies or retractions," the man continues. His accent is Welsh. "Moody, is there anything you want to say?"

Moody shakes his head. "Only that we all know the truth. You're unnatural, Mullins. Admit it and you'll save yourself a beating." Conviction rings out in his voice. He believes that he holds the moral high ground. Numerous boys nod their agreement and Lacey calls out "Hear, hear!" In my mind, I'm pummelling his face bloody.

Alfie lifts his head. "I'm not unnatural. I'm just me." His voice sounds so small, so young.

The man gives a grim smile. "No apologies or retractions then. Let's get on with it."

He holds up one hand, drops it and steps back smartly. The crowd roar their encouragement as the contenders square up to each other. Moody dances in—those big feet of his are surprisingly nimble. Alfie does his best to emulate him.

Almost immediately, Moody makes a savage jab. Alfie lunges to one side in time to avoid it.

"Come on, Moody," Lacey yells. "Show the little freak how a real man behaves!"

Alfie flinches. I think those words hurt him more than physical blows could. I glare at Lacey and promise vengeance. One day, somehow.

Alfie tries a jab of his own and looks shocked when it connects with Moody's torso. There's a little gasp from the crowd. I doubt that Moody had even considered the possibility that Alfie might actually hit him. It angers him. With narrowed eyes, he sets about my twin.

I feel every punch. A jab to his stomach causes Alfie to double over. The crowd cheers. Before Alfie has the chance to straighten up, Moody aims a punch at his chin. It catches the side of his mouth and I watch as his lip splits and blood dribbles from it. I start forward, then stop myself.

The Welsh man steps back into the ring, ringing a heavy brass bell.

"End of Round One!" he calls.

I gasp in relief.

The contenders go to their opposite corners. Alfie slumps onto the grass. Moody remains upright, talking to his supporters. Although most of the crowd are still on Moody's side, one or two have started to drift over towards Alfie's. He has gained a little respect, I think. He's putting up a better fight than expected. Someone pours him a glass of water from a stoneware jug. Alfie rinses his mouth and spits pink liquid onto the grass.

Round Two begins and Moody goes for the kill. He's merciless. I'm fighting back my tears as I watch him punch Alfie round the ring. Just before the end of the round, Moody knocks him to the ground. He falls onto his gloved hands and knees. Standing behind him, I see blood and tears dripping from his chin onto the green grass. My face is wet too. I dash the tears away and see that Alfie is doing the same thing.

"Had enough, lad?" the referee with the moustache asks. He sounds a bit kinder now. He puts a consoling hand on Alfie's shoulder. Beneath it, my brother's white skin is red with bruises that will soon bloom purple and black.

Alfie shakes his head and staggers to his feet.

The referee tousles his damp hair. "Good lad!"

Before the combatants can do more than square up to each other again, the bell rings to indicate the end of Round Two. I wonder if it's just my imagination, or has the referee called the end of the round a little early? Perhaps he's starting to feel a little sympathy for my brave twin.

Alfie staggers back to his corner. A few more boys have drifted in that direction, although most of them hang back from getting too close. I know what they were thinking—they admire his surprising courage, but they don't want their classmates to link them with someone so lacking in all the qualities they've been brought up to admire and regard as essentially British.

When Alfie pulls himself to his feet for Round Three, I know that the end is close. There's a lot of blood on him and one of his eyes has swollen closed. Strands of his hair straggle into the blood and stick there.

"Give it a rest, now, Mullins. You've proved you've got pluck," someone calls from the back of the crowd.

Alfie ignores him.

Moody's looking a little uncomfortable. I think he realises that little credit will come his way from this easy victory. What he'd wanted, I'm sure, was for Alfie to back down before the fight started—to admit that he was "unnatural" and slink away to the jeered insults of his peers. That would make Moody a hero—the boy who'd stood up for all the Virtues that had Made the Empire Great.

But Alfie won't give up and Moody is starting to come across as a bully—picking on a plucky, smaller boy.

I see the end coming, and I think that Alfie does too. For no obvious reason, Moody relaxes his guard, just for a second. Alfie risks a sharp jab towards his opponent's chest. I think he's realised, just as I have, that this is a trap. Perhaps he sees it as an honourable way out.

Moody takes a light step back and then, almost in the same movement, springs forward again. His fist swings, connecting with Alfie's cheek with tremendous force. Blood and saliva fly. Alfie is falling and hurtling backwards at the same time. He lands in a heap at the feet of the referee, who makes his decision.

"That's it. It's finished. Victory to Moody!" he calls, before Alfie can attempt to stagger to his feet again. He's finished. Beaten, bruised and bloody.

Moody raises his gloved hands in the air. The applause is subdued. I think that he realises this and, hoping to salvage his chance of a little heroism, he steps towards Alfie to help him to his feet.

Alfie's face is a streaked, puffy mask. He pushes Moody's outstretched hands away. Slowly and painfully, he straightens up.

"I'm not a coward. Or a freak. I'm just me," he says again in a mangled voice that rips into my heart.

He manages to walk away unaided, although the referee hovers around him with a blood-streaked towel. Once, my brother stops, doubles over and throws up on the grass.

The crowd drifts off quickly, leaving Moody standing alone apart from Lacey, who is flushed with the vicarious excitement of watching the boys fight each other.

"Well done," he says, clapping Moody on the back and leaving a lingering mark. "You taught him a lesson he won't forget in a hurry. The dirty little coward."

Moody looks as if the next punch he throws will be at Lacey.

"I shouldn't have listened to you," he says in a tired voice. "If there's one thing I've proved, it's that Mullins isn't a coward."

The realisation that Moody is regretting his actions makes me feel a little less antagonistic towards him. Not Lacey though. I would gladly kill him if I had the chance.

Then I make another promise, to myself and to Mother in case she is watching: I will never forget that this is all my fault, and I will never let Alfie get hurt again. Next time I will move heaven and earth to prevent it.

CHAPTER TWELVE

Cambridge, September 1914

I've left school, much to Miss Wren's relief as well as my own, and I'm wondering what to do with myself. Doing nothing is out of the question and I couldn't be less interested in the things that are supposed to be filling my head—flower arranging, flirting and fashion.

To give myself some purpose, I join the Cambridge branch of the Voluntary Aid Detachment. Most of the volunteers are women or older girls who, like me, are seeking some kind of interest outside their own homes. At the back of everyone's mind is the shadow of approaching war, and that has a big influence on the content of our meetings.

We meet in the musty hall attached to St Paul's Church and we do all sorts of fascinating things, from learning to drive to basic nursing skills—cleaning wounds, applying bandages, administering fake medicines to grinning volunteers. I enjoy most of what we learn, and it's an outlet for my restless energy.

When war is declared on a beautiful early August day in 1914, young men hurry to join up. The general belief is that there will be a brief, decisive war (which we will win, of course) and it'll all be over in a few months. If I hear some pimply idiot saying once that if they don't get in on it at the beginning, they'll miss out on all the "fun", I must hear it fifty times.

As I watch the eager boys marching through the streets of Cambridge in their brand new uniforms, I just hope that they're right. I don't want Alfie to feel pressured into getting involved. I'm also a little envious. They're escaping stuffy Cambridge for a foreign country and adventures I can only dream about.

When Alfie leaves school, he asks Father if he can spend some time in the shop. Father agrees with obvious reluctance. He wants Alfie to enter a "profession"—doctoring, or lawyering, or the navy—something that will confirm that the Mullins family are on the up. Father comes from poor stock and has worked hard to establish his business and his reputation. While we're comfortably off and secure enough in our little world of successful tradespeople and their families, he's keen for some sign of social progression too.

Alfie is given permission to help at Mullins & Son a couple of days a week, on the proviso that he starts considering which of the "professions" he wants to pursue, and begins the process of applying for it. In the meantime, Father insists on calling him his "Consulting Assistant Manager".

"He's keen to discover as much as he can about the world of commerce. He will be pursuing a career in the professions of course, but university will come first," Father explains, when some sniffy academic's wife remarks on Alfie's presence. "This is simply to keep him occupied while he prepares for adult life." According to Alfie, the look he shoots at him while he says this conveys that my brother will have little choice in the matter.

"Well, what about it?" I ask Alfie, when he tells me the story that evening. We're in my bedroom—Alfie lounging on the bed and me in a chair with my legs draped over the arms in a way that Father would say was unladylike. "I think you would enjoy being a doctor. You're good at caring."

This is true. Alfie was always there to tend to the endless cuts and scrapes I acquired when I was younger. I'm less physically active now that I'm grown up, but Alfie is still concerned about my health and welfare. When I come home exhausted from the hospital, he's often waiting with a cup of tea and suggestions as to what I can do to cope with the long, stressful days.

"A doctor," Alfie repeats. "I'd rather be a nurse, but perhaps I should. I'll look into it, although I suspect that we 'men'", he says the word with bitterness, "are going to have to put ideas of careers out of our heads for the time being. Until this war is over, the only profession deemed acceptable will be soldiering."

I carry on my voluntary work with the VAD and I enjoy it. I'm attached to the huge new First Eastern General Hospital, essentially a complex of wooden huts built on the Backs, next to the river Cam. It cares for the steadily increasing stream of injured soldiers being sent back from the Western Front.

It becomes a mini town, with its own post office, shop and even a cinema to keep the convalescing men entertained. Many of the poorer ones are cared for to a much better standard than they'd known before the war.

My favourite part of the job is helping the men out into the gardens on days when the weather is mild. I wheel them to sit by the river, or walk with them if they can manage it, and sit with them as we contemplate the slow progress of the water. I learn a lot about the war and soldiering through these lazy conversations, conducted as we watch fish darting among the weeds.

During a long shift at the hospital, I start to feel unwell in a strange way. A dull ache in my stomach and lower back that sharpens into an occasional sharp pang of pain. I feel bloated and irritable, and need to pee frequently.

"Oh. Damn," I say, when the penny drops. Gertie has warned me what to expect, and explained what I need to do when my periods begin. But I had hoped that my lack of conventional femininity and the comfort I found in men's clothes would somehow combine to prevent the curse from bothering me. That, clearly, isn't to be. I remove a field dressing from a cupboard and mutter an excuse to Nurse Poynter, who is on duty with me.

She looks at me with knowing eyes.

"Don't forget to take another safety pin," she says. "The one that comes with the dressing is never enough."

I grab an additional pin and flee. I had thought blushing was beyond me, but it seems I was wrong about that too.

As the war progresses, and more and more injured men are being shipped home, I become quite skilled at basic nursing.

This is all we VADs are permitted to do. The real nurses—the professional ones who are fully trained and paid for their skills—are the only ones deemed capable of the more complex jobs: assisting in operations, dealing with the shell-shocked and with gas burns, which are horrifically painful.

For the most part I hand out medicine, change bandages and give blanket baths. I take pride in doing my simple tasks well and in the knowledge that I'm helping the injured.

I even enjoy wearing my VAD uniform. It's not as liberating as wearing men's clothes, but at least it's free from frills and bows and has been cut to allow easy movement. It gives me a sense of purpose and, for once in my life, of belonging. Alfie likes it too, and often wears my spare apron with its big red cross on the front, and my full, white headdress.

One day he asks me whether he could take my place at the hospital for the day.

"I'm bored, just working in the shop. Nursing would be an excellent introduction to the world of medicine." He has recently sent an application to commence studies as a doctor at St Bartholomew's in London, and is waiting for a reply. They seem to be taking their time.

"No," I say immediately, imagining disastrous scenarios where my twin mixes up the medicine or bandages the wrong limb. I value my work and don't want it jeopardised.

His face drops and I feel a stab of pity for him. His interest in nursing and the sainted nurses Nightingale and Seacole goes back way longer than my own. There's no reason to think that he won't be at least as competent as I am and probably much better.

"But it's my turn to attend church parade on Sunday," I say, feeling that I need to offer him some crumb of enjoyment. "It's a bore and everyone hates doing it, so Sister has compiled a rota. Would you like to go in my place? There'll be no other VADs there."

He leaps at the idea and the following Sunday he virtually skips out of St Paul's Church and over the road to where I am loitering, dressed as a boy, waiting for him.

"Reverend Mitchell kissed my hand! I think we've got an admirer!" His eyes are bright and mischievous.

The thought of Reverend Mitchell's long, drippy nose pecking at my brother's hand is irresistible, and I laugh till my sides ache.

That gives us both more confidence and, after some home-schooling from me, Alfie begins taking some of my Sunday shifts at the First Eastern, when I know that my duties are going to be simple—on Discharge Day, for example, when all I do is help the men pack up their belongings and get them into wheelchairs, if they need them. It gives me a breather, which is very welcome.

I cut my hair as short as I dare, quoting hygiene reasons. Alfie's is a bit longer than the average young man's and, after I've cut mine, there's very little difference between our hairstyles. The headdress helps to hide any discrepancies.

Although Alfie often comes home shocked at the suffering he's witnessed, he revels in his nursing duties and quickly becomes skilled at them.

"I feel like I was born to do it!" he exclaims one day, after I tell him that a patient with badly burned legs complained that I'd handled him far more gently the previous day, when Alfie had been "me". He is proving to be a much better nurse than I'll ever be.

When he finally receives a reply from St Bartholomew's, stating that following guidance from Lord Kitchener, they are holding off training new doctors to "allow young men to fulfil their duty to their country", he isn't surprised.

"At least I have nursing," he says. "By the time they open for medical training again, I'll know enough to skip several courses."

The war has been in progress for well over a year, when Alfie comes home from one of his days in Father's shop looking stormy. At first I think he's still fretting at the recent execution of Nurse Cavell by a German firing squad. She has replaced Florence Nightingale and Mary Seacole as his new hero. But Alfie soon reveals the real reason.

"Maude Donaldson—you know, snuffly old Donaldson from Pembroke College—his squinty daughter gave me a white feather today! I'm not even old enough to enlist! Father looked furious—it was all he could do not to kick her out of the shop."

"Don't think about it," I say. "She's a mean-minded idiot. If she's so worried about the war, let her go and fight it." The thought of Maude Donaldson in a soldier's uniform makes us both laugh.

White-feathering is becoming more and more common and it's nasty. Sanctimonious girls who know they're safe are shaming young men into enlisting. They make me furious. Who are they to force other people into doing *anything* they're not cut out for?

Nonetheless, it makes me worry about Alfie even more. He's always anxious to please, to help his fellow human being and do the right thing. Every white feather he's given—and he has an unpleasant little collection of them—is a lasting reproach to him. For the first time, it occurs to me that Alfie might actually choose to go and fight. If he does, he will be killed. He simply isn't cut out for army life, for battle and all that untrammelled masculinity. His miserable experiences at school proved that. The army will likely be much worse: I can't imagine that proximity to death improves men's manners.

There and then I resolve to do anything I can to prevent Alfie from joining up. I begin to think about ways to protect him.

CHAPTER THIRTEEN

Near Passchendaele Village, Belgium, September 1917

I come round to cold darkness and relative quiet. The shells and bullets have stopped for now, but that just means that the cries of the injured men are easier to hear.

Some scream until their voices fail; until they lose consciousness or die. Others continue to call out for help. Nearby, a Tommy is talking to his mother.

"Jesus, it hurts, Mum… Make it stop, Mum. Please make it stop…"

As my eyes adjust to the dark, I vaguely recall my journey back out of the German trench. I realise that I am on my back in a shallow shell hole, my body half-submerged in muddy water. I touch my abdomen and flinch, biting my lip at the knife of pain twisting inside me. Strange that it hurts so much more now than when I was injured.

There is a man in another shell hole—about ten yards away as far as I can make out. I don't know if he's a friend or an enemy, but here in No Man's Land, that concept blurs. He's another human, hoping that today is not his last. He begins to move, inching his way out of the sheltering hole.

"Take care! Keep still!" I hiss.

As if to prove my words, a single gunshot buries itself in the mud just in front of him. He scuttles back into his hole. The movement is more animal than human. He's no different to a frightened rabbit dashing for its burrow or a hermit crab, darting back into its borrowed home.

Time feels strangely unknowable to me. I drift in and out of consciousness, only to jolt awake again, disoriented and afraid.

The voices of the injured are falling silent. I listen for sounds of movement, for recovery parties.

Nothing.

Is Liam still alive? Is Cox maintaining his amazing survival record? I hope so. My wound no longer hurts. Is that good or bad? I'm as cold as a corpse and desperately thirsty.

My mind returns to the boy I've killed. I wonder what his name was. If he'd joined the army willingly, or whether he'd been a conscript, like me. I imagine his mother at home, looking up from her book and seeing the telegram boy braking outside her home, getting off his bicycle, straightening his uniform and setting his shoulders before he approaches her door. I can see her face as she opens it, backs away from the telegram, crumples to the floor.

"I'm sorry. It was him or me. Him or me." I repeat this again and again but it doesn't stop me thinking about her agony and that of countless other mothers who have sent their sons to war with a prayer in their hearts. For the first time, I'm glad Mother is dead and safe from that gnawing fear. I vow never to marry. Never to have children. Never to swell the numbers of boys born to die young and mothers condemned to lives of grief.

Time drifts and so does my mind. I'm at home with Alfie. We're in my room, putting on clothes from our dressing-up box. The wrong clothes that are so right for us. I'm kissing my dying mother and wishing that my father could spare some of his love for me; I'm gasping as Vesta Tilley saunters around a stage; I'm watching Aunt Julia marching up our garden path, feeling that life is about to change for the better.

"Don't be scared," I murmur to my phantom brother, reaching out to touch his cheek. I don't know why he's here. He's seven again and he's crouching next to me in this shell hole, wearing that tatty feather boa from our dressing-up box. There's a string of amber beads draped over his forehead and around his hair. "You're safe… safe with me…"

I curl into a ball next to him and he gives me a little smile, stroking my hair; looking after me as usual. I slide back into sleep.

Then I'm wide awake, shivering so violently that I'm making ripples in the filthy water I'm lying in. Alfie has gone. Whatever happens to me, at least my beloved brother is safe. I wonder if I've made some kind of trade with the gods. The life of the German boy in exchange for Alfie's. Or my own. I wonder if I would do it again and know in my heart that I would. I don't regret anything except this miserable, drawn-out death.

The pain in my abdomen returns and I close my eyes and wish for sleep. For oblivion. Is death so bad? Where's my rifle? I grope around in the dark and find it. Why wait? It's coming. Speed it up. Grasp it with eager arms. Get it over with.

I'm trembling but that's cold, not fear. I'm beyond fear. How to pull the trigger? The barrel is too long. I can't reach it and point the gun at my head at the same time. A sob escapes me.

Then a hand reaches down, pulls the gun from my hand.

"This one's alive, Sergeant," someone whispers.

"This one too," another low voice from the adjacent shell hole. My neighbour must be one of ours.

I'm pulled out of my sanctuary. But instead of being lowered onto a stretcher, I'm hauled upwards until I'm dangling from the back of my rescuer. There's something about his height, smell and the shape of his body that seems familiar.

"Liam," I say, through parched lips. His head whips round for a second, but he doesn't reply.

The world becomes a jolting swirl of pain and darkness.

Then I'm back in our trench. Liam peers down at me, wiping one hand over his mouth.

"Thanks," I say, forcing myself to sit up and trying to hide the pain it costs me to do it. "I'll be fine now. Just a flesh wound. A good sleep and I'll be good as new." I'm already planning out how to treat it myself. It's important that I convince him that I'm not seriously injured. I don't want to be sent to a casualty clearing station for treatment. If that happens, the game is up.

Behind him, Sergeant Cox's impassive face appears. He's unharmed, as far as I can tell. The man must have some kind of supernatural protection.

"Let's see you stand up then, lad. If you're well enough to stand, you're well enough to stay."

I steel myself to stand, biting the inside of my cheeks to stop myself gasping at the pain.

"There you go, sir." I'm trying to sound jaunty.

Cox gives me a long look. Then he nods. "Fair enough. God knows we need every man who can hold a gun. Give your wound a good check-over and a thorough clean and we'll see how you are in the morning. Off you go, now."

I find a quiet dugout and clean my wound with rum from my hip-flask. It stings unbearably, and I can only hope that this will disinfect it adequately. Then, I reach into my pack and retrieve a field-dressing.

As I lie down to wait for sleep, I stare at the planks that are shoring up the walls to distract myself from the pain. I want to share my experiences with Alfie, but that wouldn't be wise. I'm careful to keep my letters to him light. If I didn't, he'd do something stupid like turning himself in, to "rescue" me. Next thing I know, I'll be sending my twin corny poems. The thought that I'm in danger of becoming another Venner makes me smile.

I could write to Julia, though. She's the next best thing and she can never tell our handwriting apart.

I sit up gingerly, find a sheet of paper and stare at it, wondering what I can write that will get past the censors.

Dear Aunt Julia,

Greetings from the Western Front! I hope all is well and that you haven't been arrested recently.

I grin, imagining the censor's raised eyebrows as he reads this.

I'm at the front line and we've been in action already. It's all fun and games here, and no mistake. I came through it well enough, I think, considering that I'm no one's idea of a fighting man.

Writing this seems like tempting fate, but I can't resist. Let the censor make of it what he will. Most of us are no one's idea of fighting men. Aunt Julia knows that Alfie shouldn't be here and I expect she'll take the comment at face value.

War is strange, Julia. I met a boy yesterday who was just like me, except he was German. He tried to kill me, although he didn't want to. He was crying. It was him or me. That's what I tell myself. I expect he was telling himself the same thing. I keep thinking about his mother. If I could, I would write to her and apologise.

Will that get past the censor? Who knows? It's worth a try, but I'd better not push my luck any further.

I am wounded, but it's not too bad. Just a scratch, really. What I need is for Nina to come and patch it up for me. Have you heard from her? She tells me that her nursing is going very well. I think it will be the making of her. She wasn't made for a quiet life, knitting socks and gloves for the boys at the Front.

Well, that's true enough, if you ignore the fact that Nina is really Alfie, and vice versa.

What else? I look at my letter and purse my lips. There's more blank paper than handwriting. How strange that I felt the need to communicate so strongly, but now I have the chance I don't know what to say. I wonder if Venner felt the same when he wrote those poems. Maybe he just wanted to reach out, to send something of himself to those he loved while he had the chance.

I know better than to ask you for news of Father. I haven't written to him. He seemed to be convinced that I'd be made a General after being here for a couple of weeks. I don't want to disappoint him. If you do hear from him, please send him my regards.

Keep safe and stay away from Zeppelins. Mind you, if they see you coming, they'll be turning and heading home at double speed.

Your loving nephew,

Alfie.

I imagine Julia laughing at the Zeppelin reference. The Germans are using airships to drop bombs on the people at home and, every time it happens, the newspapers are full of the horror of it: how dastardly the Germans are, and how our brave civilians would never surrender to such cowardly tactics. As for me, I think that it's sad that the new miracle of human flight is being used for such a horrible purpose.

I address my letter, hand it to Cox and manage to sleep, dreaming of Aunt Julia puncturing a Zeppelin with her umbrella and rounding up its crew single-handed, shepherding them into a prisoner-of-war camp the way a collie dog does with sheep.

CHAPTER FOURTEEN

Cambridge, April 1917

The war has become something very different to the brief battle envisaged by eager recruits in 1914. With both sides dug in, it turns into a bloody, drawn-out slog that uses up men much too quickly. More are needed. Many more. The number of dead and injured is growing at a faster rate than new recruits are joining up, so the government decides that conscription is the only way to meet the need for new soldiers. A new law is passed stating that all unmarried men and childless widowers between the ages of 18 and 41 are to register as soldiers, or have jolly good reasons why they can't. They have to be prepared to start training as soon as they're called up.

It's no longer a case of dissuading Alfie from enlisting. Now the government will compel him to become a soldier.

The call arrives in the same post as the cards marking our 18th birthday. I rush into the hallway as soon as I hear the letters tumbling onto the tiled floor. I scoop them up, smiling at the two envelopes in Aunt Julia's scrawling handwriting. She never forgets, and she always sends us individual greetings rather than treating us as a single entity. Then I spot the plain typewritten envelope addressed to Alfie. It sticks out among the handwritten ones like a crow among white doves.

My excitement dissolves into fear. I shove the letter into my skirt pocket, glancing behind me. I want to keep my brother safe just a little while longer.

It's a pointless exercise. He's standing on the stairs, gripping the banister.

"It's here, isn't it?"

I make a show of ignorance. "What? Aunt Julia's card? Yes. I hope she's chosen something a bit less controversial this year!" Last year's cards had been adorned with pictures of demonstrating Suffragettes demanding their right to vote. Father very nearly showed some emotion when he saw them. I made sure to put mine in the centre of the mantelpiece.

Alfie refuses to be diverted. "You know what I mean. My call-up. You don't need to hide it. I knew it would come, if not today then tomorrow or the next day. Looks like they can't wait to get their hands on me, eh?" He forces a smile. "They must have heard what excellent soldiering material I'll make."

His self-mockery twists in me like a knife.

"We'll fight it. Say you're needed here!"

"Needed here? For what? To advise all the war widows on their mourning outfits?" he trudges downstairs. "I won't even be able to carry on helping at the hospital. Once you go off to Brighton to be a proper nurse, I'll be redundant. I might as well go to the Front and get it over with."

I'm due to transfer to a military hospital in Brighton soon. I applied a few months previously, when I was finding my constrictive life unbearable. Since hearing that I've been accepted, I've been swinging between excitement at escaping from Father and concern about how I'd cope without Alfie. And about how he'll cope without me. I even suggested that he find an excuse to follow me, so that we could continue our dual lives. He has been trying to come up with a plan that will allow him to do that, but now it's no longer possible. He will be in a trench on the Western Front fighting for his life, long before any of that can come to fruition.

"There's the medical," I say to him. "They'll see you're not cut out to be a soldier and–"

He gives a bitter laugh and holds out his hand for the envelope—the only one that matters among the little pile of good wishes.

"If the only men in the army were the ones who were fit to be soldiers, we'd have been defeated in the first month of the war!"

I hand the envelope over and watch him tear it open. His face is expressionless as he reads the contents.

"Two weeks," he says, meeting my eyes. "I've got two weeks to get my medical. And then I've got to be prepared to leave immediately for training. It's like I said—they just can't wait to get me fighting! Fritz, you'd better watch out–here I come!"

He goes back upstairs and shuts himself in his room.

This is it. Time to tell Alfie about my plan, to sell it to him. I pace around the hall while I work out what I'm going to say. Then I follow him upstairs, knock on his door and let myself in without waiting for permission.

He's lying on his bed, arms behind his head, staring up at the ceiling. His face and lips are set.

I sit down next to him and take a deep breath.

"What are you, Alfie? Inside, I mean?"

He turns his head to look at me.

"No," he says.

"No? No, what?"

"You're not drawing me into a trap. You know what I am. I know what you are too, and I've been waiting for you to come up with some outlandish plot to get me out of conscription. I suppose I should thank you for caring about me. But I'm going. End of story."

I curse to myself: I should have been more subtle. Alfie can read my mind. But I'm not finished yet.

"The thing is, I want to go to fight. Always have—you know that. D'you remember when we were small and I'd dress as a soldier?" I see the ghost of a frown on Alfie's face. "That was fate, telling us what to do, how we should live. I honestly believe that. If you say no to me, you'll be ruining my life."

The frown clears and, for a second, I think he's going to agree with me.

"No," he says again. Nothing else. He's showing me that there's no point arguing.

Just before he closes his eyes, shutting me out altogether, he says, "It's just the way it is, Nina. I'm going and you're staying.

Now let me get some peace. While I can." He turns on his side, away from me.

He attends his medical and is passed A1. The medical officer tells him that he'll make "a fine soldier." My twin's bitter jokes about his suitability for war are coming true. Alfie is required to report to Aldershot for training at his earliest convenience.

I've already made my plan, and there's just about enough time to tidy up the loose ends.

On our final evening, Gertie pulls out all the stops to cook us a decent meal to send us off into the world with full bellies. There's duck with cranberries and new potatoes, mounds of vegetables, and a creamy trifle.

There's also wine. Lots of it for Father and Alfie, less for me.

"You won't want to risk overindulging," Father says to me, pouring me half a glass. "Especially with a long train journey ahead of you. There are bound to be many soldiers about. You'll need to stay alert."

Does Father imagine I'm going to stagger drunkenly onto my train and give myself to the nearest conscript? I wince at his low opinion of me. But I give an inward shrug too. It suits my purpose for Alfie and Father to be relaxed tonight. Let them drink themselves into oblivion.

Alfie is withdrawn, staring at his plate. Father doesn't notice. He's proud that Alfie is going off to "do his bit" and becomes quite animated.

"A soldier's life is a fine one," he says, pouring more wine. "It'll be the making of you. You'll be an officer in no time at all. And the friends you'll make. An army pal is a pal for life…"

I stifle a sarcastic retort. As if Father knows anything about war! I wonder if he has considered the implications of what he's said. In war, a pal for life could mean just a few days. The list of young men of our acquaintance who've already lost their lives is growing longer and longer. Many of Alfie's schoolmates, Moody included, have been reported killed or "missing, presumed dead."

The evening limps on, with Alfie drinking glass after glass of wine, Father encouraging him and me trying to quell my churning stomach and keep up an appearance of normality.

After what seems like an eternity, Father brings the evening to a close. "I'll say goodnight now, and goodbye," he's standing up. "I'll be gone before you in the morning. Commerce and the ladies of Cambridge wait for no man! God speed, my boy. Keep safe," he gives Alfie a hug. "And to you too, Nina. Do your best." My hug is limp and over in a heartbeat.

Alfie and I go to the kitchen to thank Gertie, who's working even later than usual because it's a "special occasion", and to assure her that we'll see her in the morning before we go our separate ways.

Before we say goodnight on the landing, Alfie gives me a long, fierce hug.

"I'll be alright, you know. You needn't worry about me," he's slurring his words.

I hug him back, just as fiercely. "I know you will," I say, and I mean it. "See you in the morning."

I go to my room and wait.

I hear the front door close behind Gertie and her exhausted yawn as she begins her walk home. Not long after, I hear Alfie snoring.

Father's room is quiet as the grave, as always. I wonder if he ever sleeps, or if he just stands, eyes open and immobile as a statue, and waits for the morning when he can begin work again.

I turn my lamp up just a little bit and get to work on making my hair even shorter.

Twenty minutes later I gather up my shorn hair, which I'll dump on the way to the railway station, and dress in men's clothes.

I creep into Alfie's room. He's curled on his side, dead to the world.

I reread Alfie's letter:

Dear A,

I've gone in your place. You can't stop me and you shouldn't try. You're going to Brighton to take up my nursing role. It's all arranged, including some nice private accommodation, so you don't have to worry about that. They're even expecting you to have short hair—I've thought of everything! If your landlord looks a bit unwelcoming, it's because I told them I'd cut mine short to prevent head lice. Sorry about that, and I hope they don't treat you like a leper! The address is attached, as well as my identity papers, letters from the hospital, etc. I've taken yours.

I want to do this and I'm cut out to do it. You're not. That's the end of it, as far as I'm concerned. If the world was a more sensible place, it wouldn't be a problem anyway.

Please don't tell anyone. If you do, I'll have to explain why I did it, which will get us both in trouble. Trust me. I'll be fine. And write to me. I'm looking forward to hearing about your nursing adventures. You were born to be a nurse, you know. And I was born to cause trouble, so this is the perfect solution.

Wish me luck.

Your loving sister,

N.

I give a nod. It'll have to do. I lack the facility to make things pretty. With his papers in my hand, and my letter on his bedside table, I steal out.

Then it's just a matter of waiting for the first inklings of dawn. I creep downstairs with my little bag of belongings. As I put on Alfie's coat and boots, I wish that I could say a proper goodbye to Gertie. She'll be hurt and she doesn't deserve to be.

Father probably won't notice that I've gone.

CHAPTER FIFTEEN

Aldershot, June 1917

After Cambridge, Aldershot comes as a shock.

It's much newer for a start. Until a few decades ago, it was nothing but a sleepy village. Now it's a busy town of red brick houses that are still being built to accommodate the swelling population. Compared to Cambridge's mellow stone buildings, the houses seem characterless and boring—indistinguishable from each other, a lot like the endless conscripts streaming into town.

Cambridge is busy, of course, especially at the end of term when the students like to let off steam, but everyone knows that life will soon settle back into its usual gentle pace. Aldershot bustles all the time, day and night. People are making a living from soldiers—catering for them, clothing them, cleaning up after them, entertaining them during their free hours, selling them books and newspapers and beer and temporary love.

There are thousands of us—new recruits, wounded veterans, artillery men, medical men, infantry men, even a cavalry brigade. I love to see them practising manoeuvres on their huge, sleek horses. Sometimes they ride into the town in their red dress uniforms, just because they can and because it gives the local children a few moments of excitement. They make the tinny cars and lorries look ridiculous. When they move in a group, they're like a force of nature. It's hard to imagine that anything could ever harm them.

I quickly discover that although we soldiers are bringing prosperity to the town, we aren't always welcome. There are simply too many of us. The barracks are overflowing and the authorities have recently taken to requisitioning schools and private houses for conscripts. It's caused a lot of bad feeling among the civilian population. More than once, a visit into town is marred by the gibes and glares of the locals. It never ends in a fight, though. We're soldiers, after all—we can take care of ourselves. And anyway, who's left to fight us? It seems as if every young man in the country has been called up to serve.

I'm quick to volunteer to be billeted in a little house not far from the railway station, in Waterloo Road. It pleases me that Alfie and I are both living in streets with military names. I decide that it's a good omen.

Most conscripts prefer to be in the big garrison buildings, where they think there's safety in numbers. I think just the opposite, and the chance of getting a bathroom that I don't have to share with dozens of men is too good to miss. The problem of how I'm going to manage bathing has been one of my biggest concerns. The only solutions I've come up with are to plead shyness or some contagious skin disease, but I don't think those excuses will last forever. I have a generous supply of field dressings for my periods, and I'm pretty sure I can get more without trouble. In a soldiers' town, they seem to be everywhere.

The thing that surprises me most about my new occupation is the language. Your average Tommy swears as naturally as he breathes, and if he doesn't when he first arrives for training, then he learns to pretty quickly. We haven't even finished putting on our uniforms for the first time before the chap in the next cubicle, a pasty-faced solicitor's clerk called Hapgood, emerges complaining that it weighs a "bloody ton". He adds that the breeches makes his balls itch like he's "got the clap".

It's the casualness of Hapgood's swearing that shocks me. It must show on my face, because he gives me a nasty little smile.

"What's wrong, mate? No one swear where you come from? Not a bloody Methodist, are you?" His accent is hard to understand. I can't place it.

I blink once. "Not bloody likely!" It feels so wrong to be swearing out loud, but exciting too. "We're Church of bloody England!" Some of the others laugh and I wonder if I've overdone it, but it's too exhilarating to stop. "I can bloody well swear till my balls drop off, when I feel like it!"

From then on, I swear freely whenever our officers are out of earshot, and under my breath when they're present. Swearing is an offence in the British Army, and I've no wish to incur a fine or to be confined to barracks. Soon I've acquired a vocabulary that would make Alfie blanch. As for Father—he'd disown me on the spot.

Alfie's first letter arrives a few days after my arrival in Aldershot and it's angry, although he's hampered by the need to be careful about what he commits to paper, in case our letters are read by censors.

What do you think you're doing? You're mad. You've no right to force my hand. You will get us both into trouble. You must *reconsider. Please. Don't do this.*

It goes on like that for quite a while.

Gertie was very sad that you left without saying goodbye. I made an excuse for you. I said that you were really nervous and couldn't sleep, and that in the end, you simply decided to get on with it. I told her that you sent her love. I was quite nervous myself when it was time to leave, but it went well.

I interpret that as meaning that Gertie hadn't noticed the swap. Good. I didn't think she would, but it's a relief to have it confirmed.

Things here are fine. My accommodation is perfectly acceptable. My room is small and a bit basic but the bed is comfy, there's plenty of hot water for baths and I certainly won't starve! Mr and Mrs Able are pleasant, once I'd convinced them that I wasn't infested with lice. Mrs A even said that short hair suited me and maybe I'll start a fashion! They're full of compliments about "the magnificent work" I'm doing for "our injured heroes".

As for the work, it's—well—it's wonderful. And it's horrible. The hospital is huge—even bigger than the First Eastern—and the bravery of the patients is astonishing. Some of the injuries…I don't know how they keep cheerful. But they do, nearly all of them. They make me worry all the more for you. Please take care. Please reconsider. If anything happened to you, I'd never forgive myself.

I put the letter aside with a sense of relief. Alfie is settling in well and he's finally living the life he deserves. I've done the right thing.

My reply is short and to the point: *It's done. This is our chance. This is the opportunity we've dreamed of since we were small, so let's make the most of it. Things are fine here. Just stop worrying about me and enjoy your new job.*

After a couple of weeks, I begin to relax. There's a lot about my new life that I enjoy. I relish the sense of belonging, the fact that for the first time ever it's not only permissible to avoid all the things that women are supposed to do that drive me mad— sitting upright, being quiet, trying to look demure and *nice* all the time—it's essential. To feel free to slouch and swear and to laugh at the others' risqué jokes, and even make my own when I'd gathered the courage, is liberating.

Finally, our training starts to get more interesting. We practise route marching—a welcome change after the endless, pointless slogging around the drill square—and go out on night ops, creeping over the Aldershot heathland with our faces blackened. The gas-helmet exercises are alarming at first, especially because I've seen what gas does to men who aren't quick enough to get theirs on. The first time I pull the cloth over my head and peer through the round eyepieces, trying to get my bearings, I feel a cold shiver of panic. You have to hold a valve in your mouth to breathe through and it's far from easy, especially when you are running or fighting at the same time.

Alfie writes a couple of times a week and it's not long before I detect a growing confidence and sense of purpose in him.

There's a chap called Brighouse—a gas case. Not enough to kill him, but it has blistered his lungs and causes him pain that I can't even imagine. Like so many of the injured, he tries his hardest not to complain. Not to make a noise, even. But then you look into his eyes when he's not expecting it and you see him trying to hold back the tears, clenching his fists until it looks like the knuckle bones will burst through his skin. It makes you want to hug him and tell him how sorry you are. But you don't. You can't. Instead, you pretend you haven't noticed, or you chide him like a child making a fuss. It's not that I'm learning not to care. I'm learning not to show that I care. Pity isn't going to help anyone.

Anyway, his pulse was much too high and his heart was pattering like a frightened bird's. And the Doctor—behind his back, we call him Doctor Death—he must have got his medical training in the Crimea—wanted to bleed him!

I persuaded him that the last thing Brighouse needed was to be weakened by blood loss on top of all his other problems. Honestly! He's supposed to be an expert! Brighouse thanked me later. He said he didn't like to speak up against a doctor, but he was worried that blood-letting would have just about finished him off...

I shake my head in wonder. Alfie is finding his voice and using it. I feel proud of him. I smile at his use of "we". It means that the other nurses have accepted him. It seems that everything is going to work out as I'd prayed it would. I'm glad that I've enforced the swap, for my sake as well as for his. Finally I'm one of the boys, and I'm enjoying it thoroughly.

Being one of the lads means being subjected to relentless ribbing without a shred of malice behind it, means making sure that I give out as much as I receive, and laughing raucously no matter what. I quickly learn to control my face when someone belches, farts, describes what they've produced in the latrines that morning, or details exactly what they want to do with the girls they spot on our trips around town. Usually, the girl in question blushes and tries to look innocent. That makes me even gladder that I've left those days behind me. A woman's life is a continual challenge to be what they think men want them to be. When—if—I return to a woman's life, I will make sure that I live it to my own standards, not those of others.

My first visit to the pub is an event I'll never forget, for more than one reason. It's been a gruelling day of training: we've learned all about gas and what it can do to you. We've all seen the evidence in the form of horrifying photographs of gassed men, and practised with our gas masks until the skin on our noses, where the rough glass eyepieces settle, is red and sore.

We've attached and removed our bayonets, stabbed at sandbags and learned that if we can channel some inner hatred as we jab away at them, we have more chance of hitting them fair and square. I resist the temptation to think about Father and conjure an image of the strutting, posturing Kaiser, instead. After a final hour of drilling—forming fours and turning left and right and standing to attention—we are released for the day.

We drift off the drill ground, stretching and swearing. There's nothing in my head except the desperate need to go back to my lodgings and have a bath. Then I feel a hand on my shoulder and turn to see Liam Talbot smiling at me.

"Hard day, today. Coming for a pint, lad?"

I open my mouth to make up some excuse, but something in Liam's smile makes me change my mind and I find myself agreeing. A group of us head to the Artillery Arms in the High Street.

I approach the pub with trepidation. I am still learning the right way for a man to behave and I'm sure that in this new environment, there will be unspoken rules that I've never had to consider before. Liam pushes open the door, with its stained-glass picture of a soldier in an old fashioned red and black uniform, and steps inside. I'm close behind him.

The pub is dingy, with sawdust on the floor and a long, oak bar. The top of it is stained and looks sticky. Behind the bar are shelves and shelves of dark bottles of alcohol I've never heard of and, in front of them, some ceramic handles projecting from a piece of furniture that looks rather like an upright piano. This is set into the bar at the same height, forming an uninterrupted surface on which various men, the majority of them soldiers like us, have set their drinks. A woman behind the bar gives us a wide smile.

"What'll you have, lads?"

Hapgood pipes up with a request for "a pint of porter" and the woman takes down a ceramic mug before pulling several times on one of the ceramic handles, releasing dark liquid into it.

Someone else asks for the same and the woman goes through the same process.

Liam requests a pint of pale ale and once again the woman takes down a china mug and fills it using a different ceramic handle.

My turn is coming. What do I say? There are brass placards in front of the ceramic handles and I scan them quickly. "Mild" sounds dull to me, and a bit too feminine for my liking. I reject the drink called "porter" because it reminds me of the dogsbodies at Cambridge Railway Station, ferrying about valises and boxes for customers who treat them like dirt. I nearly order pale ale because that's what Liam ordered, but change my mind for the same reason. I want to convince myself that I've got a mind of my own, so I ask for a pint of stout because the name brings to mind jolly characters in books by Dickens that I used to enjoy.

"Oho! Mullins, I never had you down as a hardened drinker," Hapgood says, slapping me on the back.

I smile and take a deep draft of the liquid that has just been handed to me.

It's all I can do not to gasp. The taste is dark and bitter. It reminds me of iron and ice cream at the same time, and I wonder how such a combination is possible. Controlling the urge to grimace, I sigh, as the others have done after their first taste of the contents of their mugs.

"Lovely," I say. The others laugh, so I laugh too and take another gulp.

Within minutes, I start to feel light-headed. After ten minutes I'm flushed and laughing at everything being said. Within half an hour I'm on my second pint and feeling like an immortal being.

Around this time, I begin to notice a group of half a dozen girls—factory workers by the way they are dressed—seated around a table on the far side of the room. One of them looks uneasy and I wonder if, like me, this is her first time in a pub. She keeps her eyes lowered to her glass, taking tiny sips of her drink while her friends look around, exchanging quips with the rest of the clientele. This girl looks very young and, with her soft brown hair and pink cheeks, she reminds me of the country maidens who frequently appear in newspapers to advertise butter or milk or any product that is supposed to be handmade by country innocents.

Another group of trainee Tommies are taking a lively interest in the seated girls, and soon they have drawn up chairs beside them. There is a swift exchange of insults and innuendo, and it surprises me that the girls seem to understand every comment that the Tommies make, even the obscene ones. I was brought up to believe that women were oblivious to the unsavoury workings of the male mind and needed to remain that way. The alternative is to live under a cloud, regarded as "no better than they ought to be," and to be shunned by decent men and women.

But here is a young woman who responds to a request from one of the Tommies to "show her jugs" with a spurt of laughter and a quick riposte. "Show me a shilling and I'll show you more than my jugs. I'll show you my blooming bowl as well!" This is greeted with a roar of laughter from nearly everyone in the pub. I join in. It's important that I come across as one of the lads. I'm not precisely sure what she means, but I can make a good guess.

The young woman with the pink cheeks doesn't join in, I notice. Her cheeks get even pinker and she bites her lip.

"Cheer up, Elsie," one of her friends calls out, "we're in a pub, not at a wake!"

Elsie looks up and smiles obediently, drawing the attention of one of the seated Tommies. He obviously fancies his chances with her, because he drags his chair closer to hers and drapes one arm over the back of it, which makes Elsie sit up straighter.

"Tell you what, *Elsie*," the way he enunciates the syllables of her name makes it sound as if he is biting chunks out of it, "come out back with me. I've not got a shilling, but what'll you do for tuppence ha'penny, eh? Or a farthing?"

Elsie blushes and looks around her friends for support, but they're laughing as raucously as everyone else. She mutters something that I can't hear. Whatever it is, it doesn't help and the randy Tommy takes it as encouragement.

"She says yes!" he roars. "She hasn't got change for the farthing, but I can use up the rest of the balance another time."

To cheers and jeers, the Tommy is trying to pull her out of her seat. She struggles and looks on the verge of tears. "No! Please, Joan, Connie," she begs her friends for help, but all they do is laugh.

I've downed my second pint by now, and I make a start towards her. How can all these stupid people stand there and laugh? She is clearly terrified and, judging by the blood suffusing the Tommie's cheeks, he's drunk enough to do anything.

I've only taken a couple of steps before I stop. I can't draw attention to myself this way. Imagine if I got into a brawl and was taken to hospital. The game would be over for me and for Alfie. I clench my hands into fists, wanting to help but unable to help, wondering if I dare shout to someone to come to their senses and *stop* this.

The Tommy has her halfway to the door by now and the look on his face has changed from drunken amusement to grim determination. This is not going to end well. *Why* is everyone laughing? Can't they see what is about to happen?

A figure steps in front of the struggling pair. Liam.

"I'll tell you what it is," he says to the Tommy, "I'm getting the impression that the lady isn't too keen on the idea. I heard a definite "no" from her. How about letting her go and finding someone more willing? A good-looking lad like you will have 'em queueing up, farthing or no!"

The Tommy tells Liam to mind his own business, and Liam shakes his head.

"Can't do that, mate. Call me a do-gooder, but I can't stand by while you—distress this young lady. Look at her—she's just a kid, really. And she's crying. Where's the fun in that?"

The Tommy looks mutinous but, after a long moment, he lets the girl go. She returns to her friends who have finally come to their senses and start fussing over her. The Tommy is looking Liam up and down. He takes it calmly, meeting his eyes and tilting his head to one side. It's as if he's saying, "If you fancy your chances, you're welcome to have a go at me, but I don't think it'll end well for you."

The Tommy must agree with Liam's assessment. He storms out of the pub, brushing past a policeman who must be off duty because he has a drink in his hand and showed no interest in helping.

"I was going to help her," I claim, as Liam rejoins us. "I was just waiting for—for…" I can't think of how to finish my sentence. Words seem hard to grasp at the moment, and even harder to say.

Liam gives me a brief smile. "I know, Mullins."

The barmaid, who looks to be in her thirties, with kind brown eyes and fair hair that is escaping from the pins intended to keep it tidy, has been watching me. She seems to have taken a shine to me.

"You don't get out much, do you?" she says, as she hands me my third pint. "Take this one slowly."

I stutter a denial, and tell her that, on the contrary, I'm used to spending most of my waking hours in the pub. My words seem to be running together but I think she gets the gist.

She cocks her head to one side.

"Nice young lad like you, someone needs to take you under their wing. If I was a single woman, I'd offer to do it myself, but…" she waggles her left hand with its wedding ring and nods across the room to where the policeman is glowering in our direction. "My Alfred wouldn't take too kindly to it."

Alfred! Another Alfie! Anyone called Alfred must be a thoroughly decent chap. I decide that I must say hello to him. I haven't taken more than a couple of steps before a hand on my shoulder stops me.

"Going somewhere?" Liam asks, when I turn to find out who has accosted me.

"Same name as my— as me! I need to say hello." I duck out of Liam's grasp and prepare to resume my walk, which is more difficult than usual because it's becoming a struggle to gauge directions, or even to stand up straight. The policeman's frown seems to be deepening by the second, especially when I flash a wide smile at him.

Liam moves in front of me, blocking my way.

"Take my word for it, Mullins, you're better off pursuing that acquaintance another day."

"Why? I'm being friendly. I—"

Liam is turning me round, leading me back to the others.

"He's got more pluck than sense, this one," Liam says. "We need to keep an eye on him."

I open my mouth to protest but close it again, deciding it doesn't really matter.

"Thanks, Talbot. You're a good fellow. A damned good fellow. You're all damned good fellows." I smile vaguely at the group of conscripts. "I'm damned lucky to know you all."

Hapgood places a mug into my hand and I raise it in a sloppy toast.

"To friendship. And to damned good fellows everywhere!" I announce. I catch the eye of the barmaid. "And to kind ladies who hand out *delicious* beverages. And their noble husbands who uphold the law no matter what. We're safe in our beds with fellows like that on hand to protect us! A Hun would run a bloody mile—"

The noble policeman seems less than pleased by my compliments. Perhaps he suspects me of sarcasm. He is pulling a notebook out of his tunic pocket and his face is turning as dark as the liquid sloshing around in my mug.

"Time to make a move," Liam interrupts. He threads one arm through mine and hauls me towards the door. Hapgood takes my other arm and, between them, they manoeuvre me past the scowling policeman and into the bright evening air.

"Where are your lodgings, Mullins? I'll see you safely home."

After Liam has agreed to meet up with the others later in a different pub, we set off for Waterloo Road. I weave my way happily along the streets of Aldershot, singing war songs and raising my cap to passing ladies, who either glare or smile at me.

It strikes me that I'm feeling tremendously happy. I'm thoroughly enjoying the freedom of my new life and for the first time I have friends, or at least the possibility of making them. I'm no longer the outsider; I'm one of a crowd, living and learning together, with a common goal.

"Talbot, stout is MAH-vellous. Absolutely bloody MAH-vellous." I slur.

He gives me a sideways grin and I feel my heart give a twist. I stop for a moment as I take in an unwelcome realisation. Oh no. Not that. Not now. And why him? Rescuing that girl doesn't make him a knight in shining armour. And what would I do with a knight in shining armour, anyway? I shake my head, trying to dislodge the unwelcome thoughts that threaten to destroy my newly-found sense of belonging.

Liam smiles again and gives my cheek a light, playful bash. I'm sure it's just wishful thinking that it lingers a second longer than necessary.

"You're a liability, Mullins. But I like you. God knows why. In you go, lad. I expect you won't be feeling quite so happy in the morning."

He steps back. For a moment, a look of confusion passes over his face. I can't work out why. Then he gives me a crooked smile, and slouches away.

CHAPTER SIXTEEN

Travelling to the Reserve Trenches, near Passchendaele Village, Belgium, early September, 1917

Finally, when we have learned to drill and march, to handle weapons, to carry them without injuring ourselves as we crawl on our bellies, and to dig trenches which, we are told, will become second homes to us, our training comes to an end and we are informed that we will be heading out to the front.

The announcement, made in a cheery voice by Sergeant Grimes, who has been with us since the start of our three-month stay in Aldershot, falls among men silenced by the realisation that the thing they have secretly been dreading can be put off no longer. A few minutes ago we were bantering, exchanging jokes and insults and laughing when one hit home. Now the smiles have slid from our faces and our eyes are straining to see into a future that we can't quite imagine, in spite of all our training.

We are going into battle.

As we prepare to leave Aldershot, I notice a further change to Alfie's letters. They are no longer taken up solely with hospital life. It seems that Alfie too, is finding friendship in his new role

I went out for a drink with some of the other nurses a few nights ago, he writes. *I had no idea how romantically we are regarded by many of the public. The number of times someone came up to thank us for our sacrifice! You'd think we'd just come back from the trenches! And the number of young men, soldiers most of them, who sent drinks over to our table! One of them, a young officer in a beautifully cut uniform that looked as if it had just been delivered from a high-class tailor, sent over champagne. "See you at the Front," he mouthed at us, which seemed rather negative, when you think about it. Not that we will get to the Front, of course. We're too young and inexperienced for that. Anyway, negative or not, he had curly hair, beautifully brilliantined, and deep brown eyes. He came over and kissed our hands before he left, and I'm sure that he held on to mine for longer than strictly necessary! Nancy, one of my new nursing friends, commented on it.*

I swear, dear brother, that ever since then I've been dreaming of gallant officers with brown eyes!

I'm concerned at what Alfie has written and spend much of the train journey from Aldershot to Southampton turning it over in my mind.

First, there's the risk of Alfie getting caught, if he forms a relationship with another man. Homosexuality is illegal and punishable by a prison term, but even that is preferable to the alternative. If Alfie is deemed to have deserted the army by allowing me to go in his stead, he will be shot. The closer he gets to other people, the more his risk of discovery increases.

But Alfie is sensible and sensitive, he's a good judge of character and he can be trusted not to divulge his secret to the wrong person. I realise that, more than ever before, we are utterly reliant on each other. When we were children, my happiness depended on Alfie, and his on me. Now it's more than happiness in the balance, it's Alfie's life and my freedom. I bite my lip and make a solemn vow that I will keep to my disguise no matter what.

Liam catches my expression and asks if everything is all right.

"Fine," I say, ignoring the increase to my heartbeat when I spot concern in his eyes.

"Girl trouble, I daresay." He nods at the letter that I'm twisting in my hands. "Don't let them lead you by the nose. Come back a hero and they'll be lining up to demonstrate their admiration!" He winks at me and I wrestle up a smile in response. If Liam is a knight in shining armour, then that armour is tarnished. The thought of him accepting "admiration" from gaggles of girls, who in my mind are all conventionally pretty and pliant, is not something that I want to dwell upon.

From Étaples we are moved by train to a reserve trench and given time to settle in before our first stint in the front line. Once we have grown accustomed to the barrage of ear-splitting noises, life becomes a round of mundane duties: drilling, cleaning weapons and uniforms, erecting tents, and filling sandbags. In other circumstances we might complain that the work is tedious, but, as we wait for the call to the move to the Front, we cherish it. In a few days this life of practise and polishing will, I suspect, seem very desirable. We will count the days until we are back here again, in stolid safety, doing the things that keep us busy and take our minds off life in the front line.

Another letter from Alfie arrives, even more ebullient than the last.

Brighton is a lively town and it's hard to resist its gaiety, even after a long shift at the hospital. There are weekly fundraising dances, and I must say that I am becoming rather good at the foxtrot and one-step. My dance card is usually completely full! There are countless restaurants too, and even a music hall! Perhaps, after the war, we might set up home here together.

Some of my fellow nurses have local beaux. They wait outside the hospital for them to finish work. There are a couple who are obviously shy. They hide in the doorway of a nearby hotel, clutching little posies of flowers as if they're frightened that someone will snatch them away. One of them blushes furiously if we stop to greet him. It's very sweet.

Reading between the lines, I suspect that Alfie would like a beau of his own but I hope he will think carefully before pursuing that route. While he was at school he frequently had crushes on other boys, but to the best of my knowledge none of them were requited. When it comes to love, he is as much a novice as I am. I send up a heartfelt prayer that he will be careful and that his search for love won't affect his judgment, then sit down to compose a suitably oblique response in which I try to sound encouraging at the same time as reminding him of his need for caution.

All too soon, we receive notice that we are to take up front-line duties. A contingent of our men—company commanders, weapons officers and Lewis Gun teams—are sent to the Front to prepare for our arrival. Our own journey takes place at night and we march in silence. All the things I learned in training are jostling for prominence in my head. I'm worried that, at the vital moment, I will forget everything and disgrace myself. I glance up into the face of the man marching next to me. Judging by the strain in his set face, his thoughts are equally grim.

All too soon, we reach our destination. We move into position, nodding at the men we are relieving as they hand over their weapons to us. They will take over the guns that we left behind in the reserve trench.

"Seen much action?" I ask the gangly young man who passes his rifle over to me.

"Not so much. The powers that be are saving up for the big offensive; if it's action you're after, you'll not be disappointed."

I decide to ignore the pity that I detect in his face.

I'm pretty sure no one gets much sleep that night. I spend much of it straining my eyes to peep over the top of our trench into No Man's Land. How far away is the German front line? Is there some fellow over there, peering back towards me right now, wondering the same thing?

From time to time, the wind carries snatches of German conversation to us. I don't understand the words but they sound like normal, everyday exchanges. Are they talking about their families and their hopes for the future? Perhaps they're discussing mundane things—the quality of the food, or how long they need to wait before they will be sent back for some respite. At one point, one of them laughs. His laugh sounds like any other. It's not the laugh of a cold-hearted murderer planning mayhem and destruction. Perhaps they aren't the rapacious baby-killers described to us in grim detail by Sergeant Grimes, during bayonet practice. And if they aren't, how are we going to live with ourselves when we kill them?

CHAPTER SEVENTEEN

Near Passchendaele Village, Belgium, October 1917

I t's the morning after our second attack and I am no worse, which is something. By some miracle I seem to have escaped infection. It's a quiet day, which gives me a chance to recuperate, and that afternoon there's even some good news.

"The powers that be are feeling benevolent, lads," Cox says, with his grave twinkle. "We're falling back to the Reserve Trench tomorrow. We're giving some other lucky lads the chance to be heroes for a while. And we've been given a week's leave."

"*Leave?* We've not been here five minutes," Lacey blurts out. "It must be a mistake."

"Are you complaining?" Cox asks. "Error or no, it's in writing and it's happening. Unless you want to stay behind….?" He lifts an eyebrow.

"No! Of course not," Lacey assures him. "But– leave…. Where will we go? What will we do? How will we…?" he trails off and wipes the back of his hand along his mouth.

Liam spits into a puddle.

Someone else swears under his breath.

We know what's going on in Lacey's head because we're all thinking it too: knowing what we now do about life here, how will we find the courage to come back?

Cox tries to keep the compassion from his face as he answers.

"You'd be surprised what men can do when they have to. As to the question of where you go and what you do, most men go home. A little R and R and some of your mother's home cooking will set you up a treat…."

Liam looks Lacey up and down.

"Quite a lot of home cooking, for some of us," he mutters into my ear.

I bite back a laugh, trying to ignore the stab of excitement I feel at the warmth of his breath so close.

"Where will you go?" I ask him. From what I know of Liam, he won't be rushing home to his loving parents. It's much more likely that he'll pass the week in the arms of a willing girl.

He shrugs.

"London, I think." He nods. "Yes, London. A chap can lose himself there, forget his troubles for a while." He hesitates, then smiles at me. "Want to come? I have a feeling we would rub along very well together in London. I should enjoy showing you the sights and all that."

I'm sorely tempted. It would be very easy to read too much into Liam's invitation, but spending more time than necessary with him is dangerous. For once, I regret my adeptness at playing the man. It cuts me off forever from being anything else to the only person I have ever found attractive.

So I give him a grin, and shake my head.

"I appreciate the offer," I say, "but I believe I'll go to Brighton. I'd like to surprise my sister…."

Liam opens his mouth, then closes it again. He shrugs.

"Another time, perhaps." Then he changes the subject.

Two days later, I'm waiting outside the hospital where "Nina" works.

The Royal Pavilion was once the home of a Prince with questionable taste, judging by the domes, gilding and minarets that proliferate here. Now it's a hospital for men who have lost limbs in the war. I wonder if Walter Warmsley might be inside, coming to terms with life with one arm. I make a mental note to ask Alfie to look out for him.

As I loiter in a nearby doorway, waiting for Alfie to emerge, I'm confused by the flurry of activity around me. Shops are open and the goods in their windows strike me as exotic and extravagant. Does any woman really need silk stockings so fine that they're little more than pale, weightless wisps? What kind of a man would spend three shillings on hair preparations? The bright colours of women's skirts and dresses seem garish after the muddy tones of the Front, and the noise of everyday traffic—motor cars, omnibuses, horse-drawn carts—startles me almost as much as the thunder of battle used to when I first encountered it.

In spite of this, my heart is thumping at the prospect of seeing my twin again. My mind's eye imagines him at the centre of a cluster of happy, glowing nurses. They are pushing open the door, chatting as they surge out onto the street. Then Alfie spots me, stops dead, and rushes towards me with open arms.

Of course, it doesn't happen like that.

He's with a cluster of other nurses, all right. But the one who pushes open the door—and it's not Alfie—does so as if it takes the final dregs of her strength. The group who trudge out are pale and subdued. The black smudges beneath their eyes tell their own tale.

Alfie is one of the last to emerge. He's walking with a sturdy, blonde girl who looks like a farmer's daughter. They are silent, with no energy for idle chat. He is in the act of removing his headdress and I realise that his hair has grown. He has a long fringe which trails over his face, partially obscuring it.

I've been leaning on the wall of a nearby hotel, my own cap tipped over my eyes. When I spot Alfie, I stand up straight and push it back. All of a sudden, I'm scared. What will he think of me? Say to me? Will he thank me or hate me for what I've done?

As I cross the road, flinching from horses and motorcars and dodging piles of dung, Alfie sees me.

For a second, he falters. His companion has spotted me too. There's no mistaking my identity—I can only be Alfie's twin. She gives me a tired smile, steps back, and merges into the background.

Alfie rushes towards me all right, but the expression on his face isn't exactly one of untrammelled delight. I freeze. I'm still in the road, and a red cross ambulance is forced to swerve to avoid hitting me. How ironic that would be: injured by a vehicle designed to bring succour to the wounded.

Alfie reaches me, catches my arm roughly and steers me away without a word. It's not until we're safely on the other side of the road that he swings me round so that he can stare searchingly into my face.

"You bloody, bloody idiot," are his first words. This shocks me; I've never heard him swear before.

It's not the welcome I was expecting, although I should have known better. Did I really expect Alfie to thank me? I put both of us in jeopardy. I forced him into living a lie. The fact that the lie was also the life he'd dreamed of is neither here nor there.

"Nice to see you too," I say, with my usual bravado. "How are you?"

"How am *I*? How do you think I am? I'm worried sick about you, Nina. How are you? What's it like? How do you manage?" He fires a barrage of questions at me.

"Oh," I shrug, "it's not so bad. You get used to it." He'll be on the lookout for signs that I'm not being honest with him. Well, two can play at that game. By now I'm an expert deceiver. I make sure that my eyes meet his, fair and square.

The old Alfie would be happy to take me at my word, but this new one is made of sterner stuff. His eyes are searching my face, lingering on—I'm not sure what. My tired eyes, perhaps, or the extra sharpness in my cheekbones. It's not that we don't get enough food, but army life—the physicality and the stress of it—are changing me inside and out.

He sees it. He's the one person in the world I can't fool.

He takes a deep breath. His eyes don't leave mine, but their expression becomes gentler.

"You bloody idiot," he says again, in a very different voice this time. "Come on. There's a tea house around the corner. You're going to tell me what it's like. The truth, Nina. This is me; I know when you're lying."

"My God. How can you bear it?"

Alfie is sitting opposite me in one corner of the stuffy tea house. Just behind me there's some kind of potted plant with fleshy leaves that keep falling onto my shoulder. I brush them away with an impatient hand.

"You get used to it," I say. "The things I thought would be problems—going to the lavatory—" I try to suppress a laugh at the thought of our stinking latrine trench being described as a lavatory, "—things like that—they really aren't a problem. I just choose my moment carefully. Mind you, there are things there that would make your hair curl…There was one rat. I swear it wasn't much smaller than Mr Bullock's dog—"

Alfie frowns. He picks up the tea spoon from the ridiculously ornate cup in front of him and pokes it towards me.

"You're trying to distract me," he says. "Don't. Tell me about it. You know what I mean. The important stuff, not the size of the rats."

I hesitate. What can I say? For all I've tried, I can't lie to Alfie. It would be like lying to myself.

"I've written to you about going into action," I begin, "but I can't describe it in any way that would make sense. You can watch a bullet coming towards you and see it pass you by as if time has slowed down, but at the same time hours go by—a day even—and you feel as if you've only just stepped out of your trench…. You see blood and death and heroes and cowards, and you fight boys you should be meeting on the cricket field, not a battleground. Sometimes you kill them. Sometimes they kill you. It's war."

I brush the leaves of the intrusive plant off my shoulder again. For a second it feels like the hand of a stranger, calling on me for something I don't want to do. I find that I have to steady my own hand to stop it shaking. It's a stupid idea, putting the plant where it winds up the patrons, but it's part and parcel with the rest of the décor here—all doilies, prints of Victorian children sobbing beautifully, and swan-necked ladies. I detest this place.

Alfie isn't looking at me. He's pushing a cube of sugar around the tablecloth with one finger. Then he looks up and wipes his eyes before pulling at his fringe again. It seems to be a new habit he's developed.

"Nina, you can't go back. I won't allow you to," he states.

"Nonsense. Let me tell you this…" I glance around to make sure no one is eavesdropping. "I'd rather be on the Front than doing your job. That, to me, would be as terrible as soldiering sounds to you. All those men with ruined lives, needing you, depending on you…." I shake my head. "I just couldn't do it. At least in the trenches I'm spared that. Lives end or are changed forever but we don't get involved. We can't. Over there," I point towards the hospital, "I'd drown in the flood of their need."

I'm too hot and the plant is pawing at me again. I turn around, rip the offending leaves away from the fleshy stem, crumple them up and drop them on the floor. A waitress in a pinny and a starched cap looks annoyed. She takes a couple of paces towards me and opens her mouth. I flash her a warning look. She closes her mouth and backs away.

Alfie stares at me for a long time. I meet his eyes, and this time I don't look away. Eventually he nods.

"It's terrible work," he says. "Terrible and wonderful too. Sometimes I come home crying with the horror of what I've seen. But…I make a difference, Nina, I really do."

He begins to tell me about some of his patients—a professional footballer who'd lost a leg; a farmhand who will never be able to support his huge family again; a miner who'd been called on to tunnel beneath the German trenches, only to meet a German miner intent on doing the same thing under the British front line.

"Their tunnels intersected. The German acted faster. He threw a grenade—very stupid thing to do underground, Sid says—and Sid wakes up two days later in a field hospital. It's only when he decides that he needs the lavatory and tries to stand up that he realises that he's missing both legs…"

Alfie runs out of words. He stares at me, willing me to understand.

"But you help them. Help them get used to things," I say, thinking how inadequate the words sound. To gloss over the awkward moment, I lean across the table and brush the hair from his eyes—it must be annoying him. He flinches away but he's not quick enough. I see the purple and yellow remains of a bruise around his left eye.

"What? What happened?"

Alfie shrugs.

"Oh, nothing much. A bit of an accident…"

"Don't lie. It's me, remember." I turn his own words back on him.

He looks at the tablecloth for a moment.

"I was beaten up," he says, lifting his head.

My fists clench and I'm on my feet.

"Who? Tell me."

He pulls me down again.

"Shhh!" He waits for the other customers to return to their dainty teacups before continuing in an undertone.

"I'd been working a late shift. Going home, past a pub. Some Tommies came staggering out as I passed. One decided to try his luck and found more than he bargained for…. He wasn't best pleased." Alfie's cheeks are scarlet, but he tries to smile.

I feel rage surging through me. It's a struggle not to leap to my feet again.

"The bastard. The bloody bastard," I say through my teeth. The fact that it's a fellow soldier who's hurt my twin makes me even angrier.

My brother meets my eyes and shrugs.

"It could have been worse," he says. "If he'd been sober enough to think about reporting me, I'd have been in serious trouble."

"Have you had any other injuries? Does that sort of thing happen often?"

Alfie attempts a smile.

"Not often, and usually I'm quicker at removing myself from danger…it's the effect of wartime, I think. Men who think they're about to die seem to lose all their inhibitions. They need to find a woman and lose themselves for a while."

I think of my fellow conscripts in Aldershot, earnestly pursuing every barmaid and shop girl they come across.

"They need to fuck, you mean. For some of them, it'll be their first and last time." I'm thinking of Venner and young Grindley. I'm pretty sure that they both died virgins. Neither of them had that air of being sexually experienced like some of the others. And what about me? Will I die without experiencing the pleasure of physical love? I push the thought, and treacherous ideas about Liam, to the back of my mind. "For heaven's sake, Alfie, be careful! Before I go, I'll teach you a few manoeuvres that could be useful if it happens again."

Our eyes meet and we smile simultaneously. It's the idea of me—a girl living as a man—teaching Alfie—a man living as a girl—how to defend his honour. It's ridiculous and yet it sums up our strange situation perfectly.

We grin at each other and I lean forward again to rearrange the hair over his shiner.

"I'm here for three days," I say. "I'm hoping you can show me some of those attractions you wrote about, if you're not too tired. A bit of entertainment would do me good."

Alfie sits up straighter.

"Tired? I'm never too tired to entertain my twin," he says. "I'll tell you what—there's a music hall—the Phoenix—a few streets away. We'll go there later. It'll be like reliving old times. As luck would have it, Vesta Tilley is top of the bill tonight."

Vesta Tilley. I hadn't thought about her for a long time. Those childhood days when I'd thought she was the bee's knees, and when the height of my ambition was to be accepted as a woman dressed as a man, seem to be part of someone else's life. How I've changed since then. Alfie too. Vesta Tilley's achievements seem trite now. She looked like a man but made it clear she was a woman, whereas Alfie and I not only look like members of the opposite sex, we live that way too.

Still, it seems appropriate to spend the first night of our reunion this way. The other good thing, at least as far as I'm concerned, is that music halls are rowdy and they offer no time for reflection or deep conversations.

"Actually, there'll be another kind of attraction tonight," Alfie falters, blushing. "Someone I'd like you to meet…."

My eyes fly to his but he is concentrating on stirring sugar into his tea and won't look up.

"You mean…?"

"Yes." Now he looks up. "I'll bring him along tonight."

We part shortly after and, as I walk away, my thoughts are all on what Alfie has just revealed. Who has he met? Is he safe? Does he know Alfie's full story? Alfie's story and mine too?

I get to the Phoenix a little early and take stock of it. It is much grander than the Cambridge Music Hall: at least twice the size, judging from its exterior, with no less than six glass doors flanked by a pair of classical stone columns. Through the glass I can see two huge gas chandeliers suspended from the ceiling like a giant's Christmas decorations. There's plush red carpet on the floor and wooden panels, painted with rural scenes, on the walls.

I take in this splendour in a matter of seconds and then don't give it another thought, because my attention is caught by Alfie outside, moving towards a waiting man.

He is neither tall nor short and although he is probably around the same age as us, the pain behind his eyes makes him look like he belongs to an older generation. His skin is so pale it's almost translucent and his hair is darkened by the brilliantine he uses to plaster it to his head. His suit is loose on his frame. He holds himself a little awkwardly, as if standing is difficult for him.

When he moves forward, I realise why. He walks with a pronounced limp.

Alfie has changed out of his nurse's uniform and is now wearing a dress that I recognise—cut on simple lines, it's sage green with thin cream stripes. One of my dresses from my old life. As usual, it looks better on Alfie than it did on me. He makes it elegant. On me it looked plain. I slip outside to meet them.

The man is leaning forward to give my twin a peck on the cheek. I know he has registered my presence because he stiffens a little, but doesn't turn away from Alfie. Then he looks at me properly. He starts toward me and for a moment I think he's going to greet me in the same fashion, but he checks himself. A faint flush appears on his cheeks as he holds out his right hand.

"Hello," he says, "I'm David." He is smiling, and it lifts and lightens his face, making it less serious.

I'm feeling awkward for various reasons. Apart from Great Aunt Julia, this is the first time I've met someone who knows our secret and it's unsettling. Alfie has just assured me that David is a completely safe pair of ears and that he would never dream of telling anyone, and I have to hope that my twin is correct. The damage has been done and there's nothing I can do about it.

I'm also struggling with the knowledge that Alfie has a beau. All our lives, we've shared everything. The thought of someone else being party to Alfie's secrets—of someone else having knowledge of my twin that even I don't have—is difficult for me to accept. If I'm being honest with myself, there's some envy mixed in too. Alfie is obviously in love and it seems that love is returned. I am highly unlikely to ever experience that feeling. The feelings I have for Liam will never be reciprocated. The best I can do is make sure he never realises, and try to forget about him.

But David makes my twin happy. He deserves my support. I won't say friendship, not yet. I need to get to know him a little.

So, I shake his hand and say, "It's a pleasure to meet you," and we turn and walk into the music hall, purchase tickets for the circle and make our way to our seats.

It's a slow journey. David is still adjusting to his prosthetic lower right leg and he walks haltingly. His own leg was blown off by a low flying shell outside Arras in March, Alfie tells me. Our conversation is stilted as we make our way up the wide staircase to the first circle.

I find out that Alfie and David met in hospital, where Alfie nursed him and managed to persuade him that a life with a prosthetic leg could still be a good one. He has three sisters but no brother, and his father was a vicar before his death a few years previously. His mother and sisters live in Weston-Super-Mare.

"Remind me never to go paddling in the sea there again," he says. "When the tide goes out, the mud stretches for miles. With this," he taps his right leg, "I'd never get out alive!"

We laugh, a little awkwardly. In spite of my qualms, I'm starting to warm to him. I decide that I'm not going to say I'm sorry for his injury. It's pointless and meaningless and I know if I was him, it would make me angry.

"After Weston-Super-Mare, the Flanders mud must have felt like a second home to you," I say with a smile, hoping he won't take offence.

For a second I think I've put my foot in it, but then he squeezes my shoulder.

"I just wanted to say—I don't judge or condemn what you are doing, and I hope you will return the compliment. Without Nina—," He takes my twin's hand and squeezes it— "I don't know how I'd have coped over these last months. As for your arrangement…" He makes a sweeping gesture that encompasses both of us, "no one knows better than I that not all men are cut out for battle. And if that's the case, I don't see why there can't be women who *are*. I think you're incredibly brave. It's just a pity that you have to resort to pretence in order to do it."

I can't think of a single thing to say to this and it's fortunate that by this time we've reached our row. Our awkward shuffle along to our seats is exacerbated by David's injury. He causes a minor incident by tripping over the foot of a middle-aged man with a fat face and a Kitchener moustache. The man makes a fuss, complaining to his neighbour in a beery voice about "young shirkers who should be off defending their country." David starts apologising immediately, but I'm seeing red. I put one hand on David's arm to shut him up.

"Hang on just one second," I say to the man. I grab his pudgy hand and force it downwards. I rap his hand against David's prosthetic leg, none too gently.

"Where d'you think he got that? Picking daisies at a Sunday school picnic? Tripping up a step after having a skinful in the pub?"

The man blusters a bit, but his face is bright red and he knows he's in the wrong.

"Next time you decide to have a go at someone, I suggest you make sure you've got your facts right, first. Otherwise you're in danger of making yourself look like a complete arse—"

Alfie drags me away as the people around us start to whisper. I hear the odd giggle and some clear murmurs of disapproval.

Stuttering, the man hauls himself out of his seat and pushes his way to the end of the row. I'm pleased to see that he stands on several feet on the way, raising a minor storm of protest from their owners.

"Good riddance," I call after him as he stumbles up the stairs towards the exit. Both Alfie and David take me by the arm and pull me towards our seats.

"You're just as I imagined," David says, as we sit down. We exchange a smile, still shy of each other.

Alfie shakes his head.

"You haven't changed at all," he says, making me raise my eyebrows.

As I take a deep breath and try to push the anger out of my body, the lights dim and the show begins.

By the time Vesta Tilley appears, I've regained my composure.

I've been watching the interaction between Alfie and David out of the corner of my eye and I like what I see. They lean towards each other without seeming to notice that they're doing it, and when Alfie drops his programme on the floor, David hurries to pick it up for him. They murmur to each other, commenting on the quality of the acts we're watching. Admittedly I don't have much to compare them to, but they seem comfortable and natural together.

There's the usual murmur of anticipation when Vesta Tilley is announced, with a fanfare of trumpets that seems rather military. This is different to the languid music that I've grown to associate with her. I wonder if she has introduced a new number to her repertoire.

When she appears, I understand. She's dressed as a soldier. Her uniform is pretty well the same as mine, but with one major difference: hers is pristine and it fits her like a glove. It's obvious that it has never seen the light of day, let alone a muddy, bloody battlefield. It's all for show.

To wild applause, she marches left and right, turning smartly and saluting the audience. Just like me and all the recruits I trained with, she has practised her manoeuvres. But unlike us, she'll never be called to perform them on the battlefield.

When she starts to sing, her song is about joining the army.

Boys, take my tip and join the army right away
The money's good - not much but good
Who knows, perhaps you'll be a general someday
Remember chaps - I said perhaps
But though we're in need of you
Don't think any old stuff will do
In the army, for the future, there will be
There will only be big strong chaps like me

She marches down a gangway into the audience. As she progresses, she's touching people on the shoulder. Not every member of the audience, though. Not women. Not old men or children. Only men who aren't in uniform. Men she can encourage or shame into joining the army.

I focus on one target in particular. He's underfed, sitting with an equally scrawny woman who I assume is his wife, and a boy who looks to be just entering his teens. The man is far from young—well into his forties, I estimate. But when Vesta Tilley touches him, he stands up. There's a look of determination or resignation on his face. I'm not sure which, but I know what it means—he's going to enlist. He's leaving his family, even though he doesn't need to, to face the hell of the battlefield. All because a music hall performer has singled him out for a fleeting moment, as she sings some trite song about matters she can't possibly comprehend.

I see sadness and pride on his family's faces and I'm sickened. The audience contains a generous sprinkling of men like me— in army uniform. They all know how wrong this is, but it seems to me that they are complicit in this deception. They know that the reality of war is exposed guts and mud, freezing cold and terror, chugging rum as you wait for death. But they sit by and say nothing. Some of them even applaud when someone stands up to signify that they will answer the call to enlist.

Suddenly, I want to throw up.

I lurch to my feet and shove my way to the end of the row. I'm dimly aware that Alfie and David are following me, whispering apologies to those whose view of the vile procedure has been blocked for a moment. They ought to be thanking me.

I shove through the closed doors into the corridor. Alfie and David catch up with me. I swing around to glare at them.

"It's wrong. An obscenity. I couldn't sit there and watch lambs volunteer for the slaughter…."

It's David who reaches out a hand, touches me on the shoulder.

"It's alright," he murmurs. "I understand. She's selling people the same lie that appears daily in the newspapers. How can they still believe it in the face of the losses, the terrible injuries? It's wilful blindness."

From then on, my qualms about him disappear.

CHAPTER EIGHTEEN

Brighton, October 1917

I stay in a guest house close to the railway station. Alfie introduces me to his landlord and landlady and offers to put me up, but I decline in spite of their murmurs of welcome. I don't want to cramp Alfie's style.

It turns out that David is staying at a small hotel on the front and has no immediate plans to move on.

"I've been discharged, obviously," he says, indicating his leg with a carefully nonchalant hand. "But as for going back to Mother and my sisters and stuffy old Weston—I don't think I could stand it. I've never been able to tell them about who I really am, of course. In Weston, my life will be nothing but a pretence: escorting girls who feel sorry for me to tennis parties, getting Mother's hopes up that I'm going to get married, settle down, and give her grandchildren. She longs for dozens of them. I can't bear the thought of it."

"Your sisters: could they supply the grandchildren?"

He grimaces. "Molly's fiancé died on the Front last year. Violet and Mary will be lucky to find young men at all. When this war finishes, we'll be missing a generation of them, and that's going to mean an equivalent number of spinsters who never marry. Already, I've heard talk of a glut of 'spare, unwanted women'. What a prospect to look forward to! The effects of this war will ripple for generations to come."

Unwanted women…I've been unwanted all my life, as a girl and woman. It's only when I turned to being a man that I realised I had a purpose. I don't doubt that if I decide to return to being a woman, I will be a "spare" one. Would that be so bad? Perhaps not. I imagine a future in which I become another Great Aunt Julia, fighting for women's rights and dressing in whatever I feel comfortable in. That sounds all right to me, but then I'm hardly a conventional woman. An upholder of the Miss Wren school of thought that a woman's only goal is to marry, have children, and care for a family. For women like that, the future must appear miserable, indeed.

After our evening's entertainment, I make a point of leaving David and Alfie to their own devices. I don't know what their sleeping arrangements are, and I'm not going to enquire. Alfie has always craved love, and I assume that means physical love as well as the romantic meeting of minds. I hope it makes him happy. David too. They deserve it.

The next day, while sitting on a bench with Alfie, watching the waves stir up the pebbles on the beach, I ask him about David.

"Why him? Not that there's anything wrong with him, of course: he's caring and charming. But how did it happen? What was it about him that drew you to him? Was it immediate? Love at first sight? Or did it take you by surprise, one day when you weren't expecting it?"

Alfie frowns and fiddles with his fringe.

"I wasn't expecting it… I dreamed of love, but I never thought I'd find it. I was surprised to find that there are others like me—men who are happier as women—and there are places where you can go where you are likely to meet them. But that wasn't what I wanted. And, of course, there are men who are attracted to their own sex—more than you might imagine. If it's unnatural, then all I can say is that there are an awful lot of unnatural people in the world—men and women! But David: he was interested in *me*. I mean me as a human being. Me as a woman. He used to ask me about where I grew up, about my family, my interests… I think it took his mind off his leg and the pain. When I wasn't on duty, he used to ask the other nurses where I was. They ragged me about it…."

He tails off and gives me an uncertain look.

"Are you all right, listening to this? It doesn't upset you? Revolt you?"

"Alfie, you idiot, you could never revolt me. Get on with it!"

He gives me a smile.

"It—love between men—wasn't mentioned much at school. The masters preferred to pretend that it wasn't happening, but if that wasn't possible—if some boys were discovered and it couldn't be ignored any longer, they treated those lovers as if they'd committed a terrible, terrible crime. Their fathers would be called in to see the Headmaster and the boys would be expelled in disgrace. We were all terrified of having the finger pointed at us! It's strange to be able to talk about love openly, even with you."

"You should have talked to me about it years ago," I say. "Nothing you do or think could be wrong. You're not capable of it."

That makes Alfie laugh.

"I'm glad you think so! When someone finds you really interesting, you notice them more. I started to ask David about himself and look forward to seeing him." He shrugs. "I suppose our love grew out of that."

"And, how did you tell him about…your secret?"

He blushes.

"When David was finally discharged, I made sure that I was on duty. I wanted to say goodbye in person, although I was dreading it. I helped him get his things together, sign the discharge forms, and I was walking him to the door. There was something in the air between us, but neither of us knew what to say, so I said goodbye and wished him luck and, just as I was walking back inside, he asked me to dinner. I wanted to say yes so much! But I couldn't. It wasn't fair on him, and it was a recipe for disaster! So, I stammered something about it not being a good idea. He took both my hands and said, 'There's no need to worry, you know. About anything. To me you are perfect, just as you are.' I looked into his eyes and I could see he *knew!* So that was that. We've never said any more about it."

I bless David for his understanding and delicacy. He has made things easy for Alfie. I also, however, feel a moment of unease: perhaps there are certain things that *need* to be spoken about between people in love. But when it comes to relationships, I suppose I'm not qualified to judge. All I can do is hope for the best for my beloved twin.

On the last evening of my leave, we go for dinner in the Grand Hotel. It's horrifically expensive, but David insists on paying.

"It's the least I can do," he says, as if he hasn't done enough already.

We dine on oysters followed by minted lamb, and drink a bottle of rich red wine. Alfie looks pretty in a black lace evening gown, and I resist the temptation to ask him if he's practising dressing in mourning. He's used to my black humour, but that would be a step too far. I'm not expecting him to talk about my return to the Front, and I'm happy to follow his lead. What will be, will be, and fretting about it—chewing it over and making yourself ill—changes nothing.

But then Alfie surprises me.

"Are you ready?" he asks, in the gap between the lamb and our pudding.

I know what he is referring to, of course, and I'm surprised. As a child, he preferred to avoid unpleasantness by sticking his head in the sand. It must be the sights he has seen as a nurse that have affected him this way. Avoiding reality is impossible in that situation, just as it is to we front-line soldiers. Alfie is changing in so many ways.

"Yes. I'm surprised to say that I don't mind going back. I know where I am there, and what's expected of me. I enjoy sharing a purpose. That means a great deal to me."

Alfie nods and places one hand over mine. "I'll be thinking of you every moment. Promise me you won't take unnecessary risks. Without you—I just don't know what I would do."

I promise, of course, but part of me is querying what my twin has said. Until recently I wouldn't dream of questioning it, but now he has David and, if I don't come home, David will support him. On the whole I'm glad, although I can't suppress a quiver of jealousy at the thought.

Alfie and David seem especially close this evening. They hold hands under the table and something about the looks they exchange tells me that they're sharing a secret.

A second bottle of wine gives me the courage to tackle them.

"Right, you two, out with it," I say.

Alfie doesn't play coy with me. He knows what I mean.

"We've decided," he says, "that after the war we're going to be together."

"Somehow," David adds. "Somewhere."

That's the rub, I think. Where can they be together? Not in England, that's for certain, unless Alfie can maintain his current persona forever. Would that be possible? I hope so. I pray so, if that's what it will take for him to be happy, but I'm struggling to envisage an England so enlightened that two men in love— or two women for that matter—would be accepted, let alone someone unfortunate enough to want to live as the opposite gender.

I wonder where Alfie's announcement leaves me and decide that it really doesn't matter. My chances of surviving to the end of the war are remote and if I do, I'll worry about it then. Alfie is happy. That's the main thing.

I lift up my wine glass to toast them.

"I'm delighted," I say, meaning it. "David, you've made my twin happy and no one deserves it more. I wish you a long, blissful future together."

Alfie is a little squiffy and as we chink glasses he spills red wine onto his breastbone, above the black lace of his gown. A superstitious person might think that the red droplets look like blood, that it's an ill-omen.

I've never been superstitious.

CHAPTER NINETEEN

A week after being on leave, we're at the front line again. I'm amazed to find that I'm almost glad to be back. Certainly, I feel more at home here than I did among the overheated tearooms and blaring music halls of Brighton.

Apart from all being a little less haggard and a whole lot cleaner after our time at home, nothing seems to have changed. Instinctively, my eyes seek out Liam. He lifts a hand and strolls over to me.

"Good break?" I ask him, knowing that I'm not going to like his response.

He rolls his eyes.

"Oh, you know," he says with a wink.

Yes, I think I do.

"How was yours? That sister of yours doing well as a nurse? Maybe I'll get to meet her someday."

I suppress a bitter laugh. How ironic it would be, if Liam fell for Alfie. When we were children, we used to talk about having two bodies with a single brain. Does that mean Alfie would be attracted to Liam, just as I am? Was I attracted to David? A little, perhaps, but the mild pull I felt is nothing like the rush of excitement I experience every time I see Liam.

"She's fine. She has a new beau," I say, wondering why I wanted Liam to know.

"Ah, I'm too late then." Liam gives a shrug and I wonder if he is joking. "I'd like to see your female equivalent. It's an intriguing thought...."

Feeling a slow flush begin to work its way down my body, I muster some excuse to get up and walk away.

I find that there's a letter waiting for me, from Aunt Julia. Her handwriting is as stiff and scratchy as she is. I find a quiet spot to sit and read it.

Dear Alfred,

What a surprise and a joy to hear from you. And how delighted I am to know that you are managing out there. You say that you are not a natural soldier but that makes what you're doing all the more admirable.

I have tried to read between the lines of what you've written about going into action. I think I know what you're saying, and I know how hard that must be for you. I will say nothing here about the morality of the governments of the world in forcing this situation upon you and so many others. I will simply say that they should learn from the recent revolution in Russia. If the Tsar can be toppled from his pinnacle, so can a king or an elected government. Of course, if women were in charge, war would soon become obsolete altogether. We would find other ways to settle our differences.

On the subject of reading between the lines, I must admit that I woke up last night with a startling idea in my head. I haven't heard from Nina, and it occurred to me that perhaps the reason for her silence was that she wasn't nursing at all and is somewhere much closer to you? *Just as she was at Esme's wedding? The way you spoke of your father made me wonder. I'm sure you will understand what I mean and I look forward to your response. Rest assured that whatever your reply, my lips will remain sealed and I will admire you all the more.*

As you say, I have had no word from your father and I don't expect to. The only word he wants concerning me is an invitation to my funeral, and I have no intention of obliging him in that respect for many years to come!

The news here is mainly of the war. Have you heard that Siegfried Sassoon—some kind of decorated war poet, I believe—published a declaration saying that the war is immoral, and has thrown his medal into a river? He seems sensible for a man. If you happen to come across him, do tell him that I said so and wish him luck. I wonder what he thinks about women's suffrage? I'm sure he would be a supporter. There's no reason why enlightened men shouldn't join the cause, just as long as they don't try to take it over!

The only other interesting thing to report is that the royal family have changed their name from something unpronounceable and more German than the Kaiser himself, to Windsor. That will help the war effort, I'm sure. These people have absolutely no idea about real life.

I must go. I have a meeting to attend and acts of defiance to commit. I shall write to tell you about them soon. Your father will be horrified!

Stay safe, and my love to both of you, or either of you, if more appropriate.

Julia.

So, Aunt Julia has guessed that we have swapped roles. I should have known better than to think that I could fool her. But she won't give us away. We're doing what she always told us to: having adventures. Anyway, she'll probably think that I'm doing this to further the cause of women's suffrage. I decide to send her a teasing reply.

Dear Aunt Julia,

How lovely to hear all your news. You will be pleased to know that all is well and that I'm still managing to survive in this world of extreme masculinity.

I grin as I imagine Julia's eyebrows raising as she reaches the end of the sentence.

I haven't come across the poet you mention, which isn't surprising when you think about the number of men out here—hundreds of thousands of us. I did know a chap called Venner who liked to think of himself as a poet. He wrote a lot of guff about primroses and starlings twittering in the hedgerows. He is dead, I'm sorry to say, but he didn't strike me as a Suffragette supporter. But, as you will agree, you can never know everything about someone, even when they are old friends, like we are. There are always things that people keep to themselves.

That's as close as I can get to confirming her suspicion about who is really out here doing the fighting. Knowing Julia, it will be enough.

Have you heard from Nina yet? She tells me that she is still excelling as a nurse and enjoying being distant from Father. Any opportunity that gets her away from him is good as far as she is concerned, even drastic ones. In fact, if I know Nina, the more drastic the situation, the more she will enjoy it! I'm sure that you will hear from her in due course and that she will say the same as me. Don't worry about us. We'll be just fine.

I'll write again as soon as I can.

With much love from me and Nina (in her absence),

Alfie

I smile, imagining her face when she reads it. I'm confident that she will understand what I'm trying to tell her and I look forward to her response. I also wonder what acts of defiance she is planning now. More window breaking? If it makes the papers, the royal family won't be the only ones changing their name. Father will too, if there's any possibility of the press linking her to the Mullins family. There must be no dents in his shining armour of Respectability.

Much to my annoyance, almost as soon as we reach the front line, I start experiencing grinding stomach and back pains. Can it be another period? That would be a major inconvenience. Would it be normal? My limited knowledge of "women's matters," gleaned from Gertie and the girls I went to school with, suggests that periods are monthly occurrences, but it can only be about three weeks since my last one. There's no one I can ask, so I'll just have to deal with it as best I can.

As soon as there's a quiet moment, I head for the latrines. I can check what's happening and pin a field dressing into place if necessary.

I wait until Liam has stowed his gun and helmet and is sitting down. He has a gift for swift sleep. His head touches the trench wall behind him and almost immediately it droops. I give him a couple of minutes just to make sure, then I stand up.

I pass Lacey who's just coming back from the latrines, and give him a nod which he just about returns. These days, we don't waste words on each other.

Or so I think. I'm another twenty yards along the track before something makes me turn back. Lacey is still standing where I passed him, watching me, hands on his hips.

"What?" I say.

He takes his time before answering.

"…There's something about you—something odd. I can't work out what it is, but I will…."

I catch my breath, but I can't let my concern show, so I laugh.

"Good luck with that. When you've worked it out, be sure to let me know, won't you?"

I don't wait for a response.

As usual the latrines are quiet, apart from the continual buzz of flies. It's not a place to hang around longer than you need to. I unbutton my flies and examine myself. It's as I thought—I'm bleeding again. I pull up some moss and wipe myself down, wrinkling my nose. Whoever called this "The Curse" knew what they were talking about. I toss the moss into the latrine pit.

I'm reaching into my pack for the field dressing when I hear a voice behind me.

"What in hell do you think you're doing?"

My heart plummets but I force myself not to react. I finish what I'm doing, stand up and button my fly. *Then* I turn around.

"What does it look like I'm doing?" I'm surprised at how calm I sound.

Liam strides towards me.

"A woman! A bloody woman fighting on the front line. You stupid, stupid–"

My chin goes up. "Why? Why am I stupid? Why can't women fight? I'm as capable as anyone. I've braved No Man's Land–"

He grasps my head and twists it from side to side, examining me like a cow at a livestock market.

"I'm the bloody idiot," he says to himself, softly. "And to think I was interested in meeting your sister! I think some part of my brain knew what you were. That's why I wanted to protect you, why sometimes the thoughts I had about you…."

I jerk my head out of his grip.

"I'm not a prize cow! Get off me! And as for protecting me –you can stick that where it hurts. I do very well looking after myself."

He releases my head, but grabs my arm and pulls me away from the latrines.

"What are you doing? You're not going to report me. You can't —"

He doesn't reply, just pulls me into an empty dugout.

I lean against the wall and cross my arms, determined not to be the first to speak. My heart is thumping wildly now: this could be the end for Alfie and me. I've got to convince this man not to turn me in, whatever it costs.

Liam slumps onto an upturned crate that someone has been using as a chair and for a long time he just stares at me.

"What's your name? I can't keep calling you Mullins."

"Yes, you can. Mullins is my name. Nina Mullins."

"Nina? So who is Alfred Mullins. And, more importantly, *where* is he?"

"He's my twin brother," I say. "I tricked him so that I could come in his place. He's—"

Liam is on his feet. "Tricked him? *Why?* Why would you do something so irresponsible? And how could any man let a woman stand in for him?"

Anger shoots through me and it's not just at his criticism of Alfie.

"You're like every other man I've met, assuming that women can't do anything except raise babies. To think I let myself believe you were different…I'm much more suited to being a soldier than Alfie ever was. I wanted this, and I can do it. I've killed a man, remember…" I have to clench my fists tight to prevent them from shaking at the memory.

Liam takes a step closer, his face like thunder. I stand my ground and stare up at him.

"Don't you realise—it's not just you you're endangering. It's all of us. Men who will put their own lives at risk to protect you. Or who'll think you're easy game and try to— to— ravish you."

I snort. "*Ravish* me? I'd like to see them try!"

"Believe me, you wouldn't." He grabs me by the arm again. "Come on. I'm taking you to Cox. The sooner we get you out of here, the better."

Fiercely, I shake his hand off and shove him backwards.

"Wait. Please." I look earnestly into his eyes. "Let me explain."

He throws me an irritated glare, but stops moving, waiting for me to talk.

Where to begin?

"We've always been like this—Alfie and me. He's gentle; I'm fierce. He hates trouble; I attract it. He's a healer. He's helping the wounded at the moment. Me? I'm not good at anything—"

"Well, that's a lie, for a start. There's at least one thing where you're top of the bloody class: pretending to be a man." Liam shakes his head, looking disgusted at his own gullibility.

I take a step forward. "Don't you see? It's not pretence. Not really. As a woman, I'm invisible at best, and a bloody nuisance at worst! But as a man—I'm useful. I have a place in the world, a job to do! And I'm doing no harm, not as long as the others don't realise."

I grasp his arm and look up into his eyes. The touch still feels comfortable, despite our disagreement, and perhaps I'm imagining it, but it seems to have the same effect on Liam. Am I getting through to him?

"But if you give me away, it'll be a disaster—and not just for me. I'll be sent home in disgrace. All the men who've been involved in training me will get in trouble. You're my best friend, so you'll look like an idiot! And Alfie—Alfie will be shot, and I'll never, ever forgive you. So please, Liam. You're my friend—"

"I'm not your friend! Alfie Mullins was my friend!" He throws off my arm, breaks off our moment of connection.

"Not true! You're the best friend I've ever had. You're—you're—" I stop, confused.

"What? What am I to you? Tell me what I am, apart from a prize chump." His voice sounds wistful. Is he finding that he doesn't like the idea of life without Alfie Mullins as his friend?

"Liam, please. Just let me be." I grasp his arm again and force him to look at me. "I'll look after myself. I'll stay out of trouble, I promise. You won't have to worry about me."

Liam shrugs my hand off again.

"You fucking idiot."

It's not the word that shocks me, it's the sadness in his face.

"Don't you understand? It's too late for that. I was looking out for Alfie Mullins because I liked him, maybe a little too much.... But that's changed now. I can't unknow what you are. I've got to protect Nina Mullins because she's my responsibility. I think you might end up being the death of me."

He walks away, leaving me standing there, blinking away tears of anger.

He doesn't look back.

CHAPTER TWENTY

Near Passchendaele Village, Belgium, October 1917

I spend some time pacing the dugout, wondering what Liam is up to. I'm pretty sure that he isn't going to betray me. If he was, he'd have done it immediately. I know him well enough to be confident of that.

Although I'm relieved, my heart is sinking too. I'll have to avoid him from now on. I refuse to be a millstone around anyone's neck and part of me hopes that if he doesn't see me, he'll forget his supposed "responsibility". I feel a sharp pang of sorrow at the thought of cutting Liam out of my life.

"Liam's right—you are a fucking idiot," I chastise myself. "Worrying yourself sick for the sake of a man! Forget him."

I learned early on that men were dangerous. I think of Father, stifling us all with his idea of love, never once seeing Alfie or me for who we really were. Perhaps death was Mother's only escape from him. Then I think about Alfie, placing his life in my hands, trusting me to stick to this plan. My plan. That I forced on him.

When I dare to contemplate the future, I think that perhaps I could set up a little home somewhere near Alfie and David. The idea of me and Liam tucked up in a cosy cottage is simply ridiculous, And I'm ashamed that I've even allowed the thought into my brain. Fool! Romantic fool!

In the close confines of the trench, avoiding Liam isn't easy, but I do my best. If he's brewing tea, I move away and busy myself cleaning my rifle. If he's taking a nap in our usual sleeping place, I'm shoring up the walls or volunteering to head back to the support trench for more supplies.

The days drag by without incident and soon I find out that there's only one more day to live through at the Front and then we'll be relieved. We'll fall back behind the line and I'll be able to get well away from him.

Only one more day.

Lacey seems determined to ensure that it's not a pleasant day. He looks at Liam, who has his back to me while he boils water in a can for a brew up, and then catches the way I avert my eyes when I have to pass him, and smiles.

"Don't tell me the lovers have had a quarrel?" he quips, looking from me to Liam and back. He speaks with a cigarette dangling from his lips. I think he believes that leaving it there makes him look a seasoned soldier—like Knowles' attempt to grow a moustache.

Liam just throws him a glance of contempt. I'd do the same if I was wise, but when have I ever been that? So, I look him up and down and say, "Dunno what you're talking about. Mind you, you seem very knowledgeable on the subject."

Lacey flushes. He's as foolish as I am—he should know by now that I'll give as good as I get, but still he can't resist the opportunity to throw a jibe. We seem destined to wind each other up. I wish it wasn't that way—we have enough enemies on the other side of No Man's Land, but I'm not going to back down from a fight. That would be fatal.

He starts to move away but then he looks back, frowning.

"You've changed, Mullins. At school, you wouldn't say boo to a goose."

A pang of alarm twists my guts. Liam turns sharply, but he checks himself and looks away again. I know he's still listening though.

"War changes people. Not always for the better," I say, giving Lacey a smirk to make it clear that I'm not speaking about myself.

That does the trick. Lacey's flush deepens. He needs to do something to save face, so he sneers and spits into the mud before striding away.

At last, our time in the front line ends and we're moved back. Time for some other poor sods to dance with death for the sake of a field of churned up mud and barbed wire. I suppose I should feel elated that I've survived this long, but I don't. I feel numb. I've seen too much.

But now there's a new danger to face.

It's Sergeant Cox who introduces it.

When we reach the reserve trench, Cox takes us to collect clean uniforms and then leads us behind it. Perhaps half a mile further on, he leads us down a track that culminates in a small lake.

"You're in for a treat, lads," Cox says. "A nice bath in a lovely clean lake. Wash the way that God intended! It's a chance to get rid of those bloody lice. Now don't tell me I'm not good to you."

There's a murmur of approval. In spite of our best efforts, we all stink—it's inevitable, given the conditions we live in—and we all suffer from lice that seem to find their way into every fold of our uniforms and crevice of our bodies. Already many of my companions are stripping off their filthy clothing, draping it over the bushes that line the edge of the water, and wading in.

For me, though, it's a disaster. I hunch my shoulders and turn to slink away, but Cox sees me.

"Going somewhere, Mullins?"

"The thing is, Sergeant–" I falter. I'm not prepared for this and I'm too tired to think on my feet.

"What? You smell as bad as the rest of us—don't think that you don't. Get in there, lad!"

I can't control a flush of shame at the knowledge that I smell horrible. I have an extra problem in that respect—I have to manage my period as well as the filth and mud that are our everyday lot.

"The thing is, Sarge," Liam's voice behind me startles me, "he's got a bit of a dicky tummy—probably been drinking shell hole water. You know Mullins—he doesn't have an ounce of common sense…."

I flash Liam a grateful look. He ignores it.

"He's practically living in the latrines at the moment," Liam finishes with heavy emphasis.

I take my cue and rub my stomach. "I really need to go, Sarge."

Cox nods. "You should've said so earlier, Mullins. There's no place for bashfulness in war, lad. Off you go. Wash when you get back."

Cox's comment about bashfulness makes Liam and I exchange a look. For a moment I hope that he's come round, that we can be friends again, but I see the warmth fade from his eyes and he turns away without another word.

I head towards the latrines but veer off when I'm certain that I'm no longer visible from the lake. There's an estaminet—a sort of unofficial bar—attached to a farmhouse a short distance from the camp and I head for it. I wonder that the family haven't moved away, but I suppose there's good money to be made from thirsty soldiers with time on their hands and death peering over their shoulders. Rumour has it that the farmer's wife does other things for money too.

I walk down the muddy street, touching my cap to an elderly man driving a wagon filled with milk churns. I wonder how many of his customers have remained in this desolate little village. Quite a few, as far as I can tell. Even though most of the squat houses lining the street have no windows left, and several have damaged roofs as well, the aroma of cooking wafts from many of them. Inside one house, a dog barks. From another comes the sound of someone playing a piano, rather well. Life goes on, even in a war zone.

I pass through the village and make my way up a track to the estaminet—an ugly red brick addition to the tumbledown farmhouse. I push open the rickety door and walk in. When my eyes have adjusted to the darkness, I make my way to the long, well-scrubbed farmhouse table that serves as a bar.

"Vin rouge, s'il vous plait," I say to the tired-looking woman who appears through a door that must lead into the farmhouse. At least something I learnt from Miss Wren's French lessons has managed to stick, although I can't remember her teaching us the word for wine. She was a follower of the Temperance Society. The woman reaches below the table and produces a glass beaker that looks clean enough. She pours a generous amount, takes my coins with a nod and disappears back into the house. I wonder about asking for food but I'm not really hungry and she's in no hurry to come back.

I sit on a rush-bottomed wooden chair and take a deep swig of the wine. It's heady stuff, even stronger than the stout I grew to enjoy in Aldershot.

I finish the wine and manage to attract the woman's attention to get another glassful. I'm feeling light-headed now. I should have asked for something to eat, after all. I drink this one more slowly and, as I sip it, I stare at the sawdust on the floor and think about all the things I haven't had the chance to do with my life, and probably never will now. Too many of them involve Liam. Then I think about the things that I wish I hadn't done. This second list is a lot shorter than the first.

I dump the glass back onto the counter, shout a word of thanks and then walk out, leaving the door swinging behind me.

CHAPTER TWENTY-ONE

Reserve Trenches, near Passchendaele Village,
Belgium, October 1917

I calculate that, by now, my comrades will have finished at the lake. In all likelihood most of them will be heading to the estaminet I've just left, or one of the others that make good money from bored soldiers with pay in their pockets and nothing to spend it on. To make sure I don't come across any of them and incur awkward questions, I take a different route. In spite of my trepidation, the thought of immersing my body in clean water is compelling me towards the lake, the way the Pied Piper drew the rats out of Hamelin.

The water is deserted, with that air of having been busy until very recently. I look around again and, when I'm certain that no one is lingering, begin to strip off my uniform. The smell of my own body makes me wrinkle my nose. Hurriedly, I wade into the water. Its cold clench makes me gasp, but oh, the bliss of feeling the mud and blood and sweat being stripped away. I walk out deeper and soon I am out of my depth, moving through the mud at the bottom of the lake, eyes open and looking for fish in the murk. It's a new experience and I like it. I can feel the water lifting my filthy hair and stripping away the mud and sweat and who knows what else.

Although I know how important it is that I don't take too long, I can't bring myself to get out. Slowly, I make my way to the bank, lifting one hand to watch sparkling droplets fall from it, making little splashes as they return to the lake.

I hear a cough behind me and nearly jump out of my skin. Heart thumping, I scrabble out and lunge for my clothes, hugging them to me before twisting around.

"Thank God!"

It's Liam. His hair is still wet and he's pushed it back from his face. Maybe that's why he looks a little different. Intent and unsmiling. He looks away.

"I heard you splashing around. I thought I'd better warn you—there's about fifty blokes swapping their uniforms for clean ones right now. Their sergeant was talking about bringing them here. Don't be long." He turns to leave.

"Wait!" The word is out of my mouth before I have time to think about it.

"Why?" He hasn't turned back.

"Liam, I— it's—" I don't know what I'm trying to say. All I know is that I want him to keep looking at me. For the first time in my life, I want someone to look at me with desire.

There's something that I want to ask him, but I don't know how to put it into words.

"Look at me," I say.

He isn't walking away any more, but he isn't looking at me, either.

"Please."

Slowly he turns his head. His eyes are full of fire.

"What do you see? A man? A woman? Tell me. I don't know what I am."

I drop my uniform and take a step forward, heart fluttering. I feel no shame and that astonishes me. A flush steals over his face. He clenches his fists.

"What d'you think you're doing? This isn't a bloody game— one minute you reckon you're more of a man, the next you're—" He's turning away again, face set, but I grab his right hand and pull it towards me. It comes to rest on my breast, such as it is. I'm astonished at my bravery. Perhaps it's the wine I just drank.

I feel his calloused thumb move to caress my nipple, which hardens and sends shock waves through my belly and along my spine.

I've never seen arousal before but I recognise it in Liam's hooded eyes and shortened breath. I feel it too—a slow, sensual, internal melting. I want more of it. It feels like power. Power I never knew a woman could possess. All my carefully constructed arguments for avoiding this man have disappeared like early morning dew in a heatwave.

Liam looks into my eyes for a long time before his head starts to dip towards mine. I'm reaching up to grasp it when we hear laughter in the distance.

"—uniform will stand up by itself when you take it off, Pascoe. I'm not saying you stink but…" I can't hear the rest of the words, just the sounds of a light-hearted tussle and other men egging them on.

"Shit!" Liam steps back and walks away. I grab at my uniform and fumble into it. Just in time. I'm buttoning my jacket when a dozen naked men appear. I nod at them and scuttle past.

Liam is waiting on the road back to camp, staring in the direction of the front line. The roar of battle has resumed, poor bastards. As I pass him, I put out one hand and touch his arm. He gives a little start.

"Tonight," I say.

His eyes fly to meet mine. Before he can reply, I walk away.

Immediately, I wonder what I've done. But I've got no intention of backing down. What have I got to lose? There's no time to waste, and Liam is the only person I've ever met who arouses these feelings in me. The fact that he seems to reciprocate them astonishes me. It's too good an opportunity to pass by. Before I die, I want to know what love feels like. It's something else that Alfie and I will have in common.

A group of us, Liam, me, and a couple of men from our new unit—Black, a pale Londoner, and a country lad called Simons, who used to work with horses—have agreed to go for a drink this evening. But before that, there's the rest of the day to get through.

We have a gas mask drill and some weapons checks, then some bright spark suggests a game of football. I sit on the sidelines and make encouraging noises, but my mind is lost in the evening to come. Briefly, I think back to the time when Alfie had refused to let me take his place at school so that I could learn to play football. I remember how angry I was. It all seems so unimportant now. I know what I want—I can still feel Liam's hand on me. I imagine that the marks of his fingers are still on my breast. I want to feel it again. And more. If I'm going to die, I don't want to die ignorant.

Liam is ignoring me again. He sits on the opposite side of the "pitch" and seems to be concentrating on the game. What does that mean? If he has qualms, I'll overcome them. I'm determined.

Just once, when the game stops while someone is trying to prevent the over-used football from deflating, he looks up and meets my eyes. For an intense moment, I feel that melting again, inside me. After what, in reality, is perhaps three seconds, he looks away, very deliberately, leaving me breathless. I can see the shallow rise and fall of his chest before he gets up and moves away.

At last, the shadows lengthen and lamps begin to illuminate the neat rows of tents. There's a certain magic in the sight, I think. We all meet up and begin the short walk to the estaminet. The talk is about anything except the war—football, complaints about the food, boasts about girls, jokes about anything that comes into our minds. It's mainly Simons and Black doing the talking. As we get closer to the estaminet, half a dozen Tommies stagger out. They're singing heartily, more than half-drunk: "It's a long way to Tipperary..." The sound travels past us and I wonder if some dying strain of it will reach the men on the front line, now that the din of battle has ended for the day.

The estaminet is full this evening and there's standing room only. The air is warm and thick with smoke. Men in uniform are playing cards or talking and laughing in groups, smoking their Woodbines as if this was a normal night in a normal pub. The sawdust on the floor is sticky with carelessly spilt drinks.

We buy a couple of bottles of wine and find a corner. As I reach out my glass to Black, who's pouring the wine, my arm touches Liam's and we both stiffen for a moment before moving away. The others don't notice.

I'm not that taken with Black—he's too mouthy for me—but Simons I think I could like. He lets Black do most of the talking, but when he does speak, he's often funny.

Black is describing his girl at home. Lottie, her name is, and to listen to Black, you'd think she'd stepped straight off the London stage or an advertisement for Pears Soap. "...she's like a peach—soft and ripe and ready for picking. I can't wait to get home."

Simons' smiling eyes meet mine. "Better hope no one goes scrumping while you're over here, then," he says. I grin at him and hope that Lottie is out enjoying herself.

"Or that she doesn't decide to go out and do some scrumping herself," I add.

Black scowls. He turns to Liam. "You look like a man of the world, Talbot. What's your taste in the ladies? Similar to mine, I'd bet—soft with plenty of curves."

"I'd say my taste has changed recently. In the past, I was always ready to be led astray by an hourglass figure," Liam says, straight faced. "But I think I'm growing up at last. These days, I find myself drawn to women with spirit and minds of their own. A curvy figure is fine, but once the novelty has worn off, you need something more. I'm hoping for a meeting of minds, one that will outlast simple lust. Although I wouldn't turn my nose up at some lust as well...."

I manage not to choke on my wine.

Black snorts. "A woman with a mind is a waste of time! You'll be sniffing after bloody Suffragettes next! What about you, Mullins?"

"I've got a thing for a nice brunette. Give me dark hair and a fiery attitude, and I'm happy," I say, quick as a flash. Liam splutters over his wine and I bash him roughly on the back. Even that rough contact makes my skin tingle.

This is going to be a long evening.

CHAPTER TWENTY-TWO

In the candlelight the rough red wine looks like fire in my glass. I twist it and admire the ruby liquid as I listen to Black's boasts and Simons' digs, and occasionally contribute to the conversation. Liam and I hardly say a word to each other. We don't need to.

The second bottle of wine disappears and Simons stumbles towards the bar for another, stopping to apologise for tripping over someone's outstretched legs.

I give a wide yawn.

"I'm all in. I think I'll call it a day." I look at Liam. "You stay here, mate. I can find my own way back." I'm teasing him: there's no way he's not coming with me.

He stretches and yawns too. "No, I'm just about done. I'm ready for some kip and, besides, if I leave you to get back by yourself, you'll end up in Fritz's trench by mistake!" He nods to Simons and Black. "See you later."

After putting up with some sarcastic comments from Black about being lightweights, we shoulder our way outside.

The cool night air feels welcome on my skin. I breathe in deeply and risk a quick look up at Liam. He meets my eyes for a moment before he starts walking.

Suddenly I'm nervous. Lost for words. I want this—I know I do. And I'm supposed to want it, aren't I? This must be what Alfie feels when he looks at David. I think about my parents. Surely my cold father never felt like this. Surely my mother never melted at the sight of him, or looked at his carefully-tended hands and burned to feel them against her skin.

Liam is silent too. He heads slowly towards camp, sometimes placing a hand on my back to steer me over the uneven track. His lightest touch makes me tingle. I veer away onto a less well-trodden path, heavily pocked with puddles and ruts of dried mud. He hesitates for a moment, then follows me.

Ahead of us looms the silhouette of a building—some sort of barn that I'd noticed on my last visit to the estaminet. Closer up, I see that the door is attached by a single hinge, hanging inwards. We stand for a few moments, listening for the sound of animals inside, but it's silent.

One of us needs to say something.

"Romantic," I manage.

Liam gives a short laugh.

He reaches in his pocket for a box of matches and strikes one so we can peer in. It illuminates a hard-packed earth floor with a pile of hay to one side. On the other side is a huge iron plough. A few wooden implements—buckets and hoes and a tangle of broken harness, lie against the far wall. There's a glassless window above this and the moon shines through it, onto Liam's serious face.

As the flame reaches Liam's fingers and he shakes it out, I'm reaching for him.

My mind and body leap as his lips touch my chilled face. He tastes of warmth and wine. I find myself straining against him and he's doing the same, but still it's not close enough. Our clothes become unwelcome barriers. The pile of hay is behind us and we tumble down onto it.

For a second, Liam raises his head.

"I– Nina–" He hesitates over my name. His voice sounds different—less certain—like it did when we were about to go over the top for the first time. "We shouldn't do this. You'll regret it later."

My answer is to reach for his tunic. I start to fumble with the buttons in the pitch blackness.

"Bloody things," my voice is different too—deeper and somehow more womanly.

His hands find mine and close over them.

"We can wait," he whispers. "I don't want to take advantage of you–"

I kiss him fiercely to shut him up.

With a deep, ragged breath, he pulls his head back.

"You're making this very hard. After the war, then–"

I'm reaching for his head again, arching myself against him. How do I know how to do this? I don't know. It just seems natural and right. Now that I've decided to do this, I have no qualms, no second thoughts. I want this cocky, confident, caring man with all my being.

"What do you mean, after the war?" I whisper into his ear. My warm breath makes him groan. "There's no guarantee that we'll last till the end of the month. I want this Liam. I want you. All of you. No pretence, no hiding, no holding back."

There's no more protest from him. His body descends onto mine, taking my breath away.

I revel in the feeling for a long moment and then push him backwards. I need to undo his tunic.

He laughs and tries to help me, but I swat his hands away.

"No. I want to do it. It's important," I say, although I couldn't begin to explain why.

He calls me a pain in the arse and submits to my fumbling fingers, allowing me to slip the tunic off his shoulders. I manage to pull off one of its buttons in the process, before making short work of my own clothes.

The first time our naked bodies are able to touch unimpeded makes us both gasp. Just before we meld fully, I realise I'm not nervous any more. And then, for a few minutes or a lifetime, I'm not sure which, Venner, Knowles, the German boy and Warmsley and their terrible fates, and the war, the unburied bodies and the prospect that shortly we could be adding to them, are wiped from my mind.

For the first time in my life, I feel like a sexual, sensual being. It's miraculous. I wish it would never end.

Afterwards, we're lazy and elated at the same time. We lie back on our scratchy bed, letting the air cool our bodies.

Liam is running one hand down my flank, over and over, as if he never wants to stop.

"You're not sorry?" he asks.

I shake my head. "Sorry? You're joking! The only thing I'm sorry about is that we can't do it again!"

That makes him laugh. "Tomorrow. We'll come back tomorrow." Then he sits up. "We'd better get back now. The last thing we want is to get confined to camp for staying out too long!"

He helps me dress, rebuttoning my fly and wrapping my puttees around my lower legs. We make a quick, playful search for his missing button, but it's gone.

"I'll blame the launderers and say it was missing when I was given it," he says.

As we emerge, we're surprised to find that it's drizzling.

I lie awake long into the night, listening to the patter of rain on the outside of my tent and reliving what we've done. Does it change me? Well, I'm no longer ignorant, and it turns out that I enjoy sex very much. That was something I doubted for a long time.

Does it make me want to be a proper, full-time woman? Who knows? A future in which I can do the miraculous thing that is lovemaking every night doesn't sound bad. But it's too soon to say. I spend some useless minutes imagining a different scenario, one that allows me to be with Liam *and* dress as a man when I want to. It's a struggle to abandon this delicious dream, but resolutely I push it away. That's for future consideration, if we have the luxury of a future.

Does what we have done change my feelings about Liam? Well, it confirms that I care about him. Deeply. That's all I'm willing to admit at the moment and perhaps it's all that matters. There's no point thinking beyond tomorrow when tomorrow may be our final day.

The next day brings a letter from Alfie. I feel a glow of pleasure at his firm, confident handwriting, and take the letter back to my tent to read in privacy.

Dear A,

I hope you're well and pray that you are.

Thanks to you I'm more than well. I'm happy, fulfilled even. I love my work and I'm good at it. That means so much to me.

I have some wonderful news and I want you to be the first to know. Sister Henderson called me into her office yesterday and asked me whether I'd be interested in training as a proper nurse—I wouldn't be a volunteer anymore. She says I have a vocation and that it would be a great waste if I didn't follow it!

I said yes, of course, it's a dream come true, but I said that first I wanted to get out to the Front, to experience what you're going through. I didn't say the last bit, of course, just that I wanted to help on the front line. She said no at first—I'm a good bit too young—but I got round her. I'm much more persuasive, these days! It helped that there's such a shortage of experienced nurses over there. In the end she agreed to sign off my transfer papers and actually said I'd be an asset! She's usually a bit of a dragon with a reputation for never praising her nurses, so you can imagine how I felt! So, dear A, you may be seeing me quite soon.

I talked it through with David last night, and he supports me all the way. He's worried, of course, but he understands my need to experience what both of you have seen. After all, you're the people I love most in the world.

So—life is good. I can't tell you how much I'd like to know that it is for you too. Please write to me and let me know how things are with you.

The news that Alfie is coming to the Western Front is both wonderful and terrifying. I hope we are able to meet up. The Front is hundreds of miles long and there are many, many hospitals and casualty clearing stations, but I'm sure that we can arrange a meeting.

As I dash off a quick, encouraging reply, I wonder if I should mention Liam. I decide against it. It's still too new and too precious to share. I decide it's time for another letter to Aunt Julia. She hasn't responded to my last, teasing one.

Dear Julia,

How are you? Have you completed your "acts of defiance"? I'd love to know what you've been up to—nothing too risky, I hope? Make sure you don't get shot like those Irish rebels last year, and remember you are a lady of advancing years!

Things here are not too bad, all things considered. We are in reserve at present, and it's a welcome relief after the front line. There is still a lot to do, of course, some of it very tedious, but we—the men in my platoon and me—are becoming fast friends and we manage to find time for fun and recreation too.

I am starting to think that being in the army will be the making of me. It has given me a purpose and I needed it. When the war has ended, I think you will be seeing a very different Alfie.

She will read all kinds of things into that. I wish I could be there when she opens this letter. She's probably the only person apart from Liam and David who would understand and keep our secret.

I don't know if Nina has been in contact yet? If not, I will reprimand her for you. She has some exciting news: she is being sent to the Front to nurse freshly wounded men. It's a huge honour for someone so young, and I'm very proud of her. I'm keeping my fingers crossed that we will be able to meet up out here. That would make me very happy.

Do look after yourself, Julia, and don't worry about me. Or Nina. I will write again soon.

Your loving nephew,

Alfie.

The next few days pass in a happy haze. Every time I see Liam I feel a rush of desire that takes my breath away. We spend our days being soldiers and our nights as lovers in the abandoned barn, savouring each new discovery about each other. I grasp the happiness I'm being offered with greedy hands and relish every second of it. Even Lacey, slinking around in the background like a hungry stray cat, can't dissipate a single second of it.

There's a side to Liam that I hadn't appreciated before, or even noticed. He can be gentle and serious. At night, when he removes my clothes, the look on his face makes me think of someone who's just discovered a great, undeserved treasure. I'm touched by it, and just a little bit worried. We can't become too dependent on each other, not in our situation. We need to be able to survive without each other. If my number's up, I know I'd die happier knowing that Liam is alive, cherishing memories of our time together but finding the strength to continue. He needs to feel the same way.

All too soon it's our last night before returning to the front line. We've made love and are lying wrapped around each other. I can feel Liam's heartbeat slowing down as it returns to normal. Sweat is cooling on his skin. I give a little wriggle.

"Bloody uncomfortable, this hay." I know he will hate this; I've discovered that there's a romantic streak in Liam that dislikes my prosaic comments about the straw that ends up poking us in inconvenient places, or the insects that enjoy feasting on our exposed skin. I say it anyway, partly because I think it's funny and partly because I can see that there's something on Liam's mind and I'm worried about what it might be. I'm half expecting him to say that we have to stop—that it's too dangerous to do this anymore.

His head lifts and he frowns into my eyes. I can see that he's hesitating to say what's in his head. Ignoring the dread that is clutching at my stomach, I decide to help him out.

"Come on, spit it out," I say. "I can cope," although my heart feels like it's shrivelling with dismay.

He lifts one hand to caress my cheek. "I'm thinking…I'm thinking that when the war's over, we should find a more comfortable way of doing this." He looks into my eyes. "With a proper bed and so forth."

My heart leaps with relief. He's not ending it and, more than that, he wants to carry on seeing me after the war ends.

"You mean, see each other properly? Like normal sweethearts?"

He gives a little, embarrassed laugh. "To begin with, maybe. If that's what you want. But then—we should settle down."

I laugh. I can't help it. "*Settle down?* As husband and wife? Do you think we're cut out for that?" As soon as the words are out of my mouth, I regret them. "Not that it's not a lovely idea, but –"

I see the look of hurt on Liam's face and shut up.

"You don't want to," he says flatly.

"No! I mean—I hadn't thought about it. It's such a– a *big* thought that we might even survive that long. I haven't dared…"

"*I* dare. I know what I want. I want to spend my life with you. The things we've shared—I'll never share them with another woman. They bind us forever…" He grasps me by both shoulders.

I wonder if he's going to tell me he loves me. If he does, what do I say? Do I love him? Yes, of course. I think about him constantly and I want nothing but happiness for him. But do I want to tell him that? No, not yet. It's tempting fate. And love or not, it doesn't alter the fact that I'm not cut out to be someone's wife. Until I met Liam, I dreamt of living as a man. Has that desire disappeared? I don't know. I need time to work everything out.

"I'd love to share our lives." I say it quickly, hoping to cut off a declaration of love that he might regret later. I think there's an ambiguity in my statement that'll salve my conscience a little. Saying I'd love to share our lives isn't like saying that we *will* do so. We'll cross that bridge when we come to it.

My agreement wipes the look of hurt from his face and he kisses me, long and lovingly. That arouses both of us again.

"One last time," he murmurs, raising his head from mine. "It'll have to keep us going for a while."

We've agreed that we won't attempt to do this while we're on the front line. It would be madness. We need to concentrate on surviving.

I clutch Liam's head through his thick hair and pull it towards mine.

Later we dress reluctantly, heavy with the knowledge that we won't be alone together for a while. Front-line duties are only five days long, but they're five days of terror and danger.

When we're dressed, we reach for each other in a long embrace. It feels as if we're saying goodbye.

We're both reluctant to leave the barn. It's our sanctuary. But finally, we grasp hands and walk out into the chilly night.

A shadow detaches itself from a nearby tree.

It walks towards us.

"Well, well. The lovers emerge from their little nest. A woman! A shameless slut, pretending to be a man. I'll say this for you. You've got nerve!"

It's Lacey.

CHAPTER TWENTY-THREE

Reserve Trenches, near Passchendaele Village,
Belgium, October 1917

My insides melt into panic that roots me to the spot, but only for a few seconds. Then I start towards Lacey with my fists clenched. Liam grabs my arms and pulls me back.

"He's holding a pistol, you idiot."

The moon is emerging from a cloud and I catch the dull glint of a short gun.

"He would be. Bloody coward," I spit the words towards Lacey.

"Not very ladylike," he smirks. "But then you're not, are you? I knew there was something suspicious about you. The Mullins I went to school with would have been shitting with fear the moment he set foot in Flanders."

Anger flares up again at this insult to my twin. There's nothing I can do physically to punish Lacey, but I can make him squirm.

"Or pissing himself? Like you did, when we went over the top for the first time? Like you do every time you get a bit scared?"

Lacey's swift indrawn breath tells me that I've hit my mark. I'm sure he's blushing.

"Shut up. I wasn't the only one…Anyone would've…"

"Not anyone. I didn't…Did you, Liam?"

"No, I didn't." Liam sounds reluctant to join the argument. Probably thinking that riling Lacey won't help. He's right, but the idea that this slimy little excuse for a man is judging and condemning us is intolerable.

"I assume you're Mullins' sister?" Lacey sneers. "She had a reputation as a misfit and a troublemaker. A very unnatural girl, from what I've heard." His eyes run slowly up and down my body.

Now it's my turn to blush and I hate myself for it.

I lift my chin and glare at him. Liam's fingers tighten around my arm but he needn't worry; I'm not going to show Lacey how much his words sting.

"What happens now?" Liam asks in a low voice.

My heart twists as I consider the repercussions of this exposure. An end to Liam and me, for a start, and we will both be in very serious trouble.

And Alfie. What will happen to Alfie? This may cost him his life.

Lacey pretends to consider. He prolongs our agony by pausing to light the cigarette dangling from his lips.

"Well, let's think. You," he nods at me and takes a long drag on his fag, "will be sent home. You're only a woman, so they'll just send you packing. I'd hate to be you when your stick-in-the-mud father gets hold of you, though. He'll disown you." He gives a happy sneer. "Perhaps you'll end up in a whorehouse. You obviously belong in one."

Excitement is making it hard for him to stay still. His eyes run over me again. I feel as if they're invading every cranny of my body.

"As for you, Talbot, you're for it. A court martial, I expect. If you're lucky, you'll get a few years in a military prison. If not…." he leaves the sentence hanging.

"And poor little Alfie? He'll be for it too. Desertion, that's what they'll call it, and we all know what happens to deserters, don't we?"

Yes, we do. They're shot at dawn. There was a chap from our battalion who deserted last year. He'd had enough, so I'm told— had done his best and couldn't do anymore. Who can blame him for that? Waldron, his name was. He was shot for cowardice, and rumour has it that his mother hanged herself afterwards.

Lacey smiles and nods several times as he sees that his suggestion has hit home.

"Yes, yes. That's how he'll go—crying and pissing himself as they stand him against the wall. And it'll serve him right. They'll make an example of him. Ha! Who else would send their *sister* to fight for them? Dirty little coward." He spits into the mud.

Cold terror steals over me as I imagine the scene that Lacey has described. I will do anything to protect Alfie, even grovel before this vile man.

"Please," I say, through clenched teeth. "Please don't do this, Lacey."

His head tilts to one side, his lips squirming over his teeth as he tries to control his smile.

"I'll have to consider," he says. "I *should* report you immediately. But—well, Mullins *was* a friend, of a sort…I'll give it some thought. In the meantime, you two had better stay away from each other. I'll be watching."

There's nothing we can do. We're at his mercy. He nods towards the camp and says, "Off you go, then. I'll let you know my decision in due course. And *if* I decide not to tell on you, you'd better be prepared to show your gratitude…"

I glance up at Liam's eagle profile, wondering what Lacey means by this. It sounds ominous. My lover's lips tighten and I know that he shares my suspicions.

Without another word, we do as we've been bidden and head back to camp.

CHAPTER TWENTY-FOUR

Near Passchendaele Village, Belgium, October 1917

And the next day we're back in the front line.

Fear of what Lacey is going to do exacerbates the usual mixture of terror and boredom. He seems to be everywhere, a living ghost who haunts our every waking moment.

If we are on lookout duty, he makes sure he's stationed next to us. Most of the time his eyes aren't trained on No Man's Land; they're on me, assessing and probing. It feels like a physical assault.

"Don't get any ideas," he mutters in my ear, when Liam and I forget his presence for a moment and exchange a secret smile. "If you want to stay out of trouble, you'd better show me that you've realised the error of your ways."

Liam stiffens and turns his head away. I see the flash of anger in his eyes and realise that he's thinking the same thing as me: wishing that a shell would fly just a little further and obliterate Lacey into bloody fragments. No one would miss him.

Front-line life goes on. We shore up trench walls; brew endless mugs of paraffin-tainted tea; gamble extravagant amounts of money on card games that I have to learn from scratch. I lose every time but what does it matter? No one expects these gambling debts to be honoured. Our chances of living long enough to pay them off are remote. When it rains, as it usually does, we fold in on ourselves, squatting in the mud like lumps of stone. On the rare occasions that the sun shines, we unfold like short-lived flowers. Whenever possible, we chug rum.

Sometimes a lookout gets spooked and calls out that we're under attack. When this happens, we simply drop whatever we're doing and crouch, clutching our rifles and grimacing in fear, like monkeys. War strips us of our humanity.

And all the while, there's Lacey, shadowing us, torturing us.

"Mullins, I think I'd like some tea. Just go and fetch some for me, will you?" He's smiling, showing those hateful teeth of his, daring me to refuse. I can't, of course. But as I pour it into an enamel mug, I turn my back on Lacey and spit into it. I wish that I was a snake and my spittle was venomous.

Later that same day we're snatching a couple of hours sleep, Liam and me, back-to-back and pressed into a shallow dugout. Lacey passes by. He kicks my foot, startling me back into wakefulness.

"You should move over there," he nods to another hole, a few yards away. Dully, I stumble to my feet. There's no point arguing, although as far as I can see the hole we're being directed to is no bigger or better than this one.

"Come on, Liam," I mutter. Liam mumbles in his sleep.

Lacey holds up one hand.

"Not Talbot, just you."

Liam's eyes have just opened. Now they narrow and I see fury in them, but I trudge to the hole and collapse into it. There's nothing else we can do. Despite my exhaustion, it takes me a long time to get back to sleep and when I wake up, I find that Lacey has crammed himself in next to me.

I'm on my feet in two seconds and walking away. So desperate am I to put some distance between my torturer and myself that I forget to duck. A sniper's bullet, screaming past my ear, reminds me.

Liam isn't far away and he reaches for me, dragging me down to safety. His touch sends tingles of longing through my whole body. Will we ever be alone again? We must find a way. It's a necessity, like breathing. Lacey has woken up too and, of course, he jumps to his feet and hurries towards us. I wish with all my heart that the sniper would try another shot and fell him in his tracks.

Even as Lacey is reaching to pull me away, Liam is whispering to me:

"Be careful. Make sure he never catches you unawares."

I know that he doesn't mean the sniper.

On the third day of front-line duty, Lacey intercepts me on my way back from the latrines. This is the one time that I have to be alone and he knows it. I try to pass him without comment, but he steps in front of me. His eyes fasten on my hands, busy with my fly buttons.

"I think I've made up my mind," he says, taking a deep drag on one of his eternal cigarettes. "Yes. You'll be glad to know that I've thought of a way that you can keep your brother away from the firing squad. When we're relieved, we'll go to that estaminet you're so fond of—just you and me—and, on the way back, we can stop in that barn and you can show me how grateful you are that I haven't given you away. You'd better not tell Talbot, if you want to keep him out of prison…"

Not once do his eyes leave my hands, and he continues on his way without waiting for my response. As I take in what he's suggesting, my knees buckle.

"Why?" I whisper after him. "You don't even like me."

He turns and finally meets my eyes.

He shrugs.

"Is that relevant? It's not as if there's a choice of women around here. And you've got to be better than the farmer's wife…. She's fifty if she's a day and she charges. *You* I can fuck for free." He starts walking again.

"Oh God." Horror snakes around my body as I imagine what I'll have to do to secure our safety. I'd rather die. But then, what will happen to Alfie?

For the very first time, I wish with all my heart that I'd never come here.

It's the final night of our front-line duty, and I'm dreading the moment when it ends, and the horror that is to follow. I'd rather stay for eternity in this comfortless trench, under an attack that never ends, than spend a single second in Lacey's arms.

When Liam is safely out of earshot, Lacey leans over and whispers what he is going to do to me when we are alone. And what he expects me to do to him.

"And just remember," he finishes, "you've got your brother and your lover to save as well as your own neck. So you'd better work hard and make sure I'm completely satisfied. And when we've finished, I'll expect you to thank me nicely and tell me that you're looking forward to the next time you get to please me." His pink tongue peeps out to moisten his lips.

The *next time*! I have to do it more than once! The thought brings my dinner back into my mouth and I puke it into the mud. Lacey shuffles from foot to foot, eyes gleaming with excitement. As he glides away, I curse him for bringing hatred and shame into my life.

Later, Liam and I are on sentry duty, close to a listening point.

I've done my best to hide my turmoil from him, but he knows me too well to be fooled.

"There's something you're not telling me," he mutters in my ear. "What is it? What has he said to you?" We both know who he means.

"Nothing," I say. "But he's holding our lives to ransom." I nod towards Lacey. Although there's no reason for him to be here, he's never far away. This time he's hunched on a firing step, keeping out of the drizzle. He seems to realise that we're talking about him and his eyes swivel in our direction, glinting in the wet moonlight. He stares at us and takes a long drag on his cigarette. Its tip glows like a demon's eye.

I turn my back on him and stare blindly over No Man's Land. A single bullet punctures the mud, a dozen yards to my left. Another sniper, bored and aiming at rats or unrecovered bodies. We're used to it.

My mind leaps forward to what I'll have to do tomorrow night and, for the thousandth time, I wonder how I'll be able to make myself go through with it.

Wait. I've been telling myself again and again that there's nothing else I can do, but there is. It's obvious. I'm a soldier, trained to kill. Why not kill Lacey? Thousands of good chaps are being wiped out every day. Why not add this poor excuse for a man to the tally? Why should he live, while decent people like Knowles, with his desperate, jaunty air and feeble moustache, die?

I glance down at my hands. Could they really do that?

I think about what I've experienced since I got to the Front—the deaths I've witnessed and the one I caused. Lacey is a thousand times more our enemy than that German boy.

And I think: yes, I can do this. For Liam and Alfie. For the people I love, and for me too.

I will become a murderer.

Shooting Lacey is too risky. It would provoke speculation and enquiries. But I have my bayonet.

I think back to my Aldershot training and remember the horror I felt at the thought of sliding that long blade into the flesh of another human being. Since then, I've used the bayonet and I've killed with it, but that was different.

So is this, I tell myself. Actually, it's worse. It's him or the three of us—Alfie and Liam and me. There'll be no end to this torture while Lacey is alive.

So be it.

As I acknowledge my task, I slip in the mud. Instantly Liam is by my side, hauling me up.

"You all right?" he asks.

I'm assuring him that it was just a misstep when Lacey materialises behind us, our eternal, hated chaperone.

"What's going on?" he hisses. "Mullins is fine. He doesn't need you grabbing him at the slightest excuse. Really, Talbot, if you could see yourself, pawing at him like a randy schoolboy…"

Liam drops my arm and takes a step back, glaring.

Lacey's lips squirm into a smile. He stands up straighter and takes a drag on his cigarette.

"For God's sake," Liam growls at him, "put that cigarette out. There are snipers everywhere."

And the idea comes to me. He probably won't even know what's happening. It won't actually be me who kills him, not really. I won't be the one pulling the trigger.

As Lacey stoops for cover, glaring at Liam for pointing out his fault, I'm peering around. There's no one near. No witnesses. Everyone is sheltering from the rain, well away from this desolate listening point.

Quickly, before I have time to think, I duck behind my enemy and grab him under his armpits. I haul him upright again. At the same time, I cough loudly to help the sniper locate us. I pray that he's still there, patient and still, waiting for a target.

"Wha–?" Lacey exclaims, as I pull him erect.

His cigarette is still clamped between his lips, a glowing target. He seems to be too stupefied to remove it. He comes to his senses and starts to struggle, tugging at my hands to free himself. My muscles are straining with effort. If the sniper *is* still there, I'm in his line of sight, as well. The shot, if it comes, could kill either one of us. I'm willing to make that gamble. The gods can decide which of us lives and dies.

"You! You're trying–" he starts to say. I'm glad I can't see his face. I concentrate on Liam, whose initial look of surprise changes to one of understanding and resolve. He grabs Lacey around the waist and holds him there, ducking low to avoid bullets.

"Lacey," I call out, to help the sniper and in case any of our side are within earshot, "you heard what Talbot said. For God's sake, put out that cigarette. Keep down."

"Bitch. Bastard. Murderers," Lacey whispers, spitting out his cigarette at last and straining to turn round and face me. After what seems like hours of silent struggle, he has made enough progress to reach toward me. His hands are curved into claws. I think he's planning to strangle me.

There is a rush of concentrated wind and a brief, sharp *plop!* A small hole appears, to the back of Lacey's left ear. It's accompanied by a spray of blood, black and delicate in the moonlight. Some of it showers my face and body. The sniper has found a larger rat to shoot and I am branded with the mark of Cain.

We let him go at the same time. His body topples forward against the trench wall. Slowly, it drags down the wall until it's lying in a puddle, face down. He twitches and the puddle ripples.

And then he is still.

"Oh," I say, watching the dead man. I'm half expecting him to get up and resume torturing us. Is he really dead? Or just pretending, the better to shock us when he climbs to his feet?

Finally, I gasp. I don't know if it's at the realisation that we're free or an acknowledgement that I am now a murderer. I want to reach for Liam, to feel his arms around me as I sob into his tunic, but I can't. So we lock eyes over Lacey's body and share our thoughts.

"We had to," I whisper. "He was going to make me—" I can't finish the sentence.

"I know. I guessed."

He hands me a handkerchief, our hands lingering in a touch. Then I scrub Lacey's blood from my face. I wonder why I'm not crying. I lift my head to where the pink dawn is starting to creep across No Man's Land, and offer my gratitude to whichever of the gods of war has decided that Lacey is more deserving of death than we are. It's a new lease of life for Alfie and Liam and me, and I'm so grateful.

But I wonder if I'll ever sleep again.

CHAPTER TWENTY-FIVE

Near Passchendaele Village, Belgium, late October 1917

Another five days in reserve. After our initial horror, Liam and I are exhilarated by our release from Lacey's sour presence. I make a silent resolve never to mention his name and I suspect that Liam must have done the same thing. I think about Lacey, of course, but I can't regret what we've done. He seems to have spent his whole life torturing people weaker than him. He fed off misery and I don't doubt that he would have continued to do so. It seems to me that, sometimes, law and justice aren't the same.

My lover and I can't wait for darkness to fall. On our first night behind the lines, we're so hungry for each other that we're stripping off our clothing before we even get to the barn, relying on the blackness to keep our secret safe. As we gain confidence as lovers we slow down, testing and teasing each other to the point where we both feel that we will die if our bodies aren't fully joined.

On our final night before returning to active duty, I lie in Liam's arms and listen to the never-ending rain on the ancient roof. I feel it too, dripping through moonlit gaps onto my hot skin, cooling it down.

A new emotion washes over me, one that surprises me. Hope. I think we can both survive this. Some deity must be looking out for us. Perhaps the gods of war want us to have a future.

"Liam," I run my fingers around his nipples.

"Mmmmm?" He's half asleep, too lazy to respond more fully.

"Wake up!" I give him a sharp nudge. He opens his eyes.

"What? You're a pain in the backside, you know that, don't you?"

"Yes, I know that." I kiss his chest. "Listen. I think we can do it. Survive this war. And if we do, let's do it. Settle down. We don't need to get married, not straight away. I know you won't try to stop me doing what I need to…"

His eyes blaze with life now as he pulls me closer to kiss me.

"We'll be happy as pigs in a sty," he murmurs.

"How romantic," I retort. "I shall look forward to it."

And then the idyll ends and we're back at the Front.

At first glance, No Man's Land hasn't changed at all—it's the same stretch of foul quagmire, littered with blackened gargoyles that used to be men. Then we realise that something *is* different: it looks as if the Germans have managed to mend their barbed wire in all the places we'd cut through it, so whatever pathetic progress we made has been wiped out. Our comrades have died for nothing. We curse the men we've just relieved for letting it happen.

Our trench contains the same mud, the same duckboards and funk holes, the same firing steps, listening posts, lice and endless discomfort. And the same stench of unrecovered bodies.

I think about Venner, dangling from the wire like a broken puppet and pray that we won't find him still there, reproaching us for being alive. I remember what he said about wanting to protect his younger brother, Harry, and I have the horrible thought that he's staying there, waiting to welcome Harry with bony, outstretched arms, when the boy receives his call-up papers.

I mention it to Liam, trying to keep my face blank to conceal how much the thought upsets me. I don't think he's fooled. He looks searchingly into my eyes before answering.

"They won't leave him just hanging there. It'd be bad for morale," he says.

I hope he's right.

We can't check immediately, because enemy gunfire keeps us ducking in our trench. It would be suicide for a man to raise his head higher than the top of the wall.

Eventually, Liam approaches Sergeant Cox and asks to borrow a periscope from the Officer's dugout.

"What do you want that for, Talbot?" Cox looks dubious.

"Curiosity, I suppose. Just want to check the wire, sir," Liam replies. "In case we're sent on another suicide mission."

It would be risky to say something so critical to some of the Non-Commissioned Officers, who act as if they've been born in castles with silver spoons in their mouths, but Cox isn't one of these. He can be as disparaging of our commanders as the rest of us.

"Very well. But be sensible with it, Talbot. I don't want any more casualties before we've even gone over the top!"

Liam does the honours, raising the long, rectangular box and moving it around as he searches. The glint of the glass in it attracts bored snipers, but he's safe enough as long as he keeps his head down.

He draws in his breath. One look at his face when he lowers the periscope tells me everything I need to know.

"He's still there," I mutter. "The bastards. The bloody bastards." I'm not sure who I'm referring to. The whole world maybe, carrying on regardless while a boy who wrote terrible poetry to calm his frightened brother is left to rot in a bog as a static target for sniping practice. It's the indignity of it that I hate. Returning to the earth should be a private matter, not something carried out in front of the disgusted gaze of two armies.

I try to take the periscope from Liam to look for myself, but he won't let go.

"You don't want to see," he says, struggling to keep the tenderness out of his voice.

"Not a pretty sight, eh? Not a suitable subject for one of his soppy poems!" I feel like laughing and wonder if I'm losing my mind. I bite my lip, hard. The pain and rush of warm blood bring me back to my senses. I concentrate on feeling resentful at Liam instead, for treating me like a sensitive girl.

I walk away, aware that Liam's concerned eyes are on me.

Although we're back in the front line, we're not called on to go over the top. Not immediately, anyway. Instead, we're given chores to do—reinforcing the trench walls where they've been damaged by shells is one of the more pleasant ones. Repairing the damage to the latrines makes us moan, but we all know we're complaining for the sake of it. Given the choice between shovelling shit with scarves over our noses or climbing out into No Man's Land again, there isn't a single man among us who would choose the latter.

But the following day, Cox calls us together. He needs volunteers.

"Headquarters are looking for a detailed report on the state of the enemy's trenches, all along the front line." He says in a non-committal voice. "We're required to send out a night-time party to reconnoitre and report back on how Fritz is standing up to the pressure in this part of the trench. Three or four of us should do, and I'll be one of them. Any volunteers?"

He looks at each of us in turn. Black and Simons drop their eyes. I do the same thing. Cox's eyes move on to Liam. I'm not looking at him because I know he won't be stupid enough to step forward. No one would. But then Cox says, "Good lad, Talbot," and my head swerves towards Liam, who is stepping back into line.

Immediately, I step forward too. "I'll go, sir."

Now it's Liam's turn to look dumbstruck.

"Mullins. Good man. One more." As Cox continues his search for the fourth member of the reconnaissance party, Liam glares at me, but he can't say anything, not while Cox and the rest of our unit or platoon are around.

The fourth volunteer is an older man called Douglas. I don't know much about him, except that he's planning to get married next time he's on leave. He likes to show us a photograph of his fiancée, a sad-eyed girl called Eliza, who looks as if she's been practising for widowhood for a long time.

We are told to report to Cox that night and are dismissed.

There's a look of fury on Liam's face. I move away to a quieter section of the trench, aware that Liam is just behind me. We're going to fall out and it needs to be done in private.

As soon as we're safely beyond the sharp bend, he grabs me and spins me around.

"What the fuck do you think you're doing?" he spits.

"Me? What the fuck do you think *you're* doing?"

Liam blinks. He's used to me swearing, but not using that word.

"I'm going to get Venner down off that wire. Bring him back for a decent burial. How about you?"

That shuts me up for a few seconds. Recovering Venner's body is important, but so is keeping Liam safe. There's no question as to which should come first.

"That's all very noble and heroic, but it's too bloody dangerous," I say, after I've had the chance to digest this. "Tell him you've changed your mind."

"Changed my mind? This isn't a bloody Sunday school outing. I can't change my mind. *You* tell him you're not well. Say your guts are playing up again. You're not going."

That's too much. Liam has no right to tell me what to do. No one has. I'm my own boss.

"In a pig's ear," I retort. "If you go, I'm going too. You can't stop me. Someone's got to look after you."

Liam has been staring at me with a face full of anger but, when he hears this, his face shuts down. It's as if saying that I want to look out for him is the most unforgiveable thing in the world.

It seems pointless to carry on arguing after that, so I march off. At the last moment, before I go back round the bend, a thought occurs to me and I turn back. "And Liam? If you're doing this because I was upset that Venner's still out there, and something happens to you, I'll never forgive you. Ever. Or myself."

Before he has the chance to retaliate, I've stormed away.

CHAPTER TWENTY-SIX

For the rest of the day, Liam and I avoid each other. Darkness seems to come early and soon it's time to report to Cox.

As we blacken our faces, Cox gives us our instructions.

"It's quite straightforward. We sneak up to the German trench. We find an unmanned section, slip in and have a little look around. Two of us will be checking the trench—that's you and me, Douglas."

Douglas nods, unsmiling.

"Look at its state of repair, at what weapons you can see, anything else that catches your eye. You other two—Talbot and Mullins—you keep us covered, just in case a curious Fritz comes poking his nose in. It shouldn't take more than a minute, once we're in. Then out we get, back we come and Bob's your blooming uncle!"

It's unlikely to be as straightforward as Cox says, but I appreciate his pretence. We all know that night time reconnaissance is even more dangerous than going over the top in the usual way. Both sides in this war have learned that the best time for surprise raids is after dark. They'll be watching for us.

And then there's Liam's plan to take a little detour on the way back to recover Venner's body. He doesn't mention it to Cox now and I don't think he's going to. Knowing Liam, he'll just peel away, get Venner down and then claim that he got lost and just happened to find himself there. I make a vow that whatever happens, I'll stick to my lover like glue. He won't be disappearing without me. Whatever he faces, I'll face it too.

It hasn't rained today and the No Man's Land mud has dried a little. It's still boggy, but it isn't the clinging mire that it was the last time we were out here. This makes it possible to move fairly stealthily, which is a blessing. If we're heard floundering around, we're dead.

Cox goes first. He's carrying some wire cutters, although he'll only use them in an emergency. At Aldershot, we were taught to avoid any unnecessary noise when we're out on night raids. It's astonishing how loud the act of cutting through barbed wire can be at the dead of night.

After Cox comes Douglas, then me, then Liam. Watching Cox's back ahead of me, a streak of solid blackness in the dark, I realise that I trust him. He's a good soldier, a good sergeant. He'll do all he can to get this job done and make sure we get back in one piece. Even so, my eyes and ears are straining for any indication that we've been spotted.

We're carrying handguns rather than our usual rifles. "They're easier to manage when it's dark and you're trying not to go arse over tit in the mud," Cox explains, before we set out. "And the rifle is a bit unwieldy when you've got to aim at someone in a trench."

We also leave our heavy backpacks behind, to help us move more easily.

"Place your feet carefully. And whatever you do, whatever you come across—you know what I'm talking about—don't cry out. If you do, you'll kill us all," Cox instructs.

I start by trying to feel the ground with my feet before I commit to taking a step, but it takes too long. Liam taps me on the back and his mouth touches my ear.

"Speed up," he whispers, his breath warm against my skin. They're the first words he's said to me since our argument.

I start to tread more normally. I've only gone a few paces like this before my foot comes down on something soft, almost sludgy on the outside, but harder inside. The stench coming from it is indescribable.

I have to clamp my teeth together to stifle my gasp of disgust. Trying not to speculate on whose body I've just trodden on, I force myself onwards.

To begin with, it's pitch dark and, when I'm not stumbling over bodies, I'm trying to avoid the shell holes. My eyes adjust to some extent and I can see a little more—the looming barbed wire and beyond it, the sandbags of the German trench. This isn't good. If I can see them, the Germans can see me, if they're looking hard enough.

Cox leads us along the barbed wire to the right, away from where I think Venner's body must be. I frown, but I'm concentrating too hard on survival to spare much thought to this.

We find a gap in the wire and we're through. Now it's straight on to the enemy trench. As we get closer, the boy I killed hauls himself out of the puddles at the bottom of his trench and steps inside my head. Has his body been recovered? If I find him still there, rotting, I don't know what I'll do.

A bullet whizzes past us and we freeze, waiting for more. They don't come. Just a sniper, trying to alleviate his boredom by taking random shots at nothing in particular. I wonder if it could be *the* sniper; the one who rescued us and gave us our lives back. If it is, I hope we won't have to kill him.

As soon as Cox judges that the danger has passed, he leads us on.

We approach the trench slithering on our stomachs, like worms. If I collide with a body now…I push the thought away. It's not helping. If it happens, it happens. I'll deal with it. I need to control my mind, keep my senses alert.

Startlingly close, a German voice begins speaking. No idea what he's saying, but he sounds as if he's moaning. I wonder if he's saying that he wants to go home, to leave this nightmare behind and get on with his life. Poor bugger! They're no different to us, but still we have to kill each other.

Cox looks behind at us and points to the right, then crawls in that direction. We follow. We pass a sharp zigzag in the trench and stop, listening. The voice of the complaining Fritz sounds a long way off, now. Closer to us, all is silent.

We look at Cox. He holds up one hand. He won't take unnecessary risks. He wants to wait just a little longer….

Seconds drag by. An owl hoots above us, probably looking for a tree to land in, but they've all been destroyed by shellfire. It will have to keep going. Shelter is further afield.

Cox nods and gestures forward.

The first thing all four of us do is look around, hearts thumping. The trench is deserted, as far as we can see, and it looks to be in impeccable condition. The straight stretch we've climbed into is maybe seventy-five yards long, with a sharp zigzag at each end.

Cox looks at Liam and me, and points to the ends of the straight bit. We nod and separate, me to the left and Liam to the right. Our job is to look out for approaching Germans while Cox and Douglas complete their assessment.

I stand with my back to my comrades, eyes and ears straining into the dark. It's very quiet. *Too* quiet? Perhaps, just around this bend, there's a party of Germans creeping towards me, rifles at the ready. I tense and curl my finger around the trigger of my pistol, gritting my teeth as I try to steady my nerves.

There! What was that? A muted thud, as if someone had just put his foot down too heavily. I fight to control the urge to squeeze my trigger, to fire into the dark at the ghosts in my head.

I'm scarcely breathing now, convinced that the sound of air passing through my body will be audible for hundreds of yards.

My head aches from concentrating so fiercely. The noise—whatever it is—isn't repeated.

Infinitesimally, I start to relax.

How long have we been here? It could be seconds or minutes or hours.

Eventually, I risk a glance back at my comrades. Cox is creeping towards me, beckoning. Time to leave.

I rejoin the others. When we're together again, Douglas gives us a thumbs-up. I've never seen such obvious relief on a face.

I'm first out of the trench, followed by Liam. Then comes Cox. Douglas is last. Just as I put my feet on the ladder, Douglas points at something sitting on a nearby firing step. A helmet. I recognise it as a pickelhaube, an archaic looking thing that British cartoonists always draw when they are making fun of the Kaiser. It has a ridiculous golden spike poking from the top. Douglas wants it as a trophy; a lot of our soldiers value them highly and will steal one if they get the chance. They talk about taking them home and boasting about how they acquired them, or selling them on to collectors. It's only a few steps for Douglas to reach it.

I've started to creep away when someone in the trench opens fire.

I turn back, but Liam spins me round again.

"Keep going," he shouts at me, all thoughts of stealth forgotten.

I break into a stumbling run. Liam is with me. A few yards behind him is Cox.

But no Douglas.

Bullets tear past us. Cox veers off sharply to the left. We follow him.

We reach the wire and throw ourselves into a crater, waiting for the bullets to stop.

"Douglas is dead," Cox says, unnecessarily. "That bloody helmet!" He shakes his head but whether it's Douglas' fatal greed, or the German guns, or his own guilt at losing a man that's angering him, I can't tell. Perhaps it's all three.

Cox is examining the wire, looking for a gap we can get through. There aren't any.

Liam points further to the left.

"I'm pretty sure there's a gap over there, sir. Saw it earlier, through the periscope. Wait here, I'll check." He's out of the crater and stealing away before Cox has the chance to object. I start to go after him, but Cox pulls me back.

"Wait," he says. I open my mouth to protest, see Cox's face and close it again.

We wait in silence. The Germans seem to have given up trying to kill the rest of us. Perhaps they're satisfied with Douglas. I think about his sad-eyed fiancée and wonder again if she always knew that this would happen. Cox will have to write to her.

Then I think about Liam and curse him for going without me. After what seems like hours pass, and he hasn't returned, I start praying for him. Please, let him be alright. I need him. He's a good man. Right now, I need to convince myself that the gods care, and could be swayed by entreaty.

The silence becomes a physical presence in the crater. I long to shatter it. In my mind, it becomes Liam's ghost.

Just as I think that I can't keep still for a moment longer, there's a burst of gunfire somewhere to our left. One, two, three, four separate shots. Not a machine gun, then. A pistol. Then some more.

I'm halfway out of the crater before I realise that Cox is right there beside me. We run along the wire, drawing fire, looking for Liam.

We reach the place where Venner was killed. I recognise the chest-height mass of barbed wire with the v-shaped gap in it. It was the last thing that Venner and his friend, and so many others, saw.

But Venner has gone.

And so has Liam.

CHAPTER TWENTY-SEVEN

Near Passchendaele Village, Belgium, late October 1917

We slip through the gap and head back to the safety of our trench. There's nothing else we can do. Night is beginning to give way to a grey dawn. It won't be long until we'll be visible to any German who's looking our way and then we'll be sitting ducks.

I'm hopeful and terrified as we make it back to safety. What will we find? I begin bargaining with the gods. Please let Liam be safe. If he's safe, I'll learn to be a proper woman. I'll marry him and have countless babies and learn to cook and be perfectly happy. I promise. I swear. Just do this one thing. Just this one thing for him. For me.

And there he is.

Relief floods over me.

He's half-sitting, half-lying against the back of a firing step with a grey blanket over him and no wonder, he must be exhausted. I know I am. His eyes are closed, but when he hears our approach, he opens them. He smiles.

"Liam!" I rush towards him, then I remember where I am and what I am and I slow down. I can still be pleased that my mate has survived, I just need to be careful about how I show my pleasure.

"Bloody Venner! He'd disappeared." Liam's voice is a little faint. "Recovery party must have got to him just before me... Then I stumbled into a German reconnaissance unit. Doing the same as us, I suppose."

"You bloody idiot! Rushing off like that. Thank God you're alright..."

He doesn't reply and it's only then that I notice how pale he is. I pull back the blanket. From his breastbone downwards, his tunic is completely red. I give a little moan and touch it with trembling fingers. It's warm and sticky.

"Can't stop it! But it's slowing down a bit now, I think…," his voice drifts away.

"No! Liam!" He seems to have passed out.

I whip my head round. "Stretcher! Get a stretcher! He's wounded, seriously wounded. He's–"

"They're on their way, Mullins," Cox says. He's been talking to some of the others, finding out what's happening. "They won't be long."

"He needs help. Has anyone done anything to help him, yet?"

Cox places a hand on my shoulder. "Everything possible has been done. He's had morphia, lad. He's in no pain," he says, with gentle emphasis.

Morphia! Morphia means it's bad. Morphia is what they give to men when there's no hope, when it's a case of keeping them comfortable until the end.

"No! Not morphia! He doesn't need that, you bloody idiots!"

Cox hauls me to my feet and leads me away. At first, I struggle against him, but then I realise it's because the orderlies have arrived with a stretcher, and he wants them to have clear access to Liam.

Standing next to Cox, with one of his hands on my shoulder, I watch as they examine Liam's wound. They're chatty with him, jovial, although he's barely responding. Over his head, I see them exchange a silent look, full of understanding.

I think I'm going to throw up. My legs feel as if they're going to collapse under me. As the orderlies gently lift Liam onto the stretcher and prepare to take him away, I break free from Cox's grasp and run over to my lover.

"Please. I need to say something to him. Something private." I look beseechingly at the orderly who is standing behind Liam's head. He shrugs and nods to his friend. They lower the stretcher and take a few steps back. I drop to my knees beside Liam.

"Liam. LIAM!" I have to resist the urge to shake him into consciousness. His eyes open, green and clear. Not the eyes of a dying man, I think. They'd be cloudy. That's what it says in all the books I've read: "his eyes were cloudy with pain."

"Do you ever get fed up with making a racket?" His voice is hard to hear.

My lips are shaking, but I control them and assemble a grin before putting them close to his ear.

"Listen. Listen to me," I whisper. "The answer is yes. I'll marry you. That's what I want to do. What I'd love to do." I'm trying to give him something to fight for.

He smiles back at me. "Good!" He beckons me closer again and I put my ear against his mouth. His hot breath feels like a blessing.

"You're a complete bloody pain in the arse. You know that, don't you?"

I give up my struggle to hold back scalding tears.

"Takes one to know one," I manage to say.

He's still trying to hang onto his smile when the orderlies pick him up again and, as gently as they can, carry him away. I crane my head to follow the stretcher party until they turn a corner and are out of sight.

Then I stagger to an empty dugout, where I drop to my knees and cry without restraint. It's not until later, when my tears have been replaced by a feeling of sick dread that fills every pore in my body, that I curse myself for not having the courage to tell him that I love him.

CHAPTER TWENTY-EIGHT

The news that Liam has died on the way to the Casualty Clearing Station comes the next day.

Cox takes me into a dugout to break it to me. I look at him with blank eyes, waiting for the pain to begin. He doesn't need to tell me. I knew yesterday that I was saying goodbye.

"Thank you, sir," says a voice that I recognise as my own.

I walk to the dugout's entrance and look up at the sky. Birds are wheeling, ready to start their long migration to warmer lands. I wish we could join them, Liam and I. My life without him stretches ahead like an empty tunnel. My knees buckle. I'm on the ground, looking at the wall. It's something that Liam can no longer see. How is that possible?

Cox picks me up. He doesn't rush or fuss. He must have done this many times. He sits me down on an upturned crate. Words are coming from his mouth but they must be in a foreign language, because I don't understand them. I frown at his lips, forcing myself to make sense of what he's saying.

"–that the pair of you were close, and you have my commiserations. He was a fine lad. The first time a close pal dies is always the hardest…."

I look at him and wonder how often he's been through this, how he can still be functioning as a human being.

"I'm sending you to the reserve trenches for a stretch. You need some time to come to terms with this," Cox continues. "There's some construction work about to begin. You can lend a hand with it. You've proved you're a capable soldier. We don't want to lose you as well."

The old Nina would have been delighted at Cox's compliment. But the new Nina, the one who was born yesterday, snivelling in a dirty puddle, and who wants nothing more than for the sickness and grief to stop forever, just nods. It makes no difference to me where I am sent, now that Liam is dead.

"I'd like to go to his funeral, sir," my lips say.

Cox looks away. "I'm afraid that isn't possible. He was buried this morning. You'll be able to visit his grave in due course but—"

I double over and throw up. The thought of Liam, my lover, vital and cocky and gentle in turns, lying in the Flanders mud is intolerable. I think about the expression of wonder on his face when he undressed me and about his quick anger. How can all that have disappeared? It's obscene. I puke and puke until I'm exhausted and there's nothing to bring up except bile.

Cox helps me to my feet and produces a rag to clean up my face.

"Wait in here for a bit, lad. Leave when you're ready. Make your way to the reserve trenches. Here's your orders—they'll be expecting you. I'll see you in a week." He pats me on the back and exits, leaving me to face my rising anger alone. Later on, I'm grateful for that.

The next thing I know, I'm in the reserve trenches, although I have no recollection of getting here. I report for duty, find the tent that's been allocated to me, lie down in it, and close my eyes. Someone rouses me. I get up and set to work. I labour from early morning until it's dark. I don't want to stop. I hardly talk to anyone and no one bothers with me.

My desire to see Liam is a physical need, like breathing or eating. My body aches for the feel of his. There are times when my need for him is so raw that my breasts become sensitive and sore, as they did when his mouth was on them. Our time together runs continually through my head and the realisation that it's finished forever makes me want to kill someone.

At last, I comprehend Father's grief. The way he shut us out when Mother died and his long agony of mourning in advance as she slowly died inch by inch, month by month. When death finally claimed her, he wanted to be alone with his memories, to relive them over and over again so that there was no chance of forgetting a single detail of their time together. Anyone breaking into that grief was an intruder.

I want to curl into a ball and stop. Just stop. And why shouldn't I? It would be easy enough. Accidents with guns happen here all the time.

But. There are two reasons for not doing that. If I die, the people who handle my body would find out that I'm a woman, if they're thorough about their job. And that will inevitably rebound on Alfie. There's always a chance that they might not: perhaps they just bury the dead without any kind of preparation. But I don't know.

The second reason also relates to Alfie. If I kill myself, he will think it's his fault and I don't know what he'd do then. The old Alfie, the one I tricked so easily and who always allowed himself to be pushed into the direction that I knew was right for him, would have been devastated, but in time he'd get over it and continue his new life.

But that Alfie has gone. The new one, who contradicts doctors and is considered robust enough to nurse out here, even though he's too young, is someone I'm still getting to know. I don't know what he would do. What if guilt prompted him to go to the authorities and tell them the truth. They might shoot him. It's not a risk I can take. I've lost one of the only two men I've ever loved. The other one *has* to survive.

So, I carry on. I labour all day on a new stable block until I'm too tired to do any more. Then I go to my tent and stare at the canvas walls until I fall into exhausted sleep. A letter from Aunt Julia reaches me. I open it and frown at the words as they squirm across the page.

Dear Alfred,

Thank you for your letter and for your wishes for my wellbeing. If you were here, I would demonstrate that my "advancing years" as you so kindly put it don't hamper me when it comes to dealing with impertinent young relatives!

As regards your enquiry into my recent activities, I was among a group of sisters who chained themselves to the railings outside the House of Commons, in protest at the subjugation of women. We created quite a stir, I can assure you. Mr Lloyd George himself was said to be highly offended by our presence. Quite an achievement! Several of us were subsequently imprisoned for disturbing the peace and I was quite prepared to suffer the same fate, but the magistrates decided that someone of "my age" would be better served with a suspended sentence. The impertinence! I gave them a piece of my mind and some supporters dragged me out of court before the magistrates could change theirs.

In your letters you state that being a soldier has altered you, and the letters themselves are evidence of that. You sound like a new you (not that there was anything wrong with the old one). If there is any unusual *reason for this transformation, please do let me know.*

Do write back soon, dear boy, and stop teasing me. When you return, I will take you to task over it. Have pity on your loving aunt and enjoy the book I am enclosing for your leisure hours.

Julia.

I manage a smile when I see the title of the book she has sent. It is called *The Female Soldier,* by someone called Hannah Snell. I flick it open at the introduction. It seems that Hannah Snell successfully masqueraded as a marine in the British Navy in the eighteenth century. After she was eventually discovered, she was even granted a soldier's pension. I really should write to put Aunt Julia out of her misery and spare her the effort of having to concoct any more veiled hints that she knows my true identity, but doing so seems like an enormous effort that I just don't have the energy to make.

One night, after lying awake for hours, I get up and go to the barn where Liam and I used to meet. I remember the button that I pulled off his tunic the first time we made love. I need to find it. It's something that we both touched.

I've got a box of matches and I search by the light of them, parting the hay like Rumpelstiltskin gleaning for gold. When the matches run out, I search in the dark, patting the ground, feeling in corners and under wooden implements. When at last my questing fingers encounter it, inside a bucket that's turned on its side, I feel a rush of joy. It's as if Liam left it there—a gift for me to find. I hold it to my cheek and thank him. Then I stow it carefully in my breast pocket, curl up on the hay and cry myself to sleep.

After a week or so, I notice changes in my body. The hard work is making me leaner, more muscular. I expected that. What I hadn't expected was my breasts feeling tender, and constant nausea every hour that I'm awake.

I ignore these odd changes until one evening, after throwing up yet another dinner that I'd forced down. I tumble inside my tent in an exhausted, nauseous heap. This can't last much longer, can it?

The penny drops and I sit up: this could well last nine months.

"Bloody hell, Liam," I whisper through the dark to the ghost of my lover, "I think I'm pregnant!"

CHAPTER TWENTY-NINE

When the shock has passed a little, I try to decide what I should do. The first thing has to be to work out if it's true. How I wish I'd listened to Gertie when she used to go on about her cousin, Norma, who seemed to be perpetually pregnant. At the time, it didn't seem to have any relevance to me. I was never going to be one of those foolish women who got trapped into having babies.

So, how can I find out? I can't exactly stroll up to one of the medics and ask him to examine me. A woman might be a little safer to approach, but there are so few around. There's the grim-faced woman in the estaminet, but I don't speak enough French to communicate such intimate details to her, and I'm sure she has no English. Anyway, the thought of sharing such news with a stranger is too horrible.

I could go to the nearest Casualty Clearing Station and seek out a nurse, I suppose. But try as I might, I can't think of a satisfactory story as to why I'd be asking. "My sweetheart at home thinks she's pregnant," is the best I can come up with, but it sounds lame, even to me. Why wouldn't the "sweetheart" seek medical advice herself? The idea that she'd write to a man and ask him to check for her is pure nonsense.

There's only one person I can ask: Alfie. With his nursing experience, he will know what pregnancy entails. He'll read between the lines and understand why I'm asking. And he won't condemn me or give me away.

It's difficult to get the letter right. It needs to get past the eyes of the censors. In the end, I settle for:

I need to ask you something very personal. Something I can't ask anyone else. My sweetheart is worried that she is pregnant. She feels constantly sick and throws up a great deal. Her breasts are sore to the touch. Can you think of any other explanation for her symptoms, dear N? I'd appreciate a swift response as she is very worried and doesn't know which way to turn.

The censors may think I'm an idiot for not knowing more about the workings of the human body, but I don't care about that. Or they may think that I'm a moral degenerate for allowing things to go so far with my girlfriend out of wedlock. Let them. I just need to know what's happening.

And then I'll know how I feel about it. At the moment, I don't know whether Liam's baby would be a gift or another reason to despair.

Alfie's reply comes a week later, as I'm about to rejoin my unit, who are back on the front line.

Dear A,

Your letter was a huge surprise. Not a shock, just a surprise. I had no idea that you'd found a sweetheart and I hope that you make each other happy. You deserve happiness.

I don't know if this will be welcome news to you, but I'm fairly sure from the symptoms you describe that your sweetheart is pregnant. For reasons that you'll understand, this is something that concerns me very much.

I don't believe that she can continue in her current profession if this is the case. We need to talk about this in greater detail, and you need to plan a sensible way forward with your sweetheart. This needs to happen immediately.

I will be transferring to the Front in two weeks. I was planning to surprise you by sending you a letter from somewhere very close, but this news is more important. We will meet up to discuss what you're going to do.

I'll contact you as soon as I'm able. In the meantime, you must do everything you can to keep safe.

Alfie is coming here soon! The relief makes me want to cry. I long to see him, to share my grief with him—to talk in a way that I cannot with anyone else about Liam.

I hope that he'll be able to help me decide what to do next because, for the first time in my life, I just don't know. I can't see a way forward. If I stay here, I could get killed and the baby with me. Liam's baby. If I wait, my deception will be revealed as soon as the pregnancy develops and then I'll be disgraced, and I dread to think what would happen to Alfie.

Maybe we're both wrong. Maybe I'm not pregnant, though I'm surprised to find that the thought fills me with sorrow. The idea that I might be carrying Liam's child is enormously comforting.

But it's frightening too. How would I cope with a baby? All I could teach it was how to be rebellious, how to annoy and disappoint people. I don't know how to cook and care or nourish and lead by example. Liam's child would deserve a much better mother than I could ever be.

As I double over to be sick for perhaps the tenth time that day, I decide that all I can do is wait for Alfie to come. Between us, we'll come up with a plan. In the old days, when we were children, there were few problems we couldn't solve when we put our heads together.

In the meantime, I'll do my best to stay safe for the sake of the baby I might be carrying. For Liam's sake.

CHAPTER THIRTY

S taying safe may not be easy. Although Cox, who greets me with a gruff kindness that nearly starts me crying again, tells me that there are no plans for an immediate attack, there are other dangerous tasks to perform: more reconnaissance missions (although I don't think that Cox will pick me for those) and running messages between command posts, a job that attracts the attention of every sniper in the area. Even venturing out into the listening post lays us open to gas attacks or German raiders. Anyway, we all know that what our Generals say they'll never do today will be top of their agenda tomorrow.

Black and Simons are subdued in my presence. Black looks over my shoulder, gives me a hearty slap on the back and says he hopes I'm "feeling more chipper now." Simons looks into my eyes and shakes my hand and says he's sorry "how things have turned out." More of those bloody euphemisms. Neither of them mentions Liam by name, which infuriates me. I nod and turn away, without replying.

As I move off, I hear Black mutter to Simons, "It's time Mullins hardened up a bit. Talbot was a good fellow, we all know that, but this is war and good fellows die all the time."

Our stint at the front line passes relatively quietly. Only one more day to go and we'll be relieved again, and I've got through my duties as well as I can when my mind is an aching blank and I'm constantly fighting the need to vomit.

Only one more night to get through.

And that's when it happens.

I'm on sentry duty. Most of the others are asleep, hunched on steps or huddled together in dugouts. It's a chilly, clear night and my breath is coming out in little white clouds. I don't mind the cold; it helps me stay alert and gives me something to think about other than my dead lover and my churning stomach.

As the end of my two-hour stint draws near, I look up at the stars and marvel at their beauty in this ugly place. It almost makes me believe that there's some design to the world and a purpose to the horrors we've experienced.

It's as my eyes are returning to scan No Man's Land that I think I see—what? Movement, close to the ground. Measured and furtive. Like a cat creeping up on a bird.

I peer into the blackness. The movement has stopped, if it was ever there in the first place. In my mind I note the place where I think I saw it, then look away and back again. This is a trick that Liam taught me while we were behind the lines.

"You'll be looking at it with new eyes. Sometimes, when you look at something too long, you stop seeing what's under your nose." He was standing very close behind me and pointing at a miraculous hare, motionless as marble, in the field about twenty yards away.

It doesn't work this time. Still, I see nothing. A soldier approaches to take over from me. It's Black. I point to the place where I think I might have seen something.

"Thought I saw movement over there. Keep your eyes open," I say.

He nods, blowing on his fingers, and I leave him to it.

Time to visit the latrines. I need to pee more frequently now, which is causing me problems, so I visit whenever I think it'll be quiet. I also want to throw up in peace.

The need to vomit is more pressing than the need to pee, so I do that first. Then I unbutton my trousers and squat.

It's while I'm doing this that I start to feel uncomfortable. As if I'm being watched. Again.

I look up.

A man is standing on a hillock of mud, looking at me.

Just for a moment, I think the ghost of Liam has returned to the place of our first talk as woman and man, and my heart leaps with joy. Then I take in the figure's blackened face, his muddy grey uniform and his pistol, which is pointing straight at me. It must have been him I saw out in No Man's Land—part of a German reconnaissance team, no doubt. Somehow, he's become separated from the others.

"Mein Gott," he says, which is more or less the same in English, as far as I can tell. He adds something that I don't catch but it's not hard to work out what he's saying. "A woman soldier!"

I stand up, button my trousers and raise my hands. I'm unarmed. I stowed my rifle before I came here. I take a step or two towards him. I hear a click as his finger moves on the trigger of his pistol and stop, bracing myself.

But he doesn't release the trigger.

My heart hammers as I take another step towards him, then another.

I try a smile and hope it looks reassuring rather than terrified.

When I'm about ten yards from him, I point at a fallen tree trunk.

"I'm going to sit down," I say in a low, steady voice.

I sit and then hold out my hands to show that I'm not carrying any weapons.

I pat the wood next to me. Warily, the German soldier sits down. He keeps his pistol pointed at my heart. His eyes never leave my face. He's a little older than me: 25 or so, with a thin face, smudged, weary eyes and hair in need of a wash and cut. In other words, he's another unremarkable soldier, just like me and many thousands more, on both sides of No Man's Land.

We look at each other.

"Um Himmels Willen, was machst du hier?" he says.

I lift my hands.

"Sorry, I don't speak German. What are you doing here? Are you lost?"

He frowns and shrugs. After a long moment, he transfers his gun to his left hand and holds the right one out to me.

"Werner," he says.

I shake his hand, then point to myself. "Nina."

"Soldat?" he says, pointing at me.

I nod. "It's a long story," I reply.

He shakes his head in disbelief. "Nur den verdammten Engländern würde einfallen, eine Frau in den Krieg zu schicken!"

The only word I understand is Frau. It means woman. Perhaps he thinks I'm one of many: a whole battalion of women soldiers.

"Don't worry," I say. "I'm the only one." I hold up one finger and point to myself, hoping that he understands. Then I mutter, "That I know of, anyway. The powers that be would never allow it."

"Schwanger?"

I lift my hands, palms upwards.

"Sorry. I don't understand."

He frowns, points at my stomach, then at the pit where I've just thrown up my guts. He mimes vomiting and rocks an invisible baby in his arms.

"Schwanger?" he says again.

"Ah, yes," I nod. "I think so."

He swears and puts his pistol down.

There's a question in his face.

"It's a long story," I say again. "I tricked my brother so that I could take his place. I'm more of a soldier than he is. He's a nurse. He saves lives instead of ending them. It's what he does best. I met a man—a soldier—who I– and we– and then he got killed and I think I'm having his baby. And I miss him so much–" To my horror, I feel tears starting to dribble down my face. I scrub at them with my sleeve. "Liam was his name. I want Liam back." Saying my lover's name out loud is both a torment and a luxury. "I want him to have a future. I want him to know his baby and watch it grow and be a loving father…."

Werner makes a clucking noise and looks concerned. He dips his fingers into the breast pocket of his tunic and pulls out a handkerchief. He offers it to me.

"Thanks," I say, scrubbing at my face. "I'm not much of a crier, usually…."

A little awkwardly, he pats my back.

I reflect that I could easily reach out and grab his gun now, but I don't want to. Werner is a decent man. We're encouraged to think of Germans as murderous beasts, but he's just like the rest of us: here because politicians have decided that he will be. The only differences between us are the colour of our uniforms and the language in which we curse our commanders.

I finish scrubbing and extend the handkerchief so that he can take it back.

"Thanks. You'll need to wash it."

He wrinkles his nose and laughs.

"Nein," he says, pushing it back towards me. And then he adds, "Du bist anders als ich mir die Engländer vorgestellt habe," whatever that means.

I shrug.

He hesitates, then takes a photo from his pocket and passes it to me. I think it's going to be of his wife, but it's a child, a girl of about two, with stormy eyes and a stubborn mouth.

"Elena," he says, pointing.

"Elena," I repeat. "Your daughter? Very pretty," It's not strictly true. Elena looks more stubborn than pretty. I imagine that she could be a handful. "How old? Two? Three?" I'm holding up the appropriate number of fingers.

"Nein." Werner looks very sad. "Sie is tot." He closes his eyes for a moment. Then he places one hand palm down over the photo and, with the other, makes the sign of a cross.

"*Dead?* Not dead? How can she be dead?" A new strain of sadness clutches at my heart and I hope I'm misunderstanding, but Werner nods.

"Es brach mein Herz. Und nun bin ich hier und verursache neuen Tod. Ich will, dass das alles aufhört," he says, giving his eyes an impatient wipe.

"I'm sorry, so sorry." I'm crying again, clasping Werner's hand.

He sighs and nods. "Zu viel Tod," he says.

Somehow, I know exactly what he's saying.

"Yes. Too much death. I wish I could make it stop."

We sit in silence for perhaps a minute, perhaps five, thinking about our dead loved ones. I get up and am about to tell him that he'd better be going before he runs into a proper soldier, when we hear English voices, carried towards us on the wind.

"You think he was headed towards the latrines? Cheeky bastard. Come on, let's cut him off."

Werner is on his feet too. We stare into each other's eyes.

"They're coming for you!" I strain my ears. How close are they? What direction are they coming from? I don't want to send Werner into their arms.

"Get your guns ready," one of the voices is saying. "Don't want the bastard slipping away."

The voice is much closer. Just the other side of the hedge. They'll be here in 30 seconds. No time for Werner to run away. If he's caught here, with me, it will be the end for both of us. I'll be shot for fraternising with the enemy. There's only one thing for it.

I grab Werner's pistol.

He lunges at me in alarm, but I'm faster.

I point the gun in the air and pull the trigger. The shot shatters the silence.

Then I point at the latrine trench.

"Get in there, quick."

Werner hesitates.

"*Quick*! Or die."

On the other side of the hedge, I hear an exclamation, followed by the sound of running feet.

I shove him towards the latrine. He gives a sort of despairing sigh and drops into it, sending clouds of flies buzzing into the night air.

I spin around, just as three Tommies pelt around the hedge towards me.

"There's a Fritz on the loose round here. You seen him?" one of them asks.

"Saw him? I took a shot at the bastard," I spit on the ground.

"Good man. Wing him?" the Tommy asks.

"Maybe. Too dark to be sure."

"Which way?"

I point away from the German trenches.

"Running in the wrong direction, stupid fucker," another of the Tommies says. "We'll get him. Come on, lads."

They're off again.

I count to twenty, then return to the latrine trench. Werner has surfaced. Shit drips over his face, into his eyes, which are full of a new kind of horror. His lips are clenched tightly shut, as if he never wants to open them again. I reach out a hand and he grabs it.

"Come on." I pull and he scrambles out. He stands there, dripping. His movements have stirred up the contents as well as the army of bluebottles, which had just settled again. He starts to gag. It must be catching because I do the same thing. I lean into the shit-filled trench and puke up what's left in my guts. Werner does the same.

"Sorry," I say, when we've both finished. "It was all I could think of."

I hold out his handkerchief again and this time he takes it. He wipes his face and hands, then folds the filthy cotton square neatly and tucks it back into his breast pocket, like he's dressing for an outing with a sweetheart.

The incongruity of the action makes me laugh. A second later, Werner joins in quietly.

He thanks me and adds, "Ich muss gehen."

He holds out one hand and I take it between both of mine.

"Go now. Your trench is over there." I point. "When all this is finished, maybe we'll meet again. Take care of yourself."

"Viel Glück." He gives a formal little bow and steals away.

My eyes follow him as his grey shadow merges with the deeper grey of the night, aware that this meeting has changed things for me. As I head back to my own trench, I make myself two promises: if I *am* pregnant, I will do everything I can to keep our baby safe, and no matter how long I am out here, I'll never kill another German.

CHAPTER THIRTY-ONE

We're back in reserve when I get Alfie's letter. I recognise his looping handwriting and my heart gives a little leap. I tear the envelope open. It's from No.32 Casualty Clearing Station, Brandhoek, which is only a few miles away.

I'm here. HOW have you coped? It's worse than I imagined. You probably know that this station is devoted to men with chest and abdominal injuries and some of the ones I've seen are heartbreaking. And those are simply the men who've been brought in for assessment. I haven't seen the wards or the operating theatre yet.

I can't get right to the front line. Women aren't allowed(!) but I think I can get to the reserve trenches. We should meet there as soon as possible. Write back and let me know when you can get there.

Is there any news about your sweetheart? Any changes? Whatever her situation, you don't need to worry a minute longer. I have a MAH-vellous plan!

Once again, I think about how much Alfie has changed. His letter is confident and commanding, and he expects me to do as he says. He has become formidable.

And, he has an idea to get me out of my predicament. Hope flutters inside me as I wonder what he has thought of. I haven't been able to come up with a single idea. Thank goodness for Alfie, my brother and friend; together, we can work things out.

I write back that I'm here in the reserve trench for four more days. Whenever he can get here, he'll find me. I'm not going anywhere.

Then it's a case of waiting. As I go about my duties—filling sandbags and mending wire, I find myself talking to Liam.

"You'd like Alfie. I wish you could have met him," I say, when there's no one around to question my sanity. "The old Alfie—you'd probably have scared him a bit, but this new one—he'd love you." I'm confident of that.

A new wave of nausea washes over me. "He'll make a good uncle," I tell my dead lover. "He'll help out a lot. I won't be alone." I think fleetingly about Father, then dismiss him from my mind. I just can't see him in the role of doting grandfather to an illegitimate grandchild.

Two days later, Black tracks me down to the back of camp, where I'm shovelling sand into bags.

"Mullins, visitor for you. A woman, no less! No need to ask who she is. You couldn't be much more alike, though she's prettier than you. Not that that's hard!" He says this with a smile in his eyes.

Joy surges through me. I shove my spade into the sand and straighten up. No need to make myself look a bit more presentable. Alfie wouldn't expect that.

I follow Black to the Reception area. There's Alfie, in his nurse's uniform. He's sitting in the biggest tent, drinking tea with an officer! When he sees me, he puts his cup and saucer down (Where did that come from? All we get are enamel mugs!) and deftly excuses himself.

We rush into each other's arms.

Alfie takes a step back and looks me up and down. He narrows his eyes. "How are you?"

I look over his shoulder at the officer, who's watching us. "I'm fine. It's wonderful to see you." I'm close to tears. Can't let the officer see that, so I steer Alfie away and we start to walk around the camp.

"You look Mah-vellous!" I say, and it's true. Alfie wears his uniform with flair and he looks at me with eyes that must have seen horrors, but that still have a smile in them.

"You look—tired," he says. He stops and examines me more closely. "More than tired."

He drapes one arm around my waist and we walk on. "Your sweetheart's pregnancy—it's still…ongoing?"

"Yes. Yes, I think so." I'm struggling to keep from crying. What's wrong with me? I've become pathetic.

"I thought so." He gives a decisive nod. "Right. And what does your sweetheart say about it?"

That's the straw that breaks the camel's back. I can't hold back the tears any more. "Alfie, he's dead. Liam. My Liam. Dead and buried in the mud…."

"Oh, Nina." Alfie wraps me in his arms and I collapse into them. He leads me onwards. I don't notice where we're going until I see the barn in front of us. That makes it worse. I grasp his arms and bury my face in his chest and cry, and cry, and cry. He pulls me inside the barn and lets me get on with it.

Eventually, he smooths the bedraggled hair away from my face and kisses the top of my head.

"I'm so sorry," he whispers. There are tears in his eyes too.

"Bloody war! Bloody bastard war!"

"Nina! Your language!"

I open my mouth to tell him exactly what he can do with his prissiness when I see the laughter in his face. I can't help it. I smile.

"You look hideous," Alfie says.

"Thanks!" I wipe my face on my sleeve.

"Sit down." He pulls me down to sit in the hay. "Tell me about Liam. About the pregnancy. How do you feel? And then—I'll tell you what we're going to do about it."

"Liam is–" I choke on a sob, "*was* a good man. The best." I curse myself for the inadequacy of my words. I try harder and the words tumble out.

"He was a bit of a fighter when he was a child. His parents were rough with him…. He tried to look after me, even when I didn't want him to. He looked quite fierce—like the eagle in the painting in the dining room at home. And he *could* be fierce, but not with me. He looked at me like I was the most precious thing in the world. We argued a lot, but it didn't matter. He wanted to settle down with me after the war. I didn't know whether it was a good idea or not. I'm not exactly wife material, but I'd have liked the chance to give it a try. If anyone could have made me happy with a woman's lot, it was Liam…."

That starts the tears again.

"Did he know? About the baby?" Alfie asks, quietly.

"No, and if he had, we'd have fought tooth and nail about it. He'd have insisted on my going home immediately and I would have refused."

This seems to be what Alfie is waiting for. He takes both of my hands.

"He was absolutely right. You know that, don't you?"

"Yes, but—I can't. I just can't. The trouble you'd get in…."

"You can, and you will," Alfie says, making me look him in the eye. "And there'll be no trouble at all, because we're going to swap places again."

CHAPTER THIRTY-TWO

Near Passchendaele Village, Belgium, November 1917

"**N**o! Absolutely not," I splutter.

Alfie crosses his arms and looks at me. "It's the only way," he says. "Use your brain and you'll see that."

"I'll never do that. Never. How can you even ask me?" I'm on my feet, glaring down at him. He stands up too.

"Actually, Nina, I'm not asking you. I'm telling you. For once, I'm going to be the decisive twin. It's the only way and I'm ready for it. It's what I want."

"What you want? Don't talk rubbish. You're doing what you want now." I gesture at his uniform. "And you're doing it brilliantly. I won't let you throw that away."

"The first thing is—yes, you're right. This is what I want. Not just the clothes and the job, I want the whole female package: periods and birth pains and all. But that's impossible and there's nothing you or I can do to change that. The second thing is—I'm not giving you a choice in this. If you won't agree, I'll go to the authorities and tell them the truth. I've got a niece or nephew to protect. That's my priority, now."

I gasp and glare at him. "You wouldn't," I say.

He gives me a little smile. "Believe me, I would. I've grown up. I'm not a scared child anymore. I do what needs to be done, and this needs doing."

"No! There's another way…besides, what about David?"

Alfie's face changes. "It's finished—me and David." He forces a smile. "I think the ghost of his vicar father reared up and told him to stop sinning."

"Oh no! I'm so sorry!" I curse the inadequacy of my words. "What happened?"

Alfie brushes away my apology. "David's mother came to visit, unannounced."

He sees my wide-open eyes and mouth and gives a bitter little laugh. "No, no, there was nothing sordid about it. No delicto flagrante! We were still in our separate lodgings, most of the time…. She arrived while I was on duty at the hospital. We'd arranged to meet that evening and go for dinner, David and me. At the Grand Hotel. I arrived and he wasn't there, which was unusual. So, I waited. And waited. Eventually, one of the hotel staff came over and asked me if I was Miss Nina Mullins. He gave me a note from David, apologising and saying his mother had turned up and we'd meet the following evening. I thought he meant the three of us and I was excited at the thought of meeting her. It was a good sign, I thought. A milestone in our relationship. I bought a new dress for the occasion…." He blinks rapidly. I put my arm around his shoulders.

"I was surprised the next day when he turned up alone, saying his mother had another appointment. The same thing happened the day after too. It was becoming painfully obvious to me that David was too ashamed of our relationship—of me—to allow me to meet his family. He was scared of what she'd think and say."

Alfie has been examining his hands but now he looks up.

"I was hurt. I asked him. He said no, of course he wasn't ashamed. It was just that he was worried that his mother would realise what I was…. I asked him what he meant and he stuttered something or other. But it was obvious that I was right. I ended it there and then. I won't be someone's sordid secret!"

"I don't know what to say."

I'm angry that my brother has been treated so shamefully, and sad that the relationship that made him happy has come to an end. But I'm also awed by him. I remember Lacey saying that at school, Alfie wouldn't say boo to a goose. That shy, terrified boy no longer exists. Alfie is strong and he knows how to protect himself. He won't allow himself to be mistreated. Then I think back to the school boxing match between Alfie and that other boy—Moody. Alfie wouldn't back down, even then. He stood up for himself and fought to the end, even when he was beaten and bloody. My brother has always had hidden strengths that I have failed to acknowledge. Perhaps I have underestimated him.

"There's nothing *to* say," Alfie gives me a hug. "It's over and done with, and we need to forget it. Your problem's more pressing. There's no other way. We must swap. You know it and I know it. And, if you don't mind my saying, refusing to do it is selfish."

"Selfish? I'm trying to save your life!"

"It doesn't need saving, not anymore. You've got to do whatever will keep your baby safe. Yours and Liam's. That's your priority, now." He gives a sudden laugh. "What would Aunt Julia say if she knew you were jeopardising the wellbeing of a future Suffragette leader?"

I have to smile at that. "Please," I say. "Please don't ask me to do this. I can't. You're my brother. I love you." I know that I must sound pathetic, and I hate myself for it. I step away and slump onto the floor of the barn.

Alfie drops on one knee beside me, careless of his white uniform. He puts his arm around my shoulders.

"And I love you. But it's like I said. I'm not asking, I'm telling. The sooner you get used to the idea the better. I'm giving you the rest of today. You need to tell me as much as you can about what you do, who the men in your unit are, that sort of thing. I'll come back tomorrow. We'll change over and you'll go back to the hospital. I'll tell you as much as possible about how things work there, but I've only just arrived so any mistakes you make will be understandable. Not that you'll be staying long. You're going to discover that you're pregnant and leave in disgrace. Got it?"

Suddenly, I can't argue any more. I'm exhausted mentally and physically, and I know he's right. I need to rest and to nourish the baby. It needs to live so that Liam will live. I just can't do that here.

I reach for his hand.

"Alfie, how did you get to be so wise and so forceful?"

He squeezes my hand.

"You gave me the chance to learn to be those things. You saved me from myself. Now I'm going to do the same for you."

CHAPTER THIRTY-THREE

Near Passchendaele Village, Belgium, November 1917

We spend the afternoon in the barn, telling each other as much as we can about our lives and routines. I give Alfie a lesson in weaponry too—how to fix a bayonet and fire a rifle. After that we wander around the camp and I point out the people and places he needs to know about.

"That's Sergeant Cox," I say, after I've saluted him. "He'll be in charge of you. Trust him and do as he says. He's a survivor. He was good to me when Liam died."

He's already met Black but I introduce him to Simons, who kisses his hand in an old-fashioned way and thanks him for all the hard work he does. Alfie murmurs something graceful and even manages a blush.

I don't sleep at all that night, and I'm willing to bet that Alfie doesn't, either. I go over what Alfie said again and again, and every time I reach the same conclusion—he's right. It's one thing to gamble with my own life. It's quite another to do it with my baby's.

The new Alfie will be able to look after himself in the trenches—I don't doubt it. It doesn't mean he'll be safe, of course, but we're reaching the end of 1917, and there are rumours that the Germans can't carry on much longer. One more big push, people say, and if we win they'll be finished. We have the Americans on our side now, and they're making a big difference. The end of the war is in sight. That makes me feel a little better.

The next morning is a day off from our usual duties, which is helpful. I look around my little tent and wonder if there's anything I want to take with me. There's only one thing I can't leave behind—Liam's button—and that's always with me. I tidy up and make my bed carefully. I want Alfie to be comfortable

Most of the men spend the morning playing or watching football, so I take the opportunity to have a good wash. I can't turn up at the clearing station smelling like a front-line soldier.

Then I wait.

Alfie arrives late morning. He's looking tired but composed. I give him a hug and lead him away to talk.

"You're sure? It's not too late."

"Absolutely sure. Never been surer. It's right, Nina, and that's all there is to say about it."

We walk and talk and remember our childhood escapades.

"Remember Esme's wedding? That was when we first realised that we could do this properly." I lift my uniformed arms and nod at Alfie's nurse's attire. "You could say we owe all our experiences to her."

"If she knew that, she'd die of mortification," Alfie grins. "Which wouldn't be a bad thing…."

"I was trying my hardest to look romantic as I went down that aisle," he reminisces. "I thought it would be my only chance. But I'm sure I looked more like a street urchin running after an ice cream cart!"

"You looked wonderful! And Aunt Julia! The terror we felt when she told us she'd rumbled us. But she was on our side…."

"I think she always will be," Alfie says. "Just bear that in mind, won't you? Father never appreciated you."

Our time is almost up. We stop laughing and head for the barn, where we're going to change.

A few minutes and it's done.

How strange these clothes feel, how constricting. When I move, my skirt catches around my legs, making it hard to walk. I'll have to practise, like once I practised moving like a man.

"How do I look?" I ask.

Alfie tilts his head on one side and considers.

"Very nice. The skirt's a little tight on you around the waist, and that'll get worse pretty quickly, but you won't be needing it for long."

He strikes a manly pose, folding his arms and sticking out his chest like a big game hunter with a fresh kill. "How about me?"

I nod. "You look like a soldier, ready for action. How do you feel?"

He smiles at me. "Like a man," he says. "It feels strange, but it's the right thing. For the moment, at least."

CHAPTER THIRTY-FOUR

Near Passchendaele Village, Belgium, November 1917

We say our real goodbyes in the barn, hugging each other fiercely.

"Thank you," I say to my twin. "Thank you for saving us," I touch my stomach with gentle hands.

"Look after yourself. You're carrying the future of our clan there—I won't be contributing any little Mullinses to the world!"

I hug him again. "That's a pity for the world. If there were more people like you, all this would never have happened." I gesture towards the churned-up fields and the rows of military tents and, beyond them, the roar and rumble of war.

Alfie turns to leave but there's something else I want to say, just in case this is my only chance to say it.

"You know what, Alfie? You're the bravest person I've ever known. Not just for this —" I gesture towards his uniform. "You always have been, I can see that now. I wish I was more like you. You're my hero."

Alfie wipes his eyes and gives a smile that's slightly wobbly. "If you were any more like me, we'd merge into a single person. And what a MAH-vellous person we'd make!"

A final, fierce hug and then we dry our faces and leave the barn.

The farewell we make in public is more muted but still heartfelt.

"Please," I whisper, "take care of yourself. Be safe."

"You too. It's a frightening place, England."

Before I know what's happening, Alfie bundles me into the back of an empty ambulance that's heading back to Brandhoek. He stands still, one hand raised, as the distance between us lengthens.

As we jolt away, I stand up in the back and push the canvas flaps out of the way so we can see each other for as long as possible. As I lose sight of Alfie, I find myself thinking about our childhood dressing-up box and that red soldier's tunic with its jangling medals. About how Alfie had disliked it as much as I loved it.

I have a strange thought. I think that we've been rebelling against the world and all its pointless rules. For a while we were winning but now the weight of tradition and expectation has proved too much for us. The boy who wanted to be a girl is a soldier. The girl who wanted to be a boy is carrying a child. For now at least, the world has won. But I vow that I will carry on my fight to be myself, whatever that entails. I know Alfie will do the same.

I'm jolted out of my misery as we pull into the Clearing Station. Row upon row of men are lying under blankets on stretchers, in front of the complex of tents and the occasional hut. There must be two or three hundred. They are close to filling the field.

"My God! Why aren't they inside?" The words burst from me before I remember that Alfie will already have seen this.

The driver, a woman of about forty in a knitted jacket and loose trousers, looks at me kindly. "I can tell you're new! They're waiting to be assessed and admitted. I only hope there's room for all of them, although not all of them will make it that far…."

I jump down and walk among them. Some are conscious, some not. Of the conscious ones, some bear their pain silently, while others moan or cry. Because these are men with chest or abdominal wounds, there isn't much blood to see—it's hidden beneath their blankets, although every now and then I see someone bleeding so profusely that it has soaked through.

I drop to my knees beside one of these. "Do you need anything?" I ask. When I'm closer, I realise that this is only a boy, surely too young to be out here. Although pain, blood loss and trench living have left their stamp on him, he can't be more than sixteen.

Somehow, he manages to smile at me. "Don't suppose you could run me to a warm bed with clean sheets and a pint of stout?" he asks, in a voice that is only half broken. I think that I must sound similar to him.

"The bed we can manage. The stout—you'll have to wait till you're better," I say. "Are you old enough to drink? How old are you?"

Alarm registers on his face through the pain. "Nineteen. They make 'em small where I come from."

"And give them voices that never break properly," I comment. Seeing his discomfort, I add: "Don't worry. I'm not going to give you away, unless you want me to. I've got a few secrets myself."

He lifts one hand and touches my short hair. "Been masquerading as a soldier, have you? To stay with your sweetheart?" There's a gleam of humour in his eyes.

"Something like that…let's have a look at you."

Gently I pull at his blanket and I'm looking at Liam's wound again. Another red tunic. There's nothing but oozing blood from his chest downwards. My hands shake.

"Nasty, isn't it?" There's a note of twisted pride in his voice.

"I've seen worse," I say.

Suddenly, the most important thing in the world to me is that this boy lives. I couldn't save Liam, but this one—maybe it's not too late.

I rise to my feet. "What's your name?" I ask.

"Arthur. Like in Camelot. Arthur Ryan."

"I'm going to get you some help." I'm already moving towards a pair of orderlies who are standing and smoking near the front of the row of men.

"There's a boy over there. He needs help. Come with me, please."

One of them has pale blue eyes and pock-marked skin. He must be in his mid-40s: just old enough to escape conscription. He looks me up and down. "New, are you? They all need blooming help! He'll have to wait his turn, like the rest of 'em."

I close my eyes for a second. What would Alfie do? He wouldn't take no for an answer.

"Please. I'm sure we can save him if you'll just help me get him inside."

The orderly shrugs.

"And then someone else will die. He'll be seen in due course. Now, I'd like to get on with my break, if it's all the same to you." He turns away.

Anger rushes through me and I push forward so that I can glare up at the man's face. Bugger diplomacy. "Don't think that because I'm wearing a skirt, I won't kick your scrawny bloody arse from here back to Dover if you leave that boy to die," I promise. "Come with me. Now. I won't ask you again."

His companion, who's a bit younger and has a prominent Adam's apple that reminds me of Father's old assistant in the shop, moves first. "Come on, Ted, break's more or less over anyway."

Ted throws his cigarette butt down and follows me.

"Bloody she-devil," I hear him mutter. "She's a disgrace to womankind, that one." Out loud he calls, "Here, you sure you're a blooming woman?"

"Fairly sure," I retort, over my shoulder. "Why do you have to ask? Have you never been able to get very close to one?"

That sets him muttering again, and his companion laughing, but by now we've reached Arthur Ryan. The orderlies lift him up, more gently than I thought they would, to take him inside to be seen.

"Thanks, Miss." Ryan's voice wavers towards me as he's carried off. "You're an angel."

Ted gives a sarcastic laugh and so do I. I've been called a devil and an angel in the same minute, and I agree with both.

CHAPTER THIRTY-FIVE

No. 32 Casualty Clearing Station, Brandhoek,
Belgium, November 1917

Arthur Ryan's situation looks precarious. He spends most of his first two days unconscious and I stop by frequently to check whether he's woken up. When I bump into the miserable orderly again, he greets me with elaborate politeness. I return his greeting in the same over-polite manner and he slinks away, muttering about skinny women who should know their place.

On the third day Arthur comes to. He's very weak and in a lot of pain, but it looks as if he's going to survive. I spend as much time as I can with him. Mainly I just talk to him, chatting about my brother and life in Cambridge and about Stoke-on-Trent, which is where he's from. I don't think it matters what I say. He just appreciates a friendly face and the chance to think and talk about something other than the pain he can't quite hide, or the war. I think he falls a little bit in love with me, which surprises me. What can he possibly see in me? Can't he see that I'm nothing but a shell?

When I'm sure that he's on the mend, I request an interview with Sister.

I like Sister Howard. She's patient but not *that* patient. I've seen her spend an hour picking bits of uniform out of a man's wound, and then give a doctor a rocket for forgetting to wash his hands between patients. Alfie would like and work well with her, I think, sending up a little prayer to the gods that he is thriving.

She's quite young for a Sister—about 30, I'd say—and there's a crinkle in her fair hair that she never quite manages to tame.

I knock on her door at the appointed time and march in. I've spent some time wondering what to say to her, and I've decided to come straight out with it. That will suit both of us, I think.

"Sister, I've come to tell you that I'm pregnant. And to apologise for wasting everyone's time in shipping me over here. I suppose I will have to go home."

She looks up from the papers strewn over her desk and frowns at me.

"Sit down," she says. "I'm not going to ask *how*. But I will ask *when* is it due?"

I've got this all worked out. "It was about six weeks ago. My intended was home on leave and I was about to come over here and, well, one thing led to another…."

"So, sometime late summer or early autumn next year, all being well…." She gives me a long look. "How are you feeling?"

"Sick as a pig, most of the time."

She nods. "Quite so. I'm not going to lecture you on what you get up to in private, that would be unnecessary and presumptuous. And heaven knows, the double standards in our society sicken me. What's acceptable for men should be acceptable for women too. I *will* say that it's a shame, because although your nursing skills aren't exactly top-notch, you care about the men and you get things done. Young Ryan would certainly have died if he'd been left to bleed out much longer."

"Thank you."

"You'll have to go home as soon as possible. With the strictest hygiene in the world, there are still too many communicable diseases around here for a woman in your condition. And anyway, you're pale and thin as a rake. You'll need plenty of rest and good food to ensure a healthy parturition." She sighs and reaches for a printed form. "I'm going to arrange for you to be on a boat back to Dover tomorrow. Do you wish to say your goodbyes to the other nurses, or shall I come up with an excuse for your sudden departure? A sudden family illness is always popular."

There's a glimmer of a smile in her eyes as she says this. I wonder how often she has done this before.

"I'll tell Ryan, but perhaps you could do the rest, Sister. I've had enough of goodbyes. But tell them the truth. I'm not ashamed of it. Just the opposite, actually."

She stands and shakes my hand.

"Good luck, Mullins. You're an unusual woman. I wish there were more like you."

CHAPTER THIRTY-SIX

London, late November 1917

Two days later, I'm back in England, still reeling from the shock of the sight of intact villages and towns, of clean people in civilian clothes and fields that haven't been bombed into muddy death traps. The uncorrupted air smells so fresh that I can't stop myself from taking deep lungfuls of it. After the monstrous noise of war, the sounds of everyday life—horses and motor cars and people chatting about nothing in particular and even the wind rustling the leaves of trees that have kept their leaves—unsettle me with their normality.

I make my way to Bayswater and now I'm standing outside a handsome, white, semi-detached villa. It has fir trees in the front garden and plaster pillars either side of the door and a brass doorknocker in the shape of a ferocious-looking monkey. Very appropriate for someone as fierce as Aunt Julia. I take a deep breath and rap on the door. She opens it herself and envelops me in a hug before dragging me inside.

"A baby? How marvellous. And no husband? Very sensible. He'd only get in the way—nasty, useless things, men! You'll stay here, won't you? In fact, that's not a question. I'm telling you: you're coming to live with me. There's no way that you can go back to your father, and I'm sure you wouldn't want to. He's a spineless newt of a man who would die of plague rather than harbour an unwed mother. We can raise your child to have progressive principles. Perhaps, in time, you can have more and we'll start a movement of sensible human beings. Alfred may join too. It's not his fault he's not a fully-fledged woman. And I like that Sassoon fellow too, I've got a good feeling about him."

She is glowing with purpose and excitement.

After a swift telling-off for not looking after myself, Julia leads me along a long, sparsely decorated passageway that seems refreshing after the clutter of Father's home, into a sitting room at the back of the house. The walls are lined with bookcases filled with well-thumbed books. There's a green velvet sofa that has seen better times, with embroidered cushions jumbled onto it. The rug on the floor has little burn marks on it, which I assume are from coals falling out of the unguarded fire. Mother would have had a fit. Over the fireplace hangs a large photograph of a handsome, serious-looking, middle-aged woman.

"Mrs Pankhurst," Aunt Julia explains, catching me looking at it. She says the name as if it explains everything and I suppose it does.

"Have you met her?" I ask.

"Yes. A huge honour. She lives on the run. The police and government think that if they could put her away, the Suffragette movement would collapse. It wouldn't—we're too dedicated—but it would be a huge blow. I met Mrs P on one of her flying visits to rally supporters."

Julia insists that I rest on the sofa while she makes tea and I'm grateful to do so. I'm tired and sick and grieving, and oh so relieved to find that Aunt Julia is happy to see me. I bring my legs up and curl them under me. Julia isn't the type who'll object to feet on sofas.

She brings in the tea on a tray decorated with an old portrait of Queen Victoria in the days of her grumpy widowhood. I reflect that if Aunt Julia and the old Queen had ever come to blows, I'd lay money on my relative coming out as the victor.

She settles beside me and places some cushions beneath my feet. Then she pours the tea into plain white cups.

"Sugar? ...Nonsense, one sugar isn't enough for a woman in your condition. Look at you—skinny as a rail. You'll need to build your strength up." She spoons two towering sugars into my cup and gives it a vigorous stir.

I take a few sips and sigh. Warmth is spreading through me. The only time I'd been warm at the Front was in the barn with Liam.

"That's better. You're getting some colour into your cheeks. Now, tell me the truth. You've done it, haven't you? Been to war? I *knew* those letters weren't from Alfred. You should have confided in me, you wicked girl."

I tell Julia all about my stint as a soldier, holding nothing back. I wouldn't insult her by doing so. She can barely contain her excitement.

"You've infiltrated the ultimate masculine domain," she says, dark eyes gleaming. "More than that—you've proved that women are capable of playing an active part in war. My congratulations, Nina. You've advanced the cause of women the world over. I'm so proud of you!"

I start to say that I had no such intention but she interrupts me. "It doesn't matter what you meant to do. It's the outcome that's important."

Her attitude to Liam's death surprises me.

"He sounds surprisingly decent for a man. And he had the intelligence to see the beauty and strength in you. A great pity that he didn't survive; the world needs more men like him," she says, giving me a brisk, bony hug. She produces a handkerchief and hands it to me.

"He will live on in your child. You will make him proud of both of you."

That sets me off again, of course. Being able to mourn Liam openly feels like a gift.

When it comes to Alfie, I'm concerned that she'll condemn me, not only for putting him in danger, but also for surrendering my place in the "ultimate masculine domain." But I needn't have worried.

"Dear Alfred. I always knew he had hidden strengths. He's done the right thing. Even you can't go storming around battlefields when you're carrying a child. Let's hope and pray that Alfred's strengths will carry him through. When he comes home, I'll invite him to join the Suffragette movement, as an Honorary Woman."

"He'll love that!"

When I try to thank her, she shushes me. "You're doing me a favour. This house is far too big for one. The neighbours disapprove of my Suffragette sympathies and ignore me. It'll be delightful to have you around, and if the neighbours find out that I'm harbouring an unmarried mother, they'll be utterly outraged. It will be quite *wonderful!*"

And for once, it's as easy as that.

A week or so before Christmas, we're decorating the fir tree nearest to the front door with Suffragette garlands of green, white and violet, much to the disapproval of the tubby bank manager who lives over the road and who walks past several times, muttering about "mad spinsters," when a letter arrives.

It's from Alfie.

We hurry inside to read it.

Dear Nina and Julia (I don't need to call you "Aunt" any more, do I?)

I was tickled pink to hear that you've joined forces. I do hope that Bayswater is ready for such a formidable duo! Julia, thank you. I knew that you wouldn't let Nina down.

Nina, how are you? Are you coping with pregnancy? I suspect that you'll be quite wonderful as a mother, for all the wrong reasons. Boy or girl, your child will be lucky to have you.

I'm doing well enough here, better than you might imagine. Sergeant Cox looks out for me as much as he can. I suspect that he has a bit of a soft spot for me.

I hope it won't upset you to hear that I hear very positive things about Liam. Black and Simons especially, once they'd got over the embarrassment of talking about him, like to remind me of his courage and spirit.

We went over the top last week and I won't say much about it. The worst of it was the men left wounded on the battlefield. I helped them when I could but I was hopelessly inadequate. I hated that. But at least one of our men will live to fight another day because of me. I hope he'll thank me.

I wanted to tell you about a letter I received this week. Nina, do you remember Moody? The boy who challenged me to a boxing match? Well, it was from him. He was writing from a convalescent home. He'd been in a bad way after getting knocked off his feet by a shell blast. He lost his memory, wandered a good mile down the trench from his section (the lord knows how he managed that), didn't know his own name and was sent to a hospital in England to recover and wait for his memory to come back.

In the meantime, he'd been reported missing in action and his family informed. Then, six months later, he woke up in the middle of a dream. In the dream he was a boy again, boxing. With me! He knew my name and suddenly his own name came back to him. He thinks that it's thanks to me that he knows who he is.

He got some information about "our" whereabouts from Gertie and managed to track me down. He wanted to apologise for the fight and THANK me for helping him to reunite with his family, who must have had heart attacks when he turned up again. He seems to think I'm some kind of guardian angel, which I am, obviously! War has the strangest consequences, doesn't it? I shall write back to confirm that I am indeed angelic and to accept his apologies.

Now I have an interesting story to tell you. We captured half a dozen Germans a few days ago. They were poking around by the latrines, of all places.

They handed over their weapons peacefully, and one of them—a thin fellow with fair hair—kept telling me that his name was Werner, as if he expected me to know it. His companion spoke a bit of English and he insisted that they had come to surrender to me and only me. They'd had enough. Can't blame them for that.

We treated them decently and sent them to wait out the rest of the war in a prison camp, but this Werner's friends were ragging him about something and it was obviously to do with me. In the end, he asked me to prove that I was male. I did so in the time-honoured fashion and it caused a lot of laughter from our lads and utter confusion to Werner and his pals. Nina, please write back soon and tell me what you can about this. I'll do my best to read between the lines.

Take the best of care of each other, and of the future hope of the Mullins family. And merry Christmas!

Your devoted,

Alfie.

CHAPTER THIRTY-SEVEN

Cambridge, December 1917

I've been back for three weeks and there's something that I can't put off any longer. I need to see Gertie. *Want* to see her. The news of my return will reach her soon and if she gets it second hand, she'll be upset. On top of that, Christmas is looming and I have a gift for her: a book of postcards of France and Belgium. Not as these places are now: charred and ruined, but as they were before men decided that the only way to settle their differences was to kill each other en masse. I know that Gertie would love to see a bit of the world and I'm sure she will appreciate this. I haven't bothered getting a present for Father. The only thing that I know he likes is new clothing, and he gets all he wants and more through his business connections.

Our house in Cambridge looks just the same. I find that astonishing. It seems *wrong* that only a few hundred miles away the world is all mud and death, while here the holly bush by the door is bursting with crimson berries and there is a beautifully neat red ribbon tied around the door knocker. This puts me in mind of that other, very different ribbon, that we came home to on the day that Mother died. That had been a day of misery, and I suspect that this one will prove similar.

I straighten my shoulders and knock.

Gertie answers. Although I've only been away a few months, she looks older.

"My goodness! Nina! Welcome home. Come in. Come in."

We exchange a hug and she bustles me into the house, taking my coat. I stand on Mother's Persian rug and look up to the middle stair and remember that day ten years ago when we started out being eagles and ended up finding the roles that would define our lives.

"I'm just back," I lie, "and I wanted to see you. I've missed you."

"Let me look at you. You look tired. And thin! Have they been working you too hard at that hospital?"

I hear a masculine cough from the living room and my heart sinks. Father is home, earlier than he used to be— business must be slow. That's unfortunate, but not unexpected. He comes out of the living room, pipe in hand, and looks at me with a puzzled air, as if he can't quite remember who I am. Gertie bustles off "to put the kettle on" but, really, she's trying to give us some time alone. I want to follow her, but I can't avoid this confrontation. If I'm honest with myself, part of me has been hoping for it.

"Nina! Why haven't you been in contact? I've been worried." He doesn't hug me or touch me. He extends one hand to usher me into the living room, a gesture he would make for an uninvited acquaintance.

I wonder if it's my wellbeing he has been worrying about, or the possibility that I might have been doing something that could damage the precious Mullins name.

"Didn't you get my letters?" I ask Father, now. "I was very busy at the hospital, I didn't get the chance to send many...." The truth, of course, is that I hadn't sent a single one. Why would I?

"No. And none from Alfred either, from whom I expected better."

I refuse to rise to the criticism implicit in this speech.

"I've been out to the Front, working in a Casualty Clearing Station. The things I've seen! The poor soldiers—'"

He holds up one hand. "That's enough. Women shouldn't be subjected to such sights. It's highly damaging to the female mind. And they certainly shouldn't speak about them. You've had your little adventure and now it's time to settle back into normal life. I'm sure the VAD will welcome you again, and Reverend Mitchell was enquiring after you just the other day."

I'm starting to feel sick again, but it isn't my pregnancy, it's an acknowledgement of the row that is about to happen. Father thinks I am coming back to live with him, but there's no way that I can settle back into his regime of rigid conformity and mindless feminine pursuits, and no way that he'll accept the new me, with my swearing and outspokenness. And that's before we get to the stigma of my illegitimate child.

I might as well get this over with.

"Father, I've got some wonderful news. I'm pregnant!" I announce.

He hesitates. "Pregnant? You mean you're married? Where is your husband? Is he a soldier?"

"That's a lot of questions. Do you mind if I sit down? I'm feeling quite sick." I drop onto the sofa. It has been changed since I left home. I find its softness cloyingly uncomfortable. It feels as if it's swallowing me up. I think longingly about lowering myself onto a simple firing step at the Front.

"Answer me, please, Nina. Who have you married? I assume he is an officer? Which regiment? Where is he?"

"He was a soldier, not an officer. His name was Liam. He died." I can't say it without tears pricking my eyes and a sob rising in my throat.

"I'm sorry to hear that. Very sorry indeed."

I nod, wondering if his regret is due to Liam's death or the fact that I hadn't managed to ensnare someone of the officer class.

"And you were married—where?" He won't leave the question of our marriage alone. I had expected this.

Just for a second, I consider lying and making up a wedding, somewhere out of the way. A wedding with military touches: members of my non-existent husband's regiment holding up swords to make an arch through which the happy newlyweds process. What harm would it do?

I know the answer to that. *I* would be harmed. To lie, to have to perpetuate that lie forever, for the sake of conforming to Father's stupid, narrow-minded rules. It would be a living death.

I raise my head and look him straight in the eye. He hates that.

"We weren't married. One day, perhaps, we would have been. Although we might have just lived together."

I wait for his reaction.

He doesn't fail me. He takes a step backwards, as if my presence is a contamination.

"You're telling me that–" he doesn't seem to know how to put it into words, so I decide to help him out.

"Yes, we made a child out of wedlock." That's putting it a lot more delicately than I would if I was still out at the Front.

He draws in a hissing breath.

"But that means that the child is a–"

"A bastard," I finish for him. The colour drains from his face. I wonder if it's a reaction to the indelicate word I've used, or to the thought of what I've been doing.

"Are you telling me that he raped you? Seduced you at least? Coerced you in some way?"

I snort. I can't help it and, anyway, I want to infuriate him. Compared to the yawning gulf between Father and me, the international disagreements that led to this war seem petty. Why didn't I wait until I was certain he'd be out? I know why. I came here to confront him and to sever the tenuous tie between us, once and for all. I want my life at the Home Front to be different. Before I went to war, I thought I had no choice but to accept Father's judgement of me. I was unlovable, troublesome, a fly in the ointment of his sacred Respectability. Now I know differently. I can live on my own terms, in my own way, and as for Father, he can go hang, for all I care.

So I smile to incense him some more. "None of those things. I loved every minute of it."

Father backs even further away. His face is suffused with disgust.

"The man—whoever he was—was a cad. A reprobate. God has punished him. Death is his punishment for ruining you."

That's it. I feel my anger bursting out of me like a breeched dam.

"Ruining me? He *made* me! *Don't* talk about Liam like that. He was a million times more of a man than you. He *loved* me. You—with your correctness and your buttons and bows and your what will the neighbours think—you're hardly a man at all!"

I'm shouting at him, poking him in his buttoned-up chest. He falls back onto the sofa.

"Get out. Get out of my house. You've disgraced us. You're nothing but a—'"

"—whore," I say, relishing the forbidden word and the way he flinches from it. "Yes, I suppose some people would regard me that way. Actually, it's a relief that you're one of them, not that I thought you wouldn't be. I don't love you and you don't love me. Your grandchild will be much better off without you souring its life. So yes, I'll go, after I've had a chat with Gertie and got my things together."

I leave him, speechless and fuming, and go to break the news to Gertie, who hugs and kisses me. "You were always one for doing things your own way. Where will you live? You'll keep in touch, won't you? You'll be needing all the help you can get with a new baby, and I'm a dab hand with the nippers."

CHAPTER THIRTY-EIGHT

Bayswater, Summer 1918

Soon the war will end. Everyone knows it. The German army's final gamble—an attempt to push us back to the sea—has failed. They are a spent force and the newspapers predict that the Kaiser will surrender and abdicate well before winter. Civilians in England are calling for his blood. The fools. As if the blood of one more man could make any difference.

As my pregnancy advances, I dream of the fun we will have once Alfie gets back: Christmas and snowballs, seaside holidays where we teach my child to swim, punting and picnics on the river Cam. If only Liam could be here too.

Liam's absence is a permanent, aching emptiness that never leaves me. I thank the gods for his baby and hope so much it will look like him, with dark hair and bold eyes. I vow to do my very best to be a good parent. I know that I won't be a conventional mother, baking cakes and knitting sweaters, but I have other qualities that I can pass on to my child. I will ensure that they grow up to value tolerance, that they are blessed with courage and self-belief. We will make Liam proud of us.

Alfie's letters are becoming more hopeful too. *There has been less front-line action over the past month or so,* he writes in May. *In fact, I'd go as far as to say that the ground behind the front line is actually more dangerous now. We've done terrible things to the land there, with our bombing, mining and trenches, and you never know when it is going to give way beneath your feet. You can disappear in a moment and never be found.*

I'm saddened when he writes to tell me that Black is one of those who perishes this way. It seems a ridiculous way to die, especially with the end of the war so close.

Aunt Julia is wonderful, full of dry humour and brisk kindness. She prepares a room for Alfie's return and makes sure that it has plenty of wardrobe space.

"As to what he chooses to put in it, that's his business and no one else's," she declares. I wrap my arms around her and give her a long, grateful hug until she pushes me away, dabbing her eyes and pretending it's because she has a head cold.

"Anyway, you must be careful not to squash the baby," she scolds. "I have high hopes for her."

Not long now, Alfie writes on another occasion. *I hope that soon we'll all be together and life will begin again. What a grand time the four of us will have. We'll turn staid old Bayswater on its head!*

I start to believe it. Finally, I think, there has been enough killing to satisfy the gods of war.

The telegram announcing that Alfie is missing in action arrives on June 5th, 1918. I'm out when it comes, so I'm spared the bleak little charade that surrounds the delivery of the news. I arrive home to find Aunt Julia waiting for me on the doorstep with tears streaming down her gaunt face.

"But we won't give up hope," she insists. She continues to hope as the weeks turn to months and there is still no news about Alfie. I hope too, but I keep my faith in him to myself. If I reveal it, it won't come true. It reminds me of the weeks leading up to my mother's death. We thought then that if we didn't talk about her illness, we could keep it at bay. We're supposed to learn from our experiences, to adjust our expectations in the light of them, but in this case, I refuse. If experience teaches you not to hope, what's the point of learning from it?

Eventually we receive a letter with more details of Alfie's disappearance. It's from Captain Farringdon, whom I've never heard of, stating that Alfie went missing while helping the wounded who were stranded in No Man's Land. He rolls out the usual lines about Alfie being "a gallant soldier and a gentleman to the core." The irony of that makes me laugh. Sometimes.

The next thing we learn is that my gentle, changeling brother is to be decorated. The citation for his (presumed) posthumous

Distinguished Conduct Medal records his "outstanding bravery in returning several times to the battlefield, at great personal risk, to go to the aid of those wounded in battle."

If Alfie is dead, and I think I would know if he was, at least he died doing what he loved. That's some comfort. There would also be a certain irony, I think, in the fact that it happened in No Man's Land. So much of his life has been spent wrestling with the complexities of being a man. In the end he has found his own, unique way of being. To my mind, that is his greatest, bravest, achievement.

I find myself remembering our childhood and the first time that we swapped clothes again. The red soldier's tunic that I couldn't wait to put on. The pointless medals jangling from it. Now Alfie has a real medal and I would give everything I own and will ever own to take it away again, for him to be safe in Bayswater with Aunt Julia and me, planning unconventional futures as we wait for the birth of my child.

I'm thinking about those euphemisms I used to ridicule. Dying in war is messy and drawn out and sometimes disgusting. I remember Venner twitching on the barbed wire and the boy with the choirboy's voice, screaming for hours until he couldn't scream any more. And a hundred others. But when I try to imagine Alfie's death, something stops me. It would be too much for me. The euphemisms have become my lifeline. I've *got* to believe them.

If Alfie *is* dead, then it will have been fast and easy. A shot to the heart and my beloved twin falls to the ground, eyes closed and a look of peace on his face. At last, I understand why intelligent folk embrace these tired ideas. We can't change the past. Why make the present unbearable? If we believe our loved ones died for nothing, in agony, how will we be able to face the impending peace?

Father, of course, has grasped at the image of Alfie as a dead hero with eager hands. It means that he doesn't have to be disappointed in him. He has even got some second-rate artist to paint a portrait of him in his uniform and has hung it behind the counter in his shop. There's a golden plaque beneath it, I'm told, *Alfred Mullins, DCM, 1899-1918*. I haven't seen the portrait myself because Father has disowned me and I am forbidden from sullying the sacred portal of Mullins & Son with my contaminating presence. I can't say that bothers me much.

So eager is Father to hang on to the idea of Alfie as a fallen hero, that he has organised a memorial service for him without even waiting for confirmation that he is dead. It's today. Julia and I haven't been invited but we go anyway and I stick out my huge belly every time some small-minded Mullins looks down their nose at me.

We shuffle into the row behind Father and it empties immediately, leaving Julia and I with a nice amount of space to spread out in. No one wants to be associated with the family's black sheep. I sit down with a grateful sigh.

One of those to vacate the pew is Esme, in another of her vile hats. More swathes of netting—black this time. More trawler's nets. Maybe being married to fish-faced Philip has influenced her choice of hat decoration. She scuttles past me as if I'm a leper, dragging her son with her. He's about four and he has a look of his father. Philip isn't present today. He's in hospital, recovering from a gas attack. I imagine him gasping and foundering, more fishlike than ever, as he breathes in the poisoned air. Gertie tells me that his recovery isn't certain. If only he had someone like Alfie to nurse him, he would have a much better chance.

I decide to say hello to Father, out of something like scientific interest. Will he respond? He stiffens when he hears my voice, but refuses to turn around or acknowledge me in any way. No surprise there. Julia glares at his back, and I have to restrain her from grabbing him by his stiff black coat and forcing him to look at me.

I'm surprised when a latecomer slips into our pew and settles next to me. I turn to find out who this brazen individual is.

Gertie! We exchange a long hug and then I nod silently at Father. I don't want her to get into trouble for sitting with me.

Dear Gertie raises her eyebrows and pulls a face behind his back. She's confident that she can handle him and if not, well, I will be needing a nanny soon and she would be perfect. I make a mental note to suggest it to her, soon.

I wonder if David is here. I managed to find his address (he's back in Weston-Super-Mare) and wrote to invite him. I kept the letter formal. There were no details or recriminations. I didn't want to make his life difficult for him. More difficult than it surely must be, already.

Yes, there he is at the back, with a young woman in grey on his arm. It shocks me to see that she is pregnant. She isn't as far along as me, but there's no ignoring the lump she carries so proudly. How will David cope with fatherhood? He was so set against it. His mother will be delighted, at least, at the prospect of those longed-for grandchildren. The young woman is wearing an elaborate hat that Esme would love. She fusses over David, sitting too close and picking up his hymn book when he drops it. Her action reminds me of the time when the three of us went to the music hall. *Then* it was David, fussing over Alfie. Is he remembering that evening? I see his lips tighten and his eyes flicker to me. I decide that he is. Good. I hope he's regretting giving up Alfie for a commonplace life with this commonplace girl.

Our eyes meet and we nod, but we don't speak. He has nothing to say that I want to hear and I'm fairly certain that he must feel the same.

Looking around at the assembled Mullinses, I see a young man I don't recognise. Tall. Pale. Broad shouldered but thin, troubled eyes and light brown hair brushed upwards and away from his face. He's in uniform, of course. Should I know him?

At the end of the ceremony he approaches me, clutching nervously at his cap.

"You must be Alfred's sister."

Alfred. Not a close friend, then. A close friend would say Alfie.

I nod. "I'm sorry, I don't think we've met?"

He grabs my hand and shakes it.

"My name is William Moody. I was at school with Alfred."

Moody! I pull my hand away.

"Oh yes, Mr Moody. I've heard of you." And I saw you, I think but don't say. "You beat him bloody in a boxing match that you forced on him."

He flushes. The blood in his cheeks takes a long time to disappear.

"I've regretted that for a long time and I tracked Alfred down to apologise for it. He accepted my apology."

I fold my arms across my stomach and nod. I don't see any reason to let this man off lightly, so I say nothing.

"I know this sounds like I'm trying to pass the buck, but really I was goaded into it. A boy named Lacey. Nasty sort. A bit of a weed, but he loved getting other boys into trouble, sniffing out their weaknesses and using them. He got a thrill out of it…"

I want to say yes, I know that when it came to victims, Lacey had eclectic taste.

"It's good of you to come," I say, relenting a little and wondering if I can tell him that Lacey won't be victimising anyone else. For many reasons, I decide against it.

"Don't assume Alfred is dead," Moody continues. "I was missing, presumed killed, but I wasn't, obviously. I'd lost my memory…it happens more often than you realise."

"I hope so," I feel myself warming towards this earnest man who wants to offer me a glimmer of faith in Alfie's return. "I haven't given up."

He nods, several times.

"Good. Good. I'm praying for him. For you all. That you'll soon be reunited."

That'll help, I think. But he means well, so I smile and thank him.

He looks at my stomach and my arms folded over it.

"I wonder, would you mind if I visited you? Once your child is born? I would like to see it grow up…" he's flushing even more fiercely.

He must have noticed that I don't have a wedding ring, or perhaps he's been listening to Cambridge gossip and now he wants to offer some charity to make up for what he did to Alfie. Well, he can take his charity and stuff it where it hurts.

I open my mouth to tell him this, but he interrupts me.

"You see, I'd like to keep up some connection with Alfred, if it's not too much trouble for you. I've come to look on him as a very positive influence in my life, and it would be a way of keeping the connection between us alive…. Until he comes home, I mean. It would mean a great deal to me."

"Oh…. Yes, of course. That would be fine."

I give him a card with Aunt Julia's address on it. He tucks it into his breast pocket, nods and thanks me again, and walks away to make stilted conversation with Father.

Later today, Julia and I will hold our own private ceremony at home. We'll toast Alfie with champagne and celebrate the qualities in her that so few people know about or appreciate. We'll say thanks for the real Alfie and we'll repeat our belief that we will see her again. Sooner or later.

I'm a Suffragette, now. Our neighbours are appalled to have another disreputable woman in the neighbourhood and they shun us both. We annoy them whenever we can, inviting like-minded women around for noisy meetings, painting protest placards in the front garden, even (after the tubby bank manager complained that our presence was having a negative effect on house prices) having the house painted in Suffragette colours. Very childish, I know, but irresistible. Alfie will adore it.

I keep my men's clothes close by: when the baby is born, I intend to go back to them whenever I want, for as long as I want, whatever others say. Life is short and precious and I'm not wasting mine trying to fit in. Whatever path I chose to follow, however others react, I know I'll be up to its challenges.

I spend a lot of time wondering about the baby. Will it be a boy or a girl? Or twins? One of each, to carry on the family tradition?

Usually, I hope for a boy. A boy who can live how he wishes and grow into whatever he wants to be. A boy who will never have to face the horrors of war. And if he turns out to be a girl, that's absolutely fine with me.

Maybe I'll call him Liam Alfred. Or Alfred Liam.

Or maybe I'll call him something completely different—a new name for a new, hopeful age.

Yes.

I think they'd both like that.

Acknowledgments

This story has been my labour of love for several years, born out of my fascinations for the First World War, the lives of women who disguised their sex to fight alongside men, (many of whom have been ignored by history), and the ongoing, loudly fought, battle of words on the subject of gender transitioning. This is a subject that has touched my family profoundly, and I'm proud of the united support we have offered to our much-cherished family member who took the brave decision to become what they always knew they were.

I owe a considerable debt of thanks to Carsten Polzin and Oliver Latsch, agents extraordinaire who, with rigour and humour, helped to shape my rambling manuscript into a coherent book.

Massive thanks too, to my editor, Cecilia Bennett, for their brilliant insights and suggestions, all of which have enhanced this story hugely, making it something of which I'm very proud.

Thanks, as ever, to Harry and Penny and Cat and Adrian for their patience and feedback. Penny, I owe you extra thanks for coming up with the title. The fizz is on me, next time we go out.

Finally, thanks to everyone who invests their time and energy in reading this book, and extra special thanks for those who approach it with an open mind and open heart. In days of conflict, we all need those.

About the Author

K ate Wiseman was born in Oxford, UK in the 1970s. The first in her working-class family to go to university, she graduated with a First in English and Creative Writing. Kate describes herself as a late developer. She didn't start trying to achieve her ambition of becoming a published writer until she was 50. Her debut adult novel, *The Red Tunic*, won the Eyelands Award for Historical Fiction pre-publication in 2020. Kate lives in Chichester, UK and works as a tutor in English. Her fascinations are history, English and mudlarking, and she is a licensed mudlark. Her ambition is to find an intact Bellarmine jug.

ARMY
UNIFORM

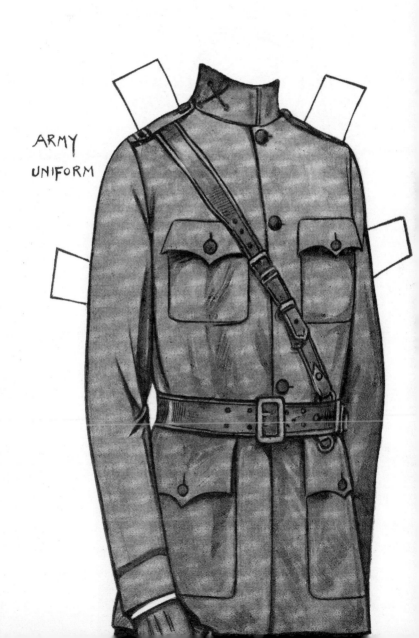

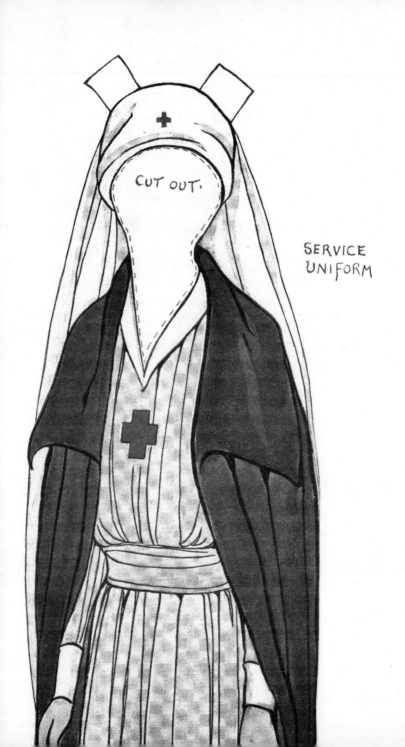